PUFFIN BOOKS
REIGNITED 2: EMERGING TECHNOLOGIES OF TOMORROW

Srijan Pal Singh is an engineer and management graduate from IIM Ahmedabad. While at the Indian Institute of Space Science and Technology, he worked with former Indian President A.P.J. Abdul Kalam as technology and policy adviser.

ALSO IN PUFFIN BY SRIJAN PAL SINGH
(with A.P.J. Abdul Kalam)

Reignited: Scientific Pathways to a Brighter Future

What Can I Give? Life Lessons from My Teacher A.P.J. Abdul Kalam

REiGNITE?

2

EMERGING TECHNOLOGIES OF TOMORROW

SRIJAN PAL SINGH

PUFFIN BOOKS

An imprint of Penguin Random House

PUFFIN BOOKS

USA | Canada | UK | Ireland | Australia
New Zealand | India | South Africa | China | Singapore

Puffin Books is part of the Penguin Random House group of companies
whose addresses can be found at global.penguinrandomhouse.com

Published by Penguin Random House India Pvt. Ltd
4th Floor, Capital Tower 1, MG Road,
Gurugram 122 002, Haryana, India

Penguin
Random House
India

First published in Puffin Books by Penguin Random House India 2019

ISBN 9780143441120

Book design by Vedanti Sikka
Typeset in Sabon by Manipal Digital Systems, Manipal

Printed at Repro India Limited

www.penguin.co.in

MIX
Paper from
responsible sources
FSC® C047271

This book is dedicated to the timeless wisdom of my teacher A.P.J. Abdul Kalam and the indomitable spirit of the Indian civilization, which inspires open thinking and indefatigable toil across generations.

The author's royalties will be donated to the Kalam Library Project, which is providing underprivileged children across India with free access to books.

Contents

Prologue

10 July 2055
0630 hours
Mars

'Trinnggg . . . Time to wake up, Ankit,' said a slightly coarse female voice.

'Ahhh! Please give me ten more minutes. Ten minutes only,' said Ankit, still not opening his eyes to the light.

'What! No way, Ankit. You are already getting a better deal than the boys on Earth, since every day you get one extra hour of sleep here on Mars. Think about those boys and get up. After all, your big mission starts today . . . If you are late, what will your team members think?'

'Okay, Mother.' Ankit gave up the struggle.

'Good boy. I will get things ready for you,' she said as she rotated the chassis of her vehicle 180 degrees and wheeled away from Ankit.

Rita was among the first generation of 300 settlers who had arrived on the red planet after a three-month-long journey from Earth. That was twenty years ago, in 2035. These initial settlers had had a hard time adjusting to the new conditions. They lived underground, in lava cubes that were the result of ancient volcanoes on the red planet. These helped them avoid ultraviolet radiation and massive sandstorms on the surface. The little houses for the first settlers were already built before they had arrived on the planet, made by an army of 1000 humanoids and rovers, which had been tirelessly working on Mars since the 2025 space missions were launched by the National Aeronautics and Space Administration (NASA), the European Space Agency (ESA) and the Indian Space Research Organisation (ISRO).

As you can guess, the most difficult challenge on the red planet was finding water. Ankit's mother, Rita, had been an expert at drilling for oil when she was on Earth. It was because of this that she had been selected for the Mars 101B mission in 2035. Her job on Mars was to detect and drill for water. Thankfully, the settlers were able to find underground rivers on the planet.

Of course, it was highly saline water but, with abundant sunshine on Mars, researchers were able to desalinate it using solar energy and also break it down to get oxygen for breathing. Under the prevailing Martian laws then, 75 per cent of the groundwater was to be used for oxygen and only 25 per cent as water. This made liquid water scarce. The daily allowance was never more than 12 litres—you could drink it, cook with it and save up some for an occasional shower. Water was the currency of exchange, and a standard 25-litre can could buy you almost anything you wanted at the Mars Store.

'Mars-born's like Ankit, who had never lived on their home planet, Earth, would often gaze at their parents' planet through a telescope. Earth looked blue from afar, and they had heard stories of natural sweet water flowing in rivers and stored in giant ponds. They had seen fascinating videos of water raining down from the skies. One could even drink this water, they'd heard. Earth seemed bountiful to Mars-borns.

Ankit's mother was an Earth-born immigrant. She was thirty-four years old when she'd arrived on the red planet, barely making the cut-off age for Martian settlers, which was thirty-five back when the programme started. Earth did not want to send older people to Mars. First, because of the harsh conditions of travel; second, because they wanted the Martian settlers to live the bulk of their lifetime on Mars so that they could contribute longer. Rita did not fare too well because of the radiation exposure she had got in the inadequately protective spaceship from Earth. Moreover, as a driller, she had to constantly enter the planet's surface, where, despite the spacesuit's protection, she was exposed to strong dust and, worse, radiation. The spacesuits provided to them in 2035 had been designed for the Moon, which was protected by Earth's magnetic cover, and were certainly not suitable for Mars. Radiation had affected many a settler, who had later been diagnosed with diseases such as blood cancer.

It was not that the Martian settlers had not been aware of the health risks they were exposing themselves to. Most of them were foremost scientists and engineers, who had chosen to bear the risks of travelling to and settling on an alien planet. After all, human exploration of new domains always came at the price of the sacrifices made by a few—and quite often the best—minds of the times. When humans ventured under the ocean for the first time, many of the best sailors lost their lives in the process, but the sacrifice was made for the discovery of seafaring. On the path to the discovery of the new continent of America, many brilliant explorers drowned in the Atlantic; and when humans aimed to fly, many scientists literally jumped to their deaths to test the wings and machines they had created. Martian settlers were only another chapter in this book of human civilization, wherein each lesson started with sacrifices and perils and ended in the conquest of a new frontier by the species. Rita was one such sacrifice.

But the Mars settlers had been given an opportunity—to be part of the first human effort towards an afterlife. Researchers at the Indian Institute of Science (IISc), along with the Harvard John A. Paulson School of Engineering and Applied Sciences (SEAS), had invented a new product. It was an electromagnetic headset that could be used to extract memories from the brain of any living being and saved on to a computer. They had been working on such a system since the year 2010, but it took them almost two decades to finally come up with a prototype that produced favourable results.

This new form of artificial intelligence, or AI, called BrainLoading, was programmed such that robots could talk, behave and even feel like the human whose thoughts were stored in its system. However, it was an alarming invention, as it could easily lead to the thoughts being stolen and traded. So its use on humans was instantly banned and declared illegal. Of course, it was still used on some animals—especially pet dogs and cats. When a pet dog would die, a robotic dog would take its place and respond in the exact same way as the earlier pet that was made of flesh and bones.

But Martian laws were not governed by the laws of Earth, and in order to give some hope to the Mars settlers, who were constantly struggling against extreme forces of nature on the lonely red planet, the laws were bent. Therefore, for the first time, in 2035, BrainLoading was made available to human Martian settlers in the event of their premature death.

In 2038, with a newborn baby in her arms, Rita was devastated to hear the news of her blood cancer. She was well aware that, with continued exposure to the radiation on Mars, she had no more than three years to live. And so she became the first applicant for the BrainLoading programme. On a designated date in 2040, when Ankit was just two years old, she transferred her memories to the humanoid robot MOTMARS, which had been imported from Earth. It was a 4-foot-tall wheel-driven machine with a screen that showed her face. It had sensors—like a camera, an odour sensor, touch sensors—and mics. They did not fit a taste sensor as MOTMARS did not need to consume anything. Anything other than electricity, of course.

But there was one problem: MOTMARS had an artificial voice that was generated by the computer. When it was activated, Rita's memories were fully revived, to everyone's relief, and the humanoid worked and behaved exactly like Rita. Except, when it spoke, it sounded like someone else. The computer-generated sound waves were humanlike, but they could not capture her original voice.

When Ankit grew up and realized the problem, he wrote to the designers of the humanoid about it. Sadly, he received a negative reply: 'If we had a large volume of her recordings saying different words, we could have uploaded it on to MOTMARS's CPU.' Alas, Rita, in her limited time, had not had the opportunity to sit down for hours every day and make these recordings.

Over the next few years, till today, in 2055, many of the Mars settlers had chosen to pass on to the afterlife in humanoid form. For a total population of about 50,000 humans, there were about 10,000 humanoids on Mars. You could see families consisting of humans and human-turned-humanoids all over the planet—in restaurants, temples and markets. Humanoids were even allowed to vote for the government on Mars. And, while still the minority in terms of overall population, it was in the year 2053 that the first humanoid prime minister of Mars was elected. A third-generation model, he was working hard to serve the planet; however, fourth-generation humanoid models had already arrived and most people had started calling the prime minister an 'outdated' model with old ideas!

• • •

The same day
0930 hours

Ankit rushed into the special seminar room ALPHA 1.

As he entered, Ankit took his helmet off, for the room was oxygen-conditioned and fully equipped with a MOXY generator, which could convert Martian carbon dioxide (CO_2) into breathable oxygen. It was always a relief to take off the airtight helmet and see the world without the glass pane in between. Ankit, like most other boys and girls his age, wondered how people could roam freely on Planet Earth without gas helmets.

In his classes, he had also learnt how, from the 1950s till about 2020, humans on Earth had destroyed much of its water and air by way of pollution—burning coal for power and oil for transportation. He always wondered at how humans valued these resources so little when they had so much of it and how now they had almost lost it all. In fact, his Mars history teacher had told him that part of the reason why humans had been sent to Mars was because they were not sure whether Planet Earth would ever recover from the pollution that was plaguing it. Ankit could not understand how short-term greed could dominate human psychology.

But now there was good news: Today's *Times of Mars* had reported that, by using nanotechnology, Earth had stored a large amount of the excess carbon dioxide deep inside the ground and that solar, hydro and tidal powers were being used as the only sources of energy now. All sources of energy were now 100 per cent green. All this had helped reverse many of the ill effects, but a lot still needed to be done to restore Earth to what it used to be some 150 years ago, when the planet was covered in plants and all water was pure and the air clean.

'Hydro and tidal! Wow! So much water,' Ankit pondered while reading the article. His thoughts were interrupted when somebody called out to him.

'Hey! Ready to climb Olympus Mons, Captain Ankit?'

Ankit turned around and saw that it was Gunjan, his medic for the expedition. Almost the same age as him, she was a well-known artist on Mars and was training to be a doctor. Gunjan was also a Mars-born, and her role was to ensure that Ankit was fully fit for the climb. For this, she would monitor his vital signs from the lab as he climbed uphill.

'Yes. Why not? We have trained for it!' he replied.

Ankit was the best known mountaineer on Mars, and his job was to explore high altitudes on the planet. His heroes were Edmund Hillary and Tenzing Norgay, the two men who had climbed Earth's highest peak, Mount Everest, way back in 1953. However, Olympus Mons was a different story. It was the largest volcano in the entire solar system.

Suddenly, the bell went off, declaring the entry of the special guest for the day. All eyes turned to the door as a 4-foot-tall humanoid wheeled in. The 100 people assembled in the room cheered. The humanoid, too, waved its hands and slowed down to greet the people in the first row. Behind him walked two guards in uniform, a human and a humanoid. This celebrity humanoid was none other than the prime minister of Mars. He had arrived to talk about the special climbing project and the prize for completing it.

'Ladies and gentlemen, humans and humanoids of Mars, welcome to Expedition Olympus. As you know, ten finalists have been selected to make an attempt to reach the top of Olympus Mons. As your prime minister, I am proud of you and hope that many of you reach the summit. As you know, Olympus Mons is the highest peak not just on Mars, but in our entire solar system. It stands at more than 2.5 times the height of Mount Everest, the highest peak any human or humanoid has climbed so far!'

The prime minister was right. Olympus Mons was more than 25,000 metres in height; compared to it, Mount Everest in the Himalayas stood at a measly 8848 metres. Also, the area that Olympus Mons occupied was almost equal to the size of the country called France on Earth. Indeed, it was a mammoth task that Ankit and the other mountaineers were about to undertake.

'But today I also want to declare a special award. Besides the cash prize for all winners, we will give a special prize to the first person to climb the mountain.' The prime minister took a pause; despite being a humanoid, he knew all the tricks of speech giving.

'It will be a trip to Earth!'

A wave of surprise rippled through the hall. This was nothing short of shocking.

'And not just that. The winner can also select one person to go with them.'

Frenzy gripped the people in the seminar room. There had been very few, practically rare, cases of citizens of Mars being sent back to Earth. The movement of people was mostly in a single direction: settlers coming from Earth to Mars. In fact, no Mars-born had ever visited Earth so far. People believed that the reason behind this was that upon seeing so much water and oxygen on their old planet, they would never want to return! Hence only the prime minister and his two ministers, for trade and for technology, had the license to travel to Earth whenever they liked.

So this was completely unexpected. The crowd was stunned, and then broke into chatter. Almost every brain (of the humans) and every processor (of the humanoids) was thinking the same thing.

What would the ancestral planet be like? Blue? Green? Brown? Was the news about nanotechnology saving the planet from pollution actually true? Would they be able to walk around without the suit and helmet? There were too many questions. Even those who had once lived on Earth had now forgotten how a gulp of natural, unprocessed water tasted, how natural the air smelled out in the open fields.

The race to Olympus Mons was now going to be all the way to the First Planet—the nickname used for Earth among the inhabitants of Mars.

• • •

19 July 2055
0700 hours
Camp 22, Olympus Mons

Ankit had fared well at Camp 22 over the past nine days, battling extreme exhaustion and very low temperatures. At 24,200 metres, Camp 22 was the last stop for climbers before the final push up the volcanic rocks on the way to the top of Olympus Mons. Out of the ten mountaineers who had started this expedition, only three remained now.

At this altitude, the rocks were frozen in the glaciers, perhaps lying motionless for over a billion years, only to be stirred by falling meteorites. In fact, more than the cold weather, the real danger so far had been the burning trails of rock particles entering the Martian atmosphere. Because of its immense height, Olympus Mons was often the first recipient of these showers.

Ankit witnessed this first-hand when one such meteorite— thankfully a relatively smaller one—landed not far from Camp 17 three nights ago. It sent shock waves into the ground, and the heat from it cracked the glaciers. Ankit wanted to venture out and check if there was water to be found, but then Gunjan, who was working with him remotely via satellite phone, advised him to stay inside the artificially pressurized tent for his own safety.

Another problem that the mountaineers were facing was that of atmospheric pressure. The pressure at Camp 22 was already below 130 pascal, which was lower than one-fourth of the pressure on the Martian surface. Ankit was aware that at the summit, the pressure would drop to 70 pascal. When Edmund Hillary had climbed Mount Everest, he had, in comparison, got a better deal—the pressure atop Mount Everest was still 32,000 pascal (it is about 1,00,000 pascal on Earth's surface). This low pressure was indeed dangerous. It meant that the mountaineers would need to be equipped for spacewalk conditions: There would be no air to conduct heat around them. Direct beams from the Sun could heat up their suits at a very rapid rate and, inversely, those patches that did not receive sunlight could be extremely cold. Every step taken by the Olympus mountaineers had to be calculated carefully, as one misstep could mean death.

As the Sun rose in the skies, Ankit stepped out of the pressurized tent. He was dressed in his heavy spacesuit. Even though the gravitational force on Mars was almost one-third of that on Earth, the 120-kilogramme spacesuit still felt like 40 kilogrammes on their backs. Walking with this load was not going to be easy.

'I must reach the top. I must go to Earth,' Ankit told himself and started walking. A distance of 800 metres vertically and some 5000 metres horizontally lay ahead of him. At this point, his mind was focused more on the peak of Olympus Mons than on the other two contestants. He could see the crest shining in the Martian skies, which were now turning from blue to yellow-brown with the rising Sun.

• • •

The same day
1700 hours

'I must reach the top. I must go to Earth. I must go to Earth!' Ankit was mumbling continuously. He was exhausted after ten hours of non-stop climbing and walking. His strong will to win the race and go to Earth was the only thing giving him the energy to keep going.

Then a voice rang in his ears.

'Ankit! Where are you? We lost communication for a while. I hope you are okay?'

It was Gunjan on satellite communication.

'Hmm . . .' Ankit could barely convey his affirmation.

'Cheer up. You are only 500 metres from the top! We are about to win! Cheer up, Ankit.'

'Five hundred metres!' exclaimed Ankit. Since his mind was focused on making it to the top, Ankit had forgotten to check the map. It was only now that he realized he was almost there! The first human to climb the tallest mountain on any planet of the solar system! He was 500 metres away from writing human history.

'Really!' Ankit found energy and renewed hope.

He looked up. All that lay ahead of him was an open gradient with shiny rocks. His mind immediately recognized these rocks; they were shergottites. Shergottites were Martian rocks, some of which were launched into space due to the impact of meteorites. These shiny pieces of rock then made a journey towards Earth and entered the atmosphere. Most of them got burnt; some of the larger ones, however, survived and fell on the surface there. The first such rock from Mars landed on Earth almost 200 years ago, in 1865, in Sherghati, India.

This was a strange coincidence. As Ankit raced up the shergottites' surface, he realized he was clearing his way to be launched to Earth . . . He was following the destiny of the rocks around him.

After seven minutes, the beeper announced the height: 25,012 metres.

This was it! Ankit had made it to the top! At 1707 hours, on 19 July 2055. His name and this date would now be immortal. He took a deep gasp of breath and fell to his knees, down on the shergottites. He wished he could touch them with his fingers, but at near-zero pressure, he couldn't even think of exposing his skin to the Martian air around him. He let out a cry of joy as he threw up his arms. Tears rolled down his cheeks. He smiled and cried at the same time as he scanned the sky to find Earth. The little blue dot was right there in the clear yellow-brown Martian horizon.

'Mom! We are going to Earth!' Ankit cried.

• • •

23 July 2055
1000 hours

At the concluding ceremony of Expedition Olympus, seminar room ALPHA 1 was filled to capacity with humans and humanoids. They were talking excitedly among themselves. Today the prime minister would be presenting two round-trip tickets to Ankit and his chosen fellow traveller.

By now everyone knew that Ankit had chosen his mother to accompany him to Earth.

'Why would he take a humanoid to Earth?' said a Mars-born.

'They can barely feel a thing. What would they do on Earth? They are afraid of water anyway!' added someone else.

A humanoid standing close to them overheard this and turned to them in dismay. It hissed, exhibiting its anger. Clearly, the two parties did not agree on this matter. But all the cacophony was soon subdued as the prime minister entered the hall. He spoke about the historic moment and how this feat could not be replicated unless humans and humanoids reached another solar system and found its highest peak.

Then the Medal of Mars was brought forth, and the prime minister put it around Ankit's neck. After this he officially announced that Ankit and Rita would be going on their month-long trip to Earth the next week. This would make Rita the first humanoid ordinary citizen to ever visit Earth. Hearing this, the humanoids in the room beeped and cheered.

• • •

30 July 2055
0700 hours

'*Trinnggg* . . . Time to wake up, Ankit . . . Time for our trip,' said the slightly coarse female voice.

This time Ankit did not need a second nudge from Rita. He sprang out of bed. Seeing him awake, Rita turned around and wheeled away to the kitchen.

With his humanoid mother out of sight, Ankit carefully leaned over the bed. His hand groped around in the narrow space under it and pulled out an old CD-ROM in a plastic case. It was at least thirty-five years old, for compact discs (CDs) were almost completely replaced by 2020, around the time scientists were still trying out ways of sending humans to Mars.

Ankit did not have a CD reader with him. In fact, there was no CD reader in the whole of Mars! 'But Earth may have one at some science museum,' he thought. After all, CDs existed about four decades ago.

Ankit knew two things about this CD he was holding. First, it was illegal. In 2055, information was a key form of currency, and carrying old information—not sanctioned by the government of Mars—was completely illegal. Under the law, he should have surrendered this CD to the government, who, in turn, would have destroyed it. If he were to be caught with it, he could be put in Martian jail for at least three years. Possessing old and unsanctioned data in 2055 was no less criminal than carrying drugs in the 2000s.

Second, its title said 'Birthday 2019: Rita'. That was the reason Ankit was taking all the risks.

This CD probably contained a video recording of his mother's birthday in 2019, when she'd turned eighteen. This meant it had her voice! Ankit was eager to hear his mother's original but now lost voice once he reached Earth. But he had planned on more than just that. He had established connection with the company that had manufactured her humanoid form. Long ago, they had emailed him that if he could get them a recording of her original voice, they would be able to reprogramme the sound system of the MOTMARS humanoid to match her voice.

The possibility of hearing his mother's voice brought out a childlike excitement in Ankit. Even when he'd been climbing Olympus Mons, he was imagining a day when he would sit with Rita and they would have long chats about stars, planets, her days on Earth and about Mars. This was his dream and passion now, and he was willing to risk everything for it.

He slid the CD into the sleeve of the spacesuit he was going to wear on his journey to Earth.

• • •

The same day
1200 hours

'Three . . . two . . . one . . . Engines ignite. Lift-off!'

Ankit, now a celebrity on Mars, peered out of the glass pane. From the launch pad, on the flat plains near the main settlement, the lift-off was smooth. And within a couple of minutes, they were zooming across the outer layers of the atmosphere and Mars soon started fading away behind them. Ankit could easily spot Olympus Mons staring at him; they were friends now.

Rita was restlessly moving around. She had the mind and memories of Earth—Rita's homeland. She remembered the meadows, the plants, the animals, the beaches, the fish, the rivers, the clouds and the rain. After twenty years, she was going to see it all again. Underneath all this joy, though, she did have one fear. How would Earth, with its human-only population, react on seeing a humanoid? Rita was hoping they wouldn't treat her like a tin robot.

● ● ●

31 July 2055
1600 hours

'Wake up, Ankit. Look, it's Planet Earth!'

Rita was peeping out of the window of the space shuttle. Ankit was only half-asleep—it was difficult to get sleep in outer space, with no gravity whatsoever. He got up and looked out of the window.

The spaceship was turning towards Earth. Ankit was seeing his ancestral planet for the first time, and it was far more beautiful than what he had seen in photographs and other visuals. It was a blue ball with white clouds moving around it like a shroud.

Over the next two hours, the ship moved closer and closer to Earth. Then came the descent. It was the most difficult part of the journey. Unlike Mars, Earth had a thick atmosphere, which resisted the entry of foreign objects with a force of friction. This friction produced a large amount of heat—enough to incinerate most metals and non-metals. But, of course, nanotechnology had been used to build Ankit's spaceship out of a special substance. A carbon compound, it was almost impossible to burn or break. The earliest form of this material was developed in the 1970s for shielding missiles, but nowadays it was mostly used in spaceships.

With a thud, orange lights came on, and an automated voiced announced, 'Prepare for landing.' It was a signal to buckle up as the turbulence phase of re-entry into Earth's atmosphere would begin. The spaceship vibrated vigorously and swivelled but remained in control. It was a very different experience from the much smoother take-off from Mars, which had a weaker gravitational pull. But the artificial intelligence piloting the ship was seasoned to handle this landing.

In the next fifteen minutes, the ship was less than 500 metres from the ground. Two large terminal parachutes were deployed to reduce the velocity. The ship then landed upright on its wheels. The GPS system of the ship told Ankit they had arrived at Dr Kalam SpacePort, New Delhi, India. Ankit knew all about A.P.J. Abdul Kalam, the prominent twentieth-century missile and space scientist, and the President of India from 2002 to 2007. Rita had even met him as a child when she had won a school science quiz in 2015.

The ship's door opened. Ankit was told that he could let go of the spacesuit and the gas cylinders. He felt jittery and anxious. He was finally here. On Earth. The planet where humans could roam around freely, breathe in fresh air without the help of oxygen tanks, masks and spacesuits, and drink as much water as they wanted.

This was nothing short of a rebirth for Ankit.

Then he took his first step. He saw a bright blue sky, scattered with clouds, and took his first deep breath on the planet.

'So *this* is fresh air. Wow!'

• • •

The same day
2000 hours
Earth

Outside the Durbar Hall of the Presidential House, Ankit stepped out of the self-driven electric car. This was the residence of the President of India, Ravi Singh, who was also the President of Earth for this term. The organization called United Nations (UN) had decided in 2025 that every year, one of the eight identified major nations will get a chance to appoint its President as President of Earth. This year it was India's turn.

A large fountain stood outside the splendid estate, throwing litres of water up in the air before it fell into a pond around it.

'Water . . . They have so much water . . . Enough to use it as a form of decoration and throw it up to the sky! This is a rich planet indeed.'

Ankit and his mother stepped on to a red escalator in the inner chamber of the Presidential House. All around them were flowers, trees and leaves dancing in the wind. The wind on Earth was far stronger than the wind on Mars, which had a much lower atmospheric density. Ankit wanted to catch the stray leaves, but Rita had already told him not to do anything childish when visiting the President of India.

Inside, Ankit was served some coffee, a traditional beverage on Earth—it was hot and delicious. Earth was blessed with so much food, of so many different varieties, it was astonishing. The food on Mars was meant only for survival, measured in vitamins and calories. The concept of eating for taste was unique to Earth.

Ankit spotted a unique framed poster hanging on the wall to his right. It read, 'How we saved Earth.' He became curious and walked up to the poster, and started reading.

The poster talked about how, after two centuries of destroying the environment of the beautiful blue-green planet, humankind had finally realized its mistake. The treaty Save Earth had been signed by all the countries of the planet in 2022, wherein they had collectively decided to completely replace fossil fuels with green alternatives within the next two years. After this, a nanotechnology-based ecological revolution had begun.

Nanotechnology was used to manufacture clean energy from the Sun and ocean tides to power the planet. Plastic, invented in the early 1900s, was abolished. In fact, large ships were deployed to dig into the oceans and drag out the billions of tons of plastic that were choking the fish and killing other undersea creatures. In place of the hazardous plastic, nanotechnologists had invented 'bio-plastic' that could decompose or be converted into rich soil in a matter of days once buried. Hence farmers on

Earth had started using bio-plastic fertilizers to grow healthy crops. Earth had also gone through a war against pollution in the next decade, and it was only around 2032 that the phenomenon of global climate change could be completely stopped and a slow reversal process was set into motion.

The poster did not fail to mention the price of this late realization by humans. Before 2022, humans polluted the planet indiscriminately and did not change their ways even after knowing the price to be paid in the near future. And by the time they realized the seriousness of the matter at hand, the impact of their actions had already caused the sea level to rise and engulf island nations such as the Maldives, the Seychelles, Sri Lanka, Britain and many more. While all the humans living on these islands had been given asylum by the United Nations in countries like India, China, the United States (US/USA), France and Australia, there had been no way to protect the local flora and fauna.

Large mammals had suffered the most. Polar bears, elephants and giant blue whales had become extinct, now existing only in photos and videos. Even smaller animals like frogs and freshwater fish suffered badly. The dwindling of these animals spelled great news for insects—especially mosquitoes, which quickly evolved into much bigger pests. These were called 'super-moskos'; up to 6 centimetres long, they attacked humans at night-time. Their bite was laden with neurotoxins, which caused widespread disease in humans and animals. The only way to keep them away was through a low-frequency sound device, which most humans always wore around their necks or as armbands.

Earth had lost a lot before humans realized the need to use technology not to consume more but to consume sustainably.

While Ankit was immersed in the article, his mind filled with thoughts of how these heavy polar bears had to have swum in icy waters, a rather cold voice rang out.

'Mr Ankit, the President wishes to see you now. But only you. There is a problem.'

Rita turned, confused. 'What is the problem?'

Ankit froze. His mind immediately went to the illegal object he was carrying in his baggage, which he had deposited at the security counter. Slowly, he followed the guard who had come to lead him away.

A couple of minutes later, the President of India and Earth stepped in. He was a tall, lean man, who briskly walked to his seat. He motioned Ankit to sit in front of him. Ankit's gaze was already downward, almost making him look guilty.

The President said, 'Ankit, what is this?'

Ankit looked up. The President was holding the CD case. They had obviously found it in his bag. A shudder of terror ran down his spine as he began to sweat.

'Sir . . . Sir . . . I am so sorry,' he mumbled. Tears began to roll down his cheeks.

'But why? You know this is a crime! And for what? We found nothing but a birthday video in this! You know that you can be deported to Mars and jailed there for years for this!' The President was getting impatient.

This was turning out to be one bad trip.

'No, sir! Please save me. I am sorry. I did not mean to steal data.' Ankit was sobbing.

'Explain yourself or we will arrest you,' said the guard behind him. He sounded angry.

The President shot him a look, indicating that he should tone it down.

Ankit was choking on his tears by now. He was scared, but more than that, he was afraid that his lifelong plan was about to be destroyed. He thought that the best course of action would be to come clean and be honest. So he began.

'Sir, I stole this old data only for one thing—my mother's voice.'

'What?' The President seemed to be amused by this.

'Sir, the girl whose birthday clip you saw on the CD is my mother. I found this CD in a box of old, discarded items, and kept it. My entire motivation of climbing Olympus Mons was to win this trip with my mother. I wanted to meet the company that designed the humanoid . . . the humanoid that holds the memories of my mother. The company once told me that if I could bring them the original voice of my mother, they would be able to programme it into the humanoid.'

Ankit paused to clear his throat and wipe his cheeks.

'Sir, I just want to hear my mother's voice. I don't remember hearing it, ever. I just want to hear my mother speak . . . Forgive me, please.'

'Oh, I see.' President Singh frowned. Though touched by this tale, he was not sure what to do. He was still bound by the rules. On the one hand, Ankit had clearly broken the law by smuggling old data, but on the other, he had an understandable reason for doing so.

While the President was pondering, the guards behind Ankit were getting ready to arrest him. They were sure Ankit would not be spared. Eerie silence hung over the room, the only sound being the soft sobs coming from Ankit.

'Young man,' finally, the President spoke.

Ankit looked up.

'You have committed a huge mistake. I cannot ignore it.'

The guards moved in closer.

'But . . .' The President took a deep breath as he signalled the guards to stand back. 'I see why you did it. So here is what I am going to do.'

He was about to give his verdict. Ankit's attention was pinned to his words.

'I will let you go back to Mars as scheduled. But this CD-ROM will be confiscated by me and destroyed as per the norms. You will not get it back. I will not speak of this incident anywhere, and I suggest, for your own well-being, that you keep quiet about it as well. I cannot protect you if this goes to the media and becomes public. Then I will be forced to arrest you, and you will be in jail, young man.' His words were cold. 'For three full years,' he further warned.

For Ankit, little choice remained. His lifelong dream was shattered. The CD-ROM that he had long cherished like a priceless treasure was about to be destroyed. He was lucky to get off free, for he could have easily landed in prison and lost everything he'd ever worked for. Yet he could only feel dejected at his fate.

The President rose. 'This case is closed. You may leave.' Saying this, he left.

Ankit wiped his tears. The guards escorted him back to the Durbar Hall, where Rita was waiting. On his way out, he asked them to lead him to the bathroom, where he washed his face and put on a fake smile. He had failed the ultimate quest, but he did not want his mother to know about his sorrow.

• • •

18 January 2056
0900 hours
Mars

Almost half a year had passed since Ankit's trip to Planet Earth.

'*Trinnggg* . . . Time to wake up, Ankit. It is your birthday!'

Ankit jerked awake. Rita's voice was not the same coarse one he was used to. He'd heard a voice that was much softer, much more human, one that echoed with love.

'Happy birthday, son!'

Ankit jumped off the bed. He was thrilled by what he had just heard. He rubbed his eyes. It was definitely coming from Rita, aka MOTMARS!

'Is that you, Mom? I mean . . . is that your voice?' he shouted with joy.

'Yes, son! It is me. I am so excited that you can finally hear me.'

Ankit raced towards her and hugged her tightly. Rita extended her metallic arms and closed them around him. Ankit was crying; she could feel the tears on her shoulder pad.

'But how did it happen?'

'Son, someone wants to grant you a special birthday wish. This email will explain it all.' She extended the touchpad to him.

Ankit grabbed it and started reading.

Dear Ankit,

Happy birthday.

That day when we met, I was deeply touched by your predicament. You risked all your fame of being the first human on Olympus Mons to hear your mother's voice. I could not forget or ignore the love you showed for your mother.

We humans have thrived on compassion, love and sacrifice. Rita deserves to have her voice back. You deserve to hear your mother speak.

After you left Earth, I got a special sanction from the United Nations to use the old CD-ROM for data extraction. This was sent to the company that made MOTMARS. It took us a few months to extract all the data from this old storage device. Boy, I wonder how people in 2019 survived with these unreliable devices!

But our engineers managed to create a complete voice map of Rita. And at the stroke of midnight, on your birthday, we upgraded Rita with this new voice map.

I hope this gift from me and Planet Earth brings you great joy and comfort.

There is no machine, no artificial intelligence and no data more powerful than human love and compassion. You taught us a new lesson.

Yours,
President Ravi Singh
Planet Earth

Introduction

Great scientists are always inspired by great purpose. Usually, the seeds of such a sense of purpose are sown early, during one's childhood or youth, and this acts as a beacon that guides all their actions throughout their lives. Their purpose may come from inspirational people they meet or from the seemingly unsurmountable difficulties they face. Even though this kind of inspiration often strikes by sheer accident, it is as if these great minds are always waiting for an opportunity to come their way.

Let me take you through the story of three of the greatest minds humankind has ever seen—their life struggles, their friendships as well as their rivalries and a tale of ultimate revenge. It is a story of how fate connected these three men, made them unique and registered their names in the pages of history forever.

A lifetime of struggle and the falling apple

In a remote village in England, called Woolsthorpe-by-Colsterworth, on the particularly cold Christmas night of 1642, a boy was born. This boy's life began with a cruel twist of fate, for his father had died two months before his birth. Thus the little boy grew up never knowing his father's love. His mother, Hannah, was under deep stress. She fought hard to raise her child but soon lost hope. When the boy was three years old, she gave up on him and moved away, leaving him in the care of his grandmother, Margery. And so the boy was stumped yet again by cruel fate; he had never seen his father and was now abandoned by his own mother.

He became a loner, barely had any friends and rarely talked to anyone. But he used his loneliness to his advantage—as a space to let his imagination wander. He tried to figure out how everything around him worked. He would attend the local school, come home for lunch and then go to the meadows and fields to observe the Sun, the sky, rainbows and trees. He would make mental notes about everything he saw in nature. Science, arising out of his imagination, became his best friend—and together they strived to better understand the world and how it worked. They would remain best friends for life.

However, often in silence, he still missed his mother. On his twelfth birthday, while he was away in the fields as usual, he saw his grandmother running towards him. Then he received news that swept him off his feet.

'Hannah is back. Your mother is back! Isaac! Your mother is back! Come home!' she repeated.

Yes! This is the story of young Isaac Newton.

After hearing this news, the young boy raced down the road to reach home, and hugged his mother. As he was embracing his long-lost mother, from the corner of his eye he saw a strange man and three young children. His mother released him from her embrace and told him that the stranger was his stepfather. She had remarried and started a new family. Newton's joy turned to ashes; his mother had come back but she was not the same to him any more.

Newton reunites with his mother

Isaac despised his new father, and the feeling was mutual. As a result, he started spending even more time away from home, in the embrace of nature and science. His mother wanted him to be a farmer, something he vowed never to become.

Time passed. Soon Newton started living in his own imaginary world. Some thought him crazy and others opined that the tragedies of his life had turned him into a private person, isolated from the world. Though Newton did not get great grades in school, he was lucky to get admission into Trinity College at the prestigious University of Cambridge in June 1661 with the help of his uncle, William Ayscough. He was admitted as a subsizar—a student whose fees were waived and, in return, they were expected to take on duties in the kitchen or for the upkeep of the college.

As a subsizar, the young man took up a job to pay for his tuition. He worked as a personal assistant to a wealthy man and made just enough to cover his education. Even at Trinity College, he was not a particularly bright student and struggled with nearly every subject. And young Isaac still did not make any friends, remaining distant and very often locked in his room. Clearly no one knew that in that dull boy lay one of the greatest scientific minds the world would ever see. Imagination in isolation was his greatest tool.

By 1665, at the age of twenty and still in college, Newton made his first discovery while poring over books and his notes.

He simplified the binomial theorem (something that is taught in class ten or so), which evolved into calculus, unravelling the mathematics of differentiation and integration. It was in this year that he completed his bachelor's degree (BA). He aimed to complete his master's (MA) soon.

But, sadly, tragedy struck again. The Great Plague ravaged England in 1665, and Trinity College was closed as a precautionary measure for two full years. All of Europe lived in fear of the deadly plague, which killed hundreds of thousands of people, and Newton, too, was forced to go back to his village. It was during these two years, in the isolation of his village, that he learnt by self-education. He worked on calculus, optics and—the most famous of his all works—gravity.

Newton's fallen apple

It was during this time, in 1666, while pondering about science under a tree, that Newton saw an apple fall to the ground, and thus the laws of gravity were revealed to humankind. Years later, the same laws would go on to define the motion of stars and planets, starting a new age of science.

The next year, in 1667, when he returned to Trinity College, Newton flourished as a successful academician, now having completed his BA and aiming to finish his MA. His binomial theory had already made him quite well known and now, with the understanding of gravity, Newton was almost a celebrity in Trinity College. When he finally completed his MA, in 1668, he was elected as Fellow of the Royal Society (FRS), a group comprising the best scientists of the time, who worked under the direct patronage of the king of England. Other members of the fellowship include Robert Boyle (Boyle's law tells us about the relationship between pressure and volume), Francis Bacon (he developed the theory of scientific methodology that was based on experimental observations), Christopher Wren (the architect of modern London), Edmond Halley (remember the famous Halley's comet?) and, of course, Robert Hooke (Hooke's law of elasticity relates the force exerted by an elastic spring with its extension).

We will come back to Newton in a while, but now I must talk about our second character.

Another genius

Nobody knows what Robert Hooke looked like, as no known portrait or statue of him has survived. Anything you find in books or on the Internet is an artistic recreation of his appearance based on descriptions by people who knew or saw him. Some say Hooke had a crooked and pale face with protruding eyes. We are not sure of this, but what we *do* know is that Robert Hooke was the most sought-after celebrity scientist of his time—and everyone wanted this genius at their party. He was said to be a 'strange genius'.

Born in 1635, Hooke was seven years older than Newton. By 1657, at the age of twenty-two, he had made a name for himself in the scientific world. He tweaked the existing design and workings of the watch and added to it a spring balance, thereby correcting an inaccuracy. Hooke perfected the watch. He was the man who enabled humanity to now track time to the exact second.

In 1660, he made a startling discovery: the law of elasticity. It related the force exerted while pulling an elastic spring to the stretching of the said spring (or a rubber band). Even today, this law is used in nearly all technologies—construction safety, surgery, space, springs, automobile shockers and countless such areas.

Robert Hooke

Five years later, in 1665, just as Newton was about to discover gravity, Hooke moved to a different field. He tried new experiments. He placed thin slices of cork under his microscope and observed them for days. He saw strange compartments in them, and drew what he observed. These sections or compartments reminded him of the bare walls of the rooms in which monks lived, so he called them cells. Thus began Hooke's quest to understand what all living beings are made up of. The scientist had opened a new avenue, which eventually shaped modern biology and medicine.

Now it is time to introduce the third and final great character in this story—Edmond Halley. But before that, we need to return to our friend Newton for a while.

Friendship, rivalry and Newton's nine sheets of gravity

As you know from a previous section, in 1667, a year after the Great Plague ended, Newton returned to college to do his MA. It was during this time that he also decided to give shape to his fascination for one of nature's most beautiful phenomena—the rainbow. Hence he started working on optics. Remember the prism experiment you probably performed in school, wherein light from one end of the triangular prism comes out from the other as an array of colours—from violet to red? Newton was perhaps the first person to perform and understand the process! In a way, that reserved boy, who had a difficult and lonely childhood, eventually discovered colours!

And this is where Newton crossed paths with Hooke, in 1671. And it was not a pleasant encounter. Hooke vehemently criticized Newton on some of his ideas about light and how colours are formed. To be honest, Hooke was a little too harsh in his analysis. Terribly insulted by Hooke's sharp disapproval, Newton, who was already a recluse, withdrew from public lectures. He isolated himself completely and withdrew into his shell of silence even further, while continuing to work on his ideas and theories, of course. Hooke's punch had thrown Newton off-balance. Nobody saw him for years afterwards; only his scientific papers told the world about his work and existence. However, interestingly, Hooke and Newton, despite not being on good terms, still read each other's scientific papers and regularly wrote letters to each other about their observations.

Eight years passed. By 1679, almost a decade later, Newton returned to the apple and started giving the concept of gravity a proper theoretical shape. Now Newton and Hooke started to discuss gravity in the letters they exchanged. In these letters, Hooke just wrote general facts and nothing new about gravity. This would later become a source of dispute between the two great minds.

During his new research, Newton started applying his theory of gravity to bodies beyond Earth. He now applied the principle to planets in the galaxy and their motion around the Sun. Around three years before this, it had already been established that planets went around the Sun in elliptical orbits. But the reason, or the 'why's, were not yet known. Around 1684, Newton unravelled this mystery by applying a very simple principle: 'Gravity decreases with the square of the distance between two bodies.' And so the law of gravity was born.

Newton's principle meant that if you increased the distance between the Sun and Earth twofold, the gravity would decrease by a factor of two multiplied by twofold—becoming one-fourth of the original gravity. This simple equation solved the mystery of why planets revolve in orbits around the Sun and how the Sun orbits the galaxy. This law of Newton remains unchanged till date.

Though Newton had made one of the most vital discoveries of human civilization, he did not want to publish this game-changing theory. After his last encounter with Hooke, he did not want to be publicly ridiculed again—by Hooke or anyone else. Then there was another problem: even if he wanted to publish his findings in a book, he'd need money to invest in it, which he didn't have. After all, back then, there were no publishing houses like we have today—like the one that made this very book and enabled you to read it. And so this game-changing law of science, handwritten in just nine sheets of paper, gathered dust in a drawer of Newton's immensely cluttered desk.

The year 1687 arrived. Three years had passed and Newton had remained out of public view. On the other side, all this while, Hooke did not advance any research on gravity and, with Newton keeping silent, the fate of gravity itself hung in the balance.

Enter Edmond Halley

Halley was a remarkable scientific mind and a great person at heart. He is renowned for not only his own works but more so for his efforts behind enabling others to take forward their research, often at his own monetary expense. Halley was also one of the very few friends Isaac Newton had. In 1687, Newton shared the nine sheets of gravity with Halley, who was immediately interested to find out how far Newton had got in explaining gravity. He beseeched Newton, 'Please work on this further and publish it as a book.'

'I do not have the resources to print it!' replied Newton.

'Don't worry, Newton. I will bear the cost of your book printing from my own pocket,' Halley reassured his nervous friend.

'And what if Hooke criticizes me again?' Newton was still in doubt.

'I will take care of it. You focus on your theory of gravity.'

Halley had just taken on a huge financial liability and risked souring his relationship with the very well-known scientist Robert Hooke.

Newton finally wrote the book, which, till date, remains one of the most significant leaps in the journey of science. It is called *Philosophiae Naturalis Principia Mathematica*. Interestingly, Newton was an Englishman, but his book was in Latin. Remember the three laws of motion? They were first expressed in this book. In this, the third law states, 'Every action has an equal and opposite reaction.' Newton's book prompted a strange reaction from our second character, Robert Hooke. He made rather baseless allegations against Newton, stating that it was, in fact, his letters about gravity in 1679 that Newton had copied to write the book. It was a serious allegation against Newton. It was only when Edmond Halley boldly faced Hooke and demanded evidence to support his charges that Hooke backed down. However, he still remained bitter towards both Newton and Halley. Had it not been for Halley's constant effort and investments, Newton and his laws of gravity and the three laws of motion would have never come to light.

But it's not that Halley himself was any less of an achiever. I am sure you have heard of Halley's comet—the most famous comet, which appears every seventy-five years. Interestingly, Halley did not really discover it, or even see it. He just predicted it!

During his research on comets, Halley pored over book after book and concluded, 'The comet seen in 1531, 1607 and 1682 were all the same comet returning to Earth's sky. Thus I predict the same comet will return in 1758.' He, a scientist, had made a prophecy that no astrologer would dare to, risking his reputation on the exactly timed occurrence of a heavenly event. Halley passed away in 1752, six years before he could actually see his prediction come true. But this prediction served as a source of inspiration to people, and the famous comet was named after him.

Edmond Halley spots Halley's comet

Humanity has always been intrigued by comets; they have instilled fear in almost all cultures—the Chinese, Indians, Babylonians, Europeans, Egyptians and Mayans. All these civilizations were terrified of spotting comets. To them it meant the death of kings, famine, disease and war. Due to these fears, ancient civilizations began tracking comets, and it is safe to say that they paused all their daily duties and activities whenever one appeared in the sky, to safeguard and ward off the 'evil' it would bring upon them. And even centuries later, countless predictions continued to be made.

And so, in one stroke, Halley had beaten these 'comet-tellers' or astrologers at their own game of prediction. The industry of false fearmongering linked to comets came to a screeching halt.

The last time we saw Halley's comet was in 1986. Ask your parents if they witnessed it—and, yes, don't miss seeing it in 2061!

A comet is not the only thing that Halley discovered. Halley was the one who discovered the pattern of Earth's magnetism while on his sea voyages. Even today, we use the magnetic map of Earth drawn by him. He also perfected the diving bell (which is a bell-shaped device that enables a human being to stay underwater for hours) and started a new technology industry of salvaging lost ship parts.

The ultimate revenge

Remember when, at the beginning, I said there was no known portrait of Robert Hooke? Well, that was not entirely true. There was, in fact, one portrait of him hanging alongside the pictures of all the other presidents and leaders of the Royal Society. It remained there until it mysteriously vanished one day, never to be found again. Can you guess who was widely thought to be responsible for the disappearance of Hooke's picture?

Isaac Newton!

Of course, nobody knew for sure. But what do you think?

● ● ●

Science and technology are born when excellent ideas meet opportunity and challenge. The greatest products around us, things we use effortlessly, have all got a history behind them. Every time you see airplanes, remember how many humans perished in order to give wings to us. The smallest bulb will remind you of the story of the 1000 failed bulbs that were made as the inventor, Thomas Edison, toiled on, unwavering in his determination to light up the world. The greatest researcher of radiation, Marie Curie—the first person to win two Nobel Prizes—eventually lost her life because of having carried radioactive substances in her pockets. Jonas Salk, the inventor of the polio vaccine, tested the first shot on himself and afterwards refused to patent (claim exclusive rights of production and sale) the vaccine, forgoing the chance to gain millions of dollars because he wanted his scientific work to benefit mankind. Even the 2005 Nobel Prize winner Barry Marshall drank a bottle of the bacteria that causes gastritis. He soon got this deadly disease, then used himself as a test subject to assess his newfound antibiotic, which proved successful. Many believe that, in 1941, the famous German physicist Werner Heisenberg knew how to build the atomic bomb but chose not to reveal the secret to Hitler and the German Nazi government, since he feared they would indiscriminately use it to wipe off cities during the Second World War, and thus saved countless lives.

One of the by-products of a life spent exploring the sciences is, of course, great prestige, honour and the ability to change the course of humankind. But it also requires a lot of patience, sacrifice and concern for the larger global good. It needs the ability to make adversity your friend. Imagine, if Newton had not turned the sadness of his childhood abandonment into a chance to explore nature, he would never have known how everything works on Earth. Had he not confined himself to the meadows and orchards or studied the rainbow, he would not have known how prisms work or seen the apple fall—which led him to discover one of the most crucial theories of science. If Edmond Halley had not sacrificed his personal goals or encouraged a reclusive Newton and egged him on to write *Philosophiae Naturalis Principia Mathematica*, the laws of motion would never have been postulated.

Remember, great scientists are very powerful as they can change the course of humankind with the knowledge they create and share. But they need to be great human beings first, so that their knowledge is deployed for good and not misused.

Now, let us start our journey to discover the emerging technologies of tomorrow.

CHAPTER 1

AUTOMOBILE TECHNOLOGY

Can you guess the number of motor vehicles presently running on the roads in the world?

Over 1.2 billion!

This amounts to one vehicle for every six humans. It includes cars, buses and trucks of all sizes. Roughly fifty years ago, in the 1960s, the number of motor vehicles on the roads was 1,26,000, which is almost one-sixth of what it is today. The boom in the automobile industry has had many effects on human civilization. Human mobility has increased from an average of 4 kilometres a day in the 1850s to over 40 kilometres a day today. Countries like the USA see an average mileage of 20,000 kilometres a year for every car, with users spending close to 4.5 hours a day on average in their cars.[1] This means that besides their homes and offices, people in many countries are spending most of their time in their cars than anywhere else. The world today has about 40 million kilometres of road network on which these wheels run. This distance is enough to go around Earth, along its equator, more than 100 times. Or it can be calculated as ten times the distance between Earth and its Moon!

But this advancement has drawbacks too. To power these vehicles, we burn over 4.5 billion litres of fuel every day, which is about 2,60,000 oil tanker trucks put together! And as we burn this fuel in vehicles, it produces 10 billion kilogrammes of CO_2, which pollutes the environment—again, on a daily basis. Transportation alone contributes to over one-third of the world's greenhouse gas emissions. And over 1.2 million people die annually in car-related accidents. But one cannot refute that cars have given us mobility and comfort like nothing else, and generated employment too. In fact, it has helped realize humankind's dream of fast locomotion.

There is no single person who can be credited with the invention of the car. Perhaps the first form of a vehicle was the wooden sledge that was invented about 9000 years ago. Sledges are still used today. They do not have wheels; they just slide. And, similarly, back then it was perhaps drawn by humans or pulled by the first animal we domesticated—the dog. It took an extraordinarily long time for wheels to be invented. We spent another 4000 years on these cumbersome and difficult-to-drag sledges. So how did humans miss out on this vital invention for so many years?

The answer is simple: wheels didn't exist in nature. The natural world has been the source of inspiration for most of our inventions throughout history. For instance, the birds soaring in the skies inspired us to invent the airplane. But the invention of the wheel was born purely out of human imagination. It is 100 per cent a *Homo sapiens* invention.

In fact, the first wheel was invented not as the keystone of transport but for pottery about 5500 years ago. It took almost another 500 years for this potter's wheel to be tied to an axle and made part of the first chariots in Mesopotamia (modern-day Iraq). The colossal pyramids of Egypt, built during the time the earliest wheels were being invented, about 4500 years ago, were also constructed without the knowledge of wheels. Imagine moving a 10,000 kg stone block across several hundred kilometres by dragging it along the ground! A typical pyramid would have taken more than 20 lakh (2 million) such stone blocks to build, which had to be dragged and accumulated for over a period of twenty years! Interestingly, the Egyptians used the pulley, which is quite similar to a wheel, to lift stone blocks up hundreds of metres to build these wonders. They also used pulleys to store pottery, made on the potter's wheel, inside the pyramid.

However, somehow, the wheel was not recognized as an integral part of transport so early on. When the chariots did finally come about, animal power was used to pull them, and the same was the case with wagons (for which horses were mostly used). Eventually these horse-drawn wagons were replaced by steam-engine cars in the early 1800s. However, the first truly commercial steam-powered vehicles came only around the 1900s. They were large and clumsy, and caused external combustion—which means that the fuel was burnt outside the engine, and that heat (often as steam) was carried in the engine to produce locomotion.

Then came three great inventors and technologists who completely transformed automobile technology.

● ● ●

In 1861, a German engineer called Nikolaus August Otto (1832–1891) invented the first internal combustion (IC) engine. Internal combustion engines are those wherein the fuel is burnt inside the engine. This helps regulate the heat flow better, reduces losses and increases the efficiency of the engine. Today, all petrol-, diesel- and gas-based cars use IC engines; but about 150 years ago, it was an unheard-of concept.

Otto lost his father the same year he was born. He lived in so much poverty in his early days that he was pulled out of school and pushed into a job. Despite lacking higher education, Otto was passionate about machines, especially those that had something to do with locomotion. His dream was to create a cleaner and more efficient engine, which would drive the cars of the future. He did not like the clumsy cars of his time, which burnt fuel—often coal and wood—in open flames, like a giant kettle, to power the wheels.

Otto's first four-stroke IC engine differed from the steam engine. In his mechanism, a mixture of fuel and air was compressed inside the engine. When ignited, the expanding gases exerted force, which moved the piston and the wheel.

Initially, Nikolaus Otto's brother and business partner, William Otto, joined him in designing this IC engine. However, this model was not successful, and Otto's first engine broke down within a few minutes of operation. This defeat discouraged William so much that he decided to abandon the project, leaving Otto alone to struggle with the invention.

Otto had to find a new partner (and funder) for his failing project and revive the IC engine. He found financial help in rich individuals who backed his ideas, and he remade the engine. He got a new business partner—Eugen Langen, who was the son of a rich sugar industrialist. With the help of Langen, Otto improved the failed engine in 1861 and, in three years, finally achieved success. By this time, in 1864, Otto had made business links with industries and prominent contemporary mechanics who had shown interest in this new engine that burnt fuel internally. Nevertheless, it would still take Otto another ten years to increase the reliability of his engine and make it really worth buying. In fact, even until 1875, he was selling only about 600 engines a year.

But, like all technologies, the IC engine started becoming more efficient, and by the year 1876 sales began to increase. In the next seventeen years, more than 50,000 internal combustion engines invented by Otto were sold. The German had made a name for himself, and even today, the four-stroke engine (used in almost all modern cars) operates on a four-step cycle called the Otto cycle.

But in those days, IC engines were hardly used in automobiles; rather, it was mostly industries such as cotton mills and paper factories that were buying these engines. The reason for this was that Otto's engine used coal gas and subsequent engines used petrol (gasoline). As you can imagine, coal gas was difficult to store in a moving automobile, compared to liquid petrol.

• • •

Otto's engine was a great innovation, but it was still not good enough to replace the prevailing steam engines. The first generation of IC engines, which ran on petrol, coal gas and even gunpowder, were woefully inefficient as they converted less than 10 per cent of the heat to useful mechanical energy. In comparison, the most efficient cars today reach up to 35–40 per cent. In addition to that, the engine was very unstable and did not operate smoothly. Therefore, even with Otto's engine around, until the end of the nineteenth century, horses were the primary 'vehicles' on the roads, with the exception of a few steam-powered cars chugging along slowly. A city like Calcutta (modern-day Kolkata) in India, with about 5,00,000 people back then, would have had about 80,000 horses for its transport. Imagine the stench in the city when each of these horses coated the streets with 15 kilogrammes of manure every day—and about 4 litres of urine!

This filth in the towns worried a twenty-something German engineer, Rudolf Diesel. Hearing about the low efficiency of IC engines in a lecture, Diesel decided to dedicate his life to changing the locomotion industry of the world—and he concluded this by the end of the discourse! Diesel realized that Otto's engine had a fundamental problem: It was mixing air and fuel and then compressing them together before igniting it. Often if the compression was too much, it led to premature ignition, which made the engine unstable.

By 1894, Diesel worked out a new design that compressed only air. Air was compressed in a small space to a high degree, and this was enough to ignite the fuel when it was injected. This way he was able to completely control the ignition process. This also ensured that the engine worked smoothly. Even today, diesel engines are designed this way and, unlike petrol engines, do not need any spark plug. A higher compression factor means a higher price for diesel engines, but in the long run they tend to be more economical.

Diesel also discovered another advantage. His engine could use fuels that were heavier than petrol, such as oils made from vegetable and other plants like corn. That was Diesel's dream: cars fuelled from farms. But another heavier fuel was derived from fossil fuels, which was discovered only after Diesel had died. This heavier fossil fuel needed less processing and hence was cheaper to manufacture. It later came to be known as 'diesel' after the inventor. A cheaper fuel, lower emission of fumes and a lower risk of explosion made Diesel's engine an essential commodity, one that was in prime demand by the military. By the early 1900s, the first submarines had started using it as well.

You might assume that, after his scientific achievement, Rudolf Diesel lived a life of riches and fame. However, that was not the case—at least not the part about the riches. His early engines were not without problems, and several of them were returned to him by customers who demanded refunds. This drove Diesel into deep financial crisis, from which he could never recover. It is quite ironic that an industrial inventor who developed the most widely used engine of our time—the engine that runs the modern economy—made so little money for himself. Rudolf Diesel saw his engine taking over the world during his lifetime but was depressed by the mounting debts he incurred. Sadly, on 29 September 1913, he took his own life by jumping off a ship into the ocean. Tragically, Diesel could never witness the commercial success of his invention. By the 1920s, his engine was running the world's trucks. By the 1930s, it was powering trains. By the year 1940, one-quarter of the global sea trade was facilitated by Rudolf Diesel's engine.

There is one more interesting anecdote about Rudolf Diesel: He never intended to run his engine on diesel, or, for that matter, on any fossil fuel at all. He was opposed to the idea of running machines on fuel dug up from the earth. His vision was to run his engine on vegetable oil. This would benefit the farmers, who would grow nuts and crops that could be converted to fuel. In fact, in 1900, he made a model that would run on peanut oil—the first biofuel engine in the world. While the machine was successful, sadly, a cheaper fossil fuel soon replaced the biofuel intended for this engine. Had Diesel's vision come true, the cars of today would not be running on petrol and diesel and fuel stations would be selling vegetable oil. Peanuts would have been the fuel of our time, and the phrase 'for peanuts' would have meant something entirely different!

• • •

While the engines were improving, cars were still beyond the reach of the masses. Imagine an everyday, low-power car, with a low level of acceleration and only four gears, having a price tag of Rs 40–50 lakh! You would probably not find this a good deal today, but it was something like this in the early 1900s, when cars first started becoming a reality. In 1907, a car fitted with IC engines would have cost about $5,00,000 or Rs 4 crore.[*]

The credit for making cars more affordable and hence an everyday comfort goes to Henry Ford of the United States of America. He established his company, Ford Motor Company, in the early 1900s with a single intent—providing quality cars to people at affordable prices. By 1903, the first Ford Model A came out. Manufacturing was very different back then. Every single car was considered a separate piece, with three to four people working all day on one car. If a part of a Model A car broke down, it could not be replaced by another Model A's similar part, as there was no interchangeability of car parts.

---

[*] All prices are in today's monetary value.

The car would then go back to the factory, where a custom part would be made and fitted. This was a frustrating cycle.

Ford realized he needed to transform this process of making cars. By 1908, Model A had evolved to Model T. This new model was cheap, strong and reliable. It cost about $21,000 to own a car (about Rs 15 lakh). Ford got so many bulk orders for this new model that he had to set up multiple new plants to meet the demand. So this is when the real automobile revolution happened. Henry Ford decided to try a fresh trick in manufacturing technology. In 1910, at his new plant in Michigan, Ford changed the method of a dedicated team assembling a single car from start to finish. He invented something called assembly line manufacturing, which is used till date to manufacture not just cars and other vehicles, but also mobile phones, televisions, washing machines, for packaging food . . . In fact, nearly all consumer goods are made using this method.

Ford realized that the entire process of making a car from scratch involved eighty-four steps. Model T came with a pioneering feature—interchangeable parts. This made any one Model T car exactly similar to another car of the same model. Ford used this aspect to his advantage. He made a manufacturing plant, where the chassis (the sturdy metallic frame of a car, on which the engine, outer body, etc. are placed) of Model T cars moved along a 150-foot conveyor belt with 140 people working along it. As the chassis moved, each of the 140 workers applied their specific parts to the chassis. Other workers fetched additional parts for these primary assemblers so that they did not run out. This significantly improved the speed of production. And since each worker soon became an expert at doing his piece of work, the overall quality of the cars improved dramatically. Henry Ford had just revolutionized the modern manufacturing process. His new plant was churning out a new car every ninety-three minutes! Compare that to a car a day!

As a result, the eventual price of a Model T car dropped to less than $3500 (Rs 2,50,000). The workers' wages shot up with the additional profits, and for the first time they were able to earn enough to afford a car themselves. In the next fifteen years, more than 1.5 crore Model T cars were sold, making it the highest-selling car of its time.

If Rudolf Diesel made little money for his work, Henry Ford had a completely different financial destiny. He rose to become one of the richest men of all times, and in today's terms his net worth was $188 billion (thrice as much as Bill Gates')!

The future of automobiles

Are you a fan of Batman? Do you follow the comics, and have you seen the Batman movie called *The Dark Knight*? If you have, then you must have noticed that the superhero owns many innovative gadgets and drives around in a cool machine called the Batmobile. This 15-foot-long, 500-horsepower armoured vehicle is strong enough to break through walls and has, besides excellent agility, the ability to lift off the ground. In its attack mode, it has two auto-cannons in the front and a small rocket launcher. In short, the Batmobile is a one-of-a-kind, state-of-the-art military vehicle and counted among the most interesting automobiles to exist in fiction.

Or is it? In this case, reality may be closer to fiction than you might imagine. Take the world's fastest armoured troop carrier, the Russian-made ZiL Punisher. It is especially designed to run on plains, snow and grass with equal efficiency. The engine of the Punisher is even better than Batman's favourite car—it has 730 horsepower. It is bulletproof; even an AK-47 cannot damage it. It is also mine-blast-resistant. And while the Batmobile can usually carry only Batman, the Punisher can carry up to ten soldiers and protect them from gunfire. The Punisher weighs a whopping 11,000 kilogrammes, almost as much as a bus. Yet it can go up to a speed of over 150 kilometres per hour. What is the price of this real-life Batmobile? It's about Rs 1.5 crore. Of course, you cannot own one yet as the Russian military does not sell it to anyone!

This is one possible future of automobile technology, wherein you can be expected to design the next generation of military vehicles that are bigger, safer, more rugged and multipurpose.

Let us discuss some other automobile trends of the future.

What was first designed by Otto, developed further by Diesel and brought to the ordinary people by Ford—the IC-engine-based compact, cheap (relatively speaking) car—is now facing its biggest threat: electric cars. You may have heard of cars powered by electricity. If you are reading this book in its publication year, 2019, the chances of you owning an electric car are very slim. But if you are reading this book in 2024 or later, there is a strong likelihood that you already own or have recently exchanged your IC-engine petrol or diesel car for a new electrical vehicle.

An automobile that is propelled by electric motors is called an electric car. The energy used by these vehicles for locomotion is stored in rechargeable batteries. In 2017, the total number of electric cars on the roads and in showrooms was over 2 million—about 2 per cent of the total number of vehicles. Of course, this share is rapidly increasing. Do you know which country has the maximum share of electric cars worldwide?

It is Norway! Over one-third of the total number of cars sold in Norway are electric. India is aiming to sell 10 million, or 1 crore, electric cars by 2030. Now, if you are planning to be an automobile designer or technologist, this is one fact you must keep in mind, shouldn't you? Also, several nations that lack petroleum are planning to ban all forms of petrol and diesel. For instance, the United Kingdom (UK) and France plan to ban these fuels by 2040. In fact, the biggest petroleum companies of the world, ExxonMobil and British Petroleum (now called BP), have estimated that there will be around 100 to 250 million electric cars in the world by then. After almost 150 years of dominating the way we've travelled, petrol and diesel engines will almost certainly bid us goodbye.

So how do these electric cars perform, you ask? Well, let us deal with that in a later section of this chapter. For now let us move on to something even more exciting.

Have you watched the movie *Transformers*? Do you recall that yellow robot in it? Remember its name? Yes, it was Bumblebee. Bumblebee is an Autobot transformer, which is a shape-shifting robot—it can operate like a human or a robot (only it's much taller and stronger), or it can change into an amazing yellow Chevrolet Camaro (or a Beetle, if you read the older comics). This Bumblebee, the car, carries its owner and lead character of the movie, Sam Witwicky, around his town and college. The catch is, Bumblebee usually takes control of the car while Sam just sits in the driver's seat, holding the steering wheel. So it is Bumblebee that goes about undertaking the tasks of regulating speed and direction, avoiding collisions and, occasionally, taking on evil Megatrons.

What Bumblebee does as a car is essentially similar to the self-driving cars of today and the future. Self-driving cars are also known as autonomous cars or robotic cars. The earliest experiments in self-driving go as far back as 1977 in Japan. By early 2017, Audi's A8 model was able to automatically drive at a speed of up to 60 kmph. However, it still needed a driver in the driver's seat, 'just in case'. But the real breakthrough in autonomous vehicles happened only towards the end of 2017, when Google announced that it had started testing a driverless car called Waymo without a backup driver in the seat. In the next few months, by the time this book was being written, in April 2018, these Waymo cars had travelled over 10 million kilometres—all without anyone in the driver's seat. Well, Bumblebee is not far away!

Essentially, self-driven cars have six levels:

- **Level 0:** These are cars that only issue warnings about collision and cannot perform any action on their own. A car-backing assistant in your everyday car is one such example.
- **Level 1, 'Hands on':** In these cars, the controls are shared between the machine and the human. Here the car can cruise on its own, but the driver needs to be constantly vigilant to take over control.
- **Level 2, 'Hands off':** Here the computer takes over the braking, accelerating and steering functions, and the driver only needs to monitor these in case the automated system fails.

- **Level 3, 'Eyes off':** Such self-driven cars allow the driver to look elsewhere, maybe watch a movie or play computer games, without watching the road. The 2018 Audi A8 is a Level 3 car.

- **Level 4, 'Mind off':** In these cars, the driver can safely go off to sleep while the car drives itself; the driver's seat can be left vacant too. Waymo cars are operating at this level. When the car needs to, it will stop, wake up the human driver with a message and alarm, and ask them to take over control or provide instructions.

- **Level 5, 'No steering wheel':** In the case of this version of self-driven cars, 100 per cent of the control will be with the machine. There will be no room for humans to take any control. The car will be like an automated taxi. This is still in test phase. The company Uber has deployed about 150 such cars on American roads. These are self-driven taxis with no driver at all, and passengers can sit in the rear. So if you are in Pittsburgh and have called a taxi from your app, chances are that the driver's name reads Computer.

Now, obviously Level 4 and Level 5 cars are still under development, and it will take some time to invent a truly self-driving car without a steering wheel. In this test phase, there have been issues, such as accidents, which will take time to resolve. Maybe you can be the one to do these tweaks!

You may wonder what makes such self-driving possible. Well, it is a combination of several sensors, such as GPS, radar, laser light sensing, odometry and computer vision. What is certain about future consumer vehicles is that they will run electrically and, in most cases, be self-driven to some extent. If this career excites you and you wish to follow in the footsteps of the icons of the modern automobile—Nikolaus Otto and Rudolf Diesel—remember these two aspects and prepare for them.

Another aspect will shape this sector in the future. But it has nothing to do with the way the car is designed, but with the way it is manufactured.

Have you heard of 3D printers? Well, it is a new kind of printer that even you can buy from Amazon.com or any other website. This printer uses a special plastic filament (or even metal) instead of ink. The 3D designs are fed into it by a computer programme, and the printer then moulds the material according to the design with perfect precision. Till 2015, it was exclusively used to make small parts, but since then, scientists have ventured into bolder and bigger objects like industrial components, parts of aircraft and drones.

Towards the end of 2015, US-based Local Motors introduced the world's first 100 per cent 3D-printed car. A small two-seater called Strati. Made from carbon-fibre-reinforced plastic, this car costs about Rs 3,00,000 and is expected to get cheaper.

Imagine how the future car showrooms will look like! They may have no cars on display but holographic images of all the different cars that exist in the world. Can you picture clipping on your Google Glass and watching a car survey, thanks to the wonders of virtual reality? Each showroom could have a 3D printer installed. You could select a model, its colour, pick an engine, add special shapes and patterns and several other customizations and pay for it using your credit card. The 3D printer will then automatically print your selected car—exactly the way you want it. In such a world, there will be fewer large automobile plants and little need to transport manufactured cars from factories to cities. Everything will be in real time, from selection and purchase to manufacturing (printing, actually) and delivery.

Thus, after more than 100 successful years of the universal way of manufacturing, the assembly lines for cars will finally halt. Finally, we will bid farewell to our third stalwart of the automotive industry—Henry Ford.

What should I do to become an expert in the automobile industry?

The automobile sector is one of the most formidable sectors to have a career in. Automobiles are not just limited to cars, but also span two-wheelers, large vehicles, transportation vehicles like trucks, and even railway engines and wagons.

An expert in automobiles should definitely have excellent knowledge of the sciences, especially the physics of motion and friction. You need to go beyond textbooks and read articles on the Internet about the latest trends in cars, especially electrical engines and the computer programmes that enable cars to self-drive. Several free car magazines are also available online, and you can find them in libraries too. These will keep you updated on the latest in the world of motion.

I cannot precisely predict everything that you may do as an expert in the automobile sector in the future, but I would expect you to be, in twenty to thirty years from now, designing cars that not only drive on the roads but are airborne as well—and perhaps also those that travel to the Moon, maybe even to Mars! Man took a very long time to discover the wheel. Are we still missing something as revolutionary as the wheel? You find out!

 ## CONVERSATIONS WITH A SCIENCE TEACHER

Which is the fastest car in the world?

One of the constant quests in the domain of cars has been the need for speed. In 1894, the world's first commercially available mass-produced car came out—the Benz Velo (and the company, Mercedes-Benz, still exists, even after all these years!). The car, which looked more like today's rickshaw, used an IC engine and could run at a speed of up to 20 kmph—a startling figure in those times.

In 1949, the 200 kmph top-speed barrier was broken for the first time by Jaguar's XK120. The company sold over 12,000 cars of this model. By 1982, the Lamborghini Countach LP500 almost scaled a top speed of 300 kmph (295 kmph, to be exact) and sold about 2000 cars of the model. The first car to break the 400 kmph limit was the Bugatti Veyron in 2005, which registered a top speed of 405 kmph and then scaled to 415 kmph in 2010. It would cost you Rs 10 crore to buy this car—though, with taxes and duties, the actual price would be more like Rs 25 crore in India. The bigger question is, where will you find the road to zoom at that 400 kmph speed?

Today, the fastest commercially available car is not American or German or Japanese but Swedish. It is the Koenigsegg Agera RS. This car has a top speed of 458 kmph. It comes with a 5000 cc engine and seven gears. It is actually cheaper than the Veyron, priced at Rs 8.4 crore (and if you were to import it to India, with taxes and duties it would cost about Rs 20 crore). Comparatively, the fastest Formula One (F1) racing car reached a speed of 413 kmph on a straight-line drive. This was done by the Honda team. You may wonder how a custom-designed F1 racing car is slower in top speed than a commercially available car. The answer is: F1 cars are designed to run on curved roads—that is how race tracks are designed. Hence their strength is in quickly accelerating and decelerating and handling road bends at relatively higher speeds—something automobile scientists call cornering.

Why do racing cars have wings on their front and back?

Formula One racing cars have wings both in the front and the rear. These are also called airfoils, and their function is similar to that of wings on an aircraft, but in reverse. While in case of an aircraft, wings provide the necessary boost for the upward lift, in a racing car the wings are curved the opposite way and hence provide downforce, forcing the car to stay on the ground even at high speeds and difficult turns. If you remove these wings from a racing car, the car will fly off every time it tries to turn at high speed.

A word of caution, do not confuse spoilers with wings, as many people tend to do. Spoilers are mounted on ordinary cars, usually at the rear, as an attachment. Spoilers are smaller in size and aren't really aerodynamically designed to provide any downforce. They just change the pattern of airflow to reduce the horizontal drag (which opposes the motion of the car) and thereby reduce fuel consumption.

Which is the heaviest vehicle ever built?

From the company Tenova TAKRAF of Germany came the world's heaviest land vehicle ever built, the Bagger 293 excavator, in 1995. This giant machine cost about $100 million to construct and took ten years to reach the roads (five years to design and manufacture, and five years to assemble). It is 96 metres tall (the Guinness World Record for the highest terrestrial vehicle). It weighs more than 14,200 tons and is of the size of a thirty-storey building. It is capable of excavating 2,40,000 tons of coal per day—the equivalent of a football field dug 30 metres (98 feet) deep. Parked in a brown coal mine in Hambach, Germany, the Bagger 293 is now awaiting the day it will again be free to roam the Earth.

Military tanks also tend to be very heavy because of their thick armour and heavy cannons. The Germans built the world's biggest tank in 1944, during the Second World War. It was the Panzer VIII Maus, which weighed about 188 tons (1,88,000 kilogrammes). It could carry more than 4200 litres of fuel in all its fuel compartments combined and run at a top speed of 20 kmph—that's less than what a bicycle can manage! Even with full fuel, the tank could only cover about 75 kilometres in one go before needing to refuel. The German army built only two such tanks.

How do electric cars operate? How do they compare with petrol or diesel cars?

We had briefly discussed electrical cars earlier in this chapter. Did you know that the very first electric car was built way back in the 1830s? This was at least forty years before the first petrol car was tested. In fact, by 1900, 38 per cent of all cars on the road were electric, with only steam cars being more in number. But then two things happened.

First, the cost of petroleum went down. This fuel offered a better way to run cars over longer distances. In a country like the USA, where trains were rare (even now passenger trains are quite few in the USA), petrol cars won over electric cars in this race for range. The second event was Henry Ford choosing to make petrol cars. Ford gave petrol cars optimum price and efficiency, and this wiped out electric cars in the early 1900s.

But then in the 1990s and onwards, there grew concern over the environmental impact of using petrol in vehicles, and electricity became cheaper with the advent of renewable sources and better transmission systems that reduced the wastage of electricity in wires. It was then that electric cars returned for their second innings.

Electric cars are simpler in design than fossil fuel cars. They essentially use a battery and electrical motors in place of the more elaborate set-up used in a petrol car, like an IC engine, a fuel tank, a carburettor, a silencer and an exhaust. The battery powers the motor, which turns the wheel.

How long can an electric car run before its battery drains out?

The range of an electric car, which is determined by the size of its battery, has historically been the limiting factor for them. The earliest cars, in the early 1900s, could run for not more than 50–60 kilometres before they would need to be recharged (which would often take hours). Once the road quality between cities improved, there was a greater emphasis on cars that could travel long distances without the need to refuel or recharge. Electric cars were beaten by petrol cars in this range race.

From the 1990s onwards, due to the increasing worry surrounding depleting underground oil reserves and steep oil prices, electric cars once again rose in research priority and market share. The best electric car, in terms of range, available today is the Tesla Model S. It has a range of 540 kilometres and a battery of about 100 kilowatt-hours (1 kilowatt-hour/kWh is what we call one unit of electrical energy. Now you can check your electricity bills!). General Motors' Bolt has a range of about 350 kilometres with a 60 kWh battery.

The battery is a major cost component in any electric car, accounting for about one-third of the total cost. The cost of these batteries, however, is on a downward curve, which is great news. In 2007, the cost of a battery was Rs 80,000 per kilowatt-hour. It came down to Rs 34,000 per kilowatt-hour in 2012 and is currently Rs 20,000 per kilowatt-hour. These prices are expected to fall below Rs 10,000 by 2020.

Can we design cars that use nuclear fuel?

During the 1940s and 1950s, with the development of nuclear-powered submarines and ships, researchers began to think of nuclear-powered cars. Fuelled by a nuclear reaction, theoretically they would release no harmful gases that could potentially cause air pollution. Even though such cars were never driven on the roads, many designers and engineers came up with prototypes and models for atomic transportation. But there were just too many conceptual problems with the design of the vehicles.

First, the powerhouse would be too small to carry out a nuclear reaction to fuel the car, unless it contained dangerous fissionable nuclear material like uranium and plutonium. Doing so would mean that one car breaking down could lead to a nuclear catastrophe and blow up the entire city!

Second, there was a problem with protecting the people inside the car from radiation. Initially engineers thought of a lightweight material that would act as a shield for the passengers against the radiation (we still haven't invented this). According to studies, to prevent such exposure, a 50-ton lead barrier is required. Not even a tank can provide this much safety.

However, engines powered by thorium lasers have kept alive our hopes of seeing a nuclear-powered car on the road. Researchers at Laser Power Systems have come up with a new turbine electric generator system, powered by a thorium-based laser. The principle is very simple: the laser produced from tiny pieces of thorium heats water, which produces steam and powers a mini turbine to produce electricity. Also, only a layer of aluminium foil is required to protect passengers from thorium radiation. Hence it is thought to be an ideal element for mobile power generation. Current prototypes of the engine weigh around 200 kilogrammes and are suitable for the conventionally designed vehicle.

So, for now, nuclear cars remain thoroughly unfeasible, but they might not always be so. Maybe you can change this. Will you?

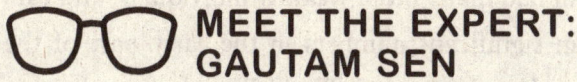 ## MEET THE EXPERT: GAUTAM SEN

Gautam Sen is an automotive design consultant, journalist and writer. Presently, he is also the vice president (communications and external relations) of the Fédération Internationale des

Véhicules Anciens (FIVA), the international federation for historic vehicles. He is also the founder editor of *Indian Auto*, the country's first automobile magazine.

Q. How is the history of vintage cars in India different from that of the rest of the world?

The history of the automobile in India has been fairly unique and very different from the rest of the world's. Within Asia, no other country has had as rich an automobile history as we have had. This is primarily because of two reasons: first, we were under the British Raj and, second, a fairly significant section of our society was very rich. Several other parts of the world were under British rule too, such as the many African nations, but their local rich were relatively fewer in number; in India, there were more than a handful of very wealthy people who could afford to buy some of the finest cars in the world. This made our history quite different from that of other Asian nations. China, for instance, has been predominantly poor too and, though they did have a feudal class, they weren't into buying fancy automobiles. On the other hand, Japan had many more wealthy individuals, and cars were imported in significant numbers in the early part of the twentieth century. But the Second World War destroyed many of the pre-war automobiles in Japan.

A significantly large number of cars survived in India as our country didn't see similar levels of devastation during the

Second World War. Europe, home to some of the greatest automobiles, saw many destroyed during the war. Thus not many automobiles survived in Germany. In France, though, there were many more survivors, as aerial bombing was limited to a few of the port cities of the country.

India has managed to secure a unique place in the history of the automobile industry, partly because of its European influences and partly because there was a certain section of rather wealthy, educated people—lawyers, doctors and engineers—who acquired some of the more tasteful cars during the early years. Many of them, as well as some of the 'princes', were educated in Europe, and most brought back a classy car or two when they returned to India. These are some of the factors that contributed to India's rich and distinctive automotive history.

Q. Which are your favourite vintage cars?

At the outset, it may be pertinent to clarify the more recent use of the term 'historic vehicles' instead of 'vintage cars'. Vintage cars are specifically those from the years 1919–1930. The English also use words such as 'veteran', 'classic', 'Edwardian' and so on as nomenclature for other periods. Americans prefer using the term 'classic', and this word applies to a very specific list of models. The Germans use the words 'oldtimers' and 'youngtimers', as well as *klassik*. With so much variation—and so much confusion—FIVA decided to club all classics, vintages, veterans, oldtimers et al. under historic vehicles. Thus FIVA defines a historic vehicle as one that is a mechanically propelled road vehicle, at least thirty years old, preserved and maintained in historically correct conditions and not used as a means of daily transport.

As regards my favourite historic vehicles, my first pick would be what I believe is one of the most beautiful automobiles ever made: the 1939 Delahaye 135M. For the better part of six decades, this car has been owned by 'Maharaja' Dalip Singh of Jodhpur. His father, Maharaja Hanwant Singh, bought this car in 1948. Eleven cars, with this specific body (designed and coach-built by the French coachbuilder Figoni et Falaschi), were produced by the French manufacturer Delahaye, out of which just five survive today. Two of these five were in India at one time. One was smuggled out of the country and is now in the US, in the famous Mullin Automotive Museum in Los Angeles. And then there is this one, in Jodhpur. Not only is the car stunningly beautiful, it also has an absolutely fascinating history.

The second automobile is another beautiful French car, also bodied by the same French coachbuilder, Figoni et Falaschi. This one is a Delage D8 S from 1933. It was, at that point of time, one of the most powerful and advanced cars. Very few numbers of the Delage D8 S were ever produced, yet two of them survive in India. One is in Gujarat, and the other—which I consider an all-time favourite—is in Delhi. The rarity of this car was a technological marvel in the 1930s, as well as the fact that it was one of the fastest and most beautiful vehicles of its time. All these factors combine to make the Delage a truly remarkable automobile indeed.

My third choice is a very different kind of car. It is not expensive, neither is it fancy—and not one bit rare, since it was produced in the thousands. It is the Wanderer W24, from 1937, produced by the German manufacturer Auto Union, which had four brands under it, Audi being one of them. The Wanderer marque was meant for the middle-class market. A few of them must have come to India; however, today just one is known to have survived. The interesting story associated with this one survivor is that it was in this very car that Netaji Subhas Chandra Bose escaped from house arrest in Calcutta, in 1941, eventually sneaking his way out of India. The Wanderer (the car also played a role of sorts in India's independence) is now on display at Netaji Bhawan, Kolkata.

Q. You played an instrumental role in the design and development of India's first sports car, the San Storm. Please tell us more about your experience and about the San Storm.

I have always been fascinated by the design of cars. Before the San Storm, I had decided to design my own car. In 1990, I had designed a motorcycle for myself. Thereafter I designed several motorcycles and mopeds for Hero Motors and a few other Indian manufacturers. But I still wanted to design my own car, so I bought a Sipani Dolphin and decided to modify it into a sports car. I chose this car because it had a separate body, which was bolted on to the chassis. So you could separate its body from the chassis, which is what I did. Then I designed the body, which was that of a two-seater sports convertible. This was then bolted on to the rolling chassis of 'my' Dolphin. A friend, Milind Thakker, who owned a company called San Engineering and Locomotive, saw it and acquired it, with plans to develop the design for series production. But his engineers struggled for almost two years to make the car producible, without much success.

Meanwhile, while on my travels in Europe (I wanted to meet many of my 'design heroes'), I realized that it would be much wiser to have the car redesigned from scratch by people who had been designing cars all their lives, in order to make the vehicle a world-class product as well as easier to produce. So we decided to approach a design group in France, the Le Mans Design Group, as they had a fine reputation for developing specialized cars for small-volume production. Since we were starting from scratch, we decided to develop a car that was modular in design and worked on engineering a brand-new chassis as well as a body. It was a very small team of a dozen-odd technicians, with most of the members having decades-long experience. It was quite a learning period for me; even though I had designed my 'own' car, I could see that the correct process was markedly different.

Once the prototype of the new car was ready, we realized that the engine of the Dolphin, even after much technological modernization, was just not good enough to power this pretty little car. So we had no choice but to rethink our power train strategy. As I knew the senior managers at Renault, we got in touch with them and successfully inked a deal to source a more modern, cleaner power train from them. But this necessitated a complete redesign of the chassis to fit the new engine. After some desperate, last-minute blood, sweat and tears, we had the first two prototypes of the coupe and the convertible ready, just in time to be flown directly to Delhi for the January 1998 edition of the Delhi Auto Expo. The two cars—the convertible and the coupe versions of the San Storm, one in yellow, the other in red—were very enthusiastically received at the show. The response was such that San believed the initial plans to produce at the rate of 200–300 cars per year was not enough, and that as many as 1000 could be sold every year.

After the unveiling, my involvement with San Engineering and Locomotive dwindled as I went on to lead other design and vehicle development projects. It took more than three years for the series production of the San Storm to start, with the first convertibles rolling out in late 2001.

Q. What are the key challenges faced by the automobile industry in India?

There are several of them, though the most detrimental may be the term 'frugal engineering'. Since a famous CEO of an international major coined the phrase, it has become a favourite buzzword of the Indian automobile industry. But frugal engineering, unfortunately, has pushed the Indian industry down the path of excessive cost-cutting, so much so that quality has been significantly compromised in many cases. Penny-pinching can compromise the final product, which, in turn, compromises the chances of success that the product can have. This has been the story of the Tata Nano—a brilliant idea that was poorly executed by being dictated by penny-pinching philosophy at its extreme. The number of Nanos sold from the start of production in 2009 until July 2018, when production stopped, was less than 2,74,000 units—this kind of figure ought to have been the average annual production of the Nano. The story of the San Storm was not dissimilar. The total number of Storms sold over a decade was what should have been in production every year. But quality issues ruined reputation and crippled sales.

Thus the lessons to be learnt from the San Storm and other projects are: first, entrepreneurs need to have very deep pockets to be in this industry; second, quality must not be sacrificed at any cost; and last, it is important to have a thinking that is borderless, because technology is borderless. Technology can be acquired from anywhere in the world, and for every project one must think of acquiring and accessing the very best, instead of having a penny-wise-pound-foolish approach of doing everything locally despite the inherent lack of knowledge and experience. As cost is a consequence of scale, once you start with quality materials and get the quantity right, the cost will automatically come down. Hence cost-cutting should be done in the production stages, not in the initial design and development stages, as intelligent design, even if a bit expensive to start with, can help bring costs down.

Q. You are the vice president of the Fédération Internationale des Véhicules Anciens. Please tell us more about what FIVA does, as well as your work there.

Established in 1966, FIVA is a global organization that is a sort of 'club of clubs', one that encourages the safe use of historic self-propelled, mechanical vehicles on the road, while remaining focused on preserving and promoting the very culture of motoring. There are thousands of clubs across the globe for historic vehicles. FIVA is the one that gets them together.

Let's take Chennai, for example. Chennai has a club called the Madras Heritage Motoring Club (MHMC). The collectors of historic vehicles in Chennai had got together years ago and formed this club, which organizes rallies and meets throughout the year. The Karnataka Vintage and Classic Car Club (KVCCC) is another such club for historic vehicles, based in Bengaluru. Clubs such as these have all banded together to create a national federation, the Federation of Historic Vehicles of India (FHVI). This federation interacts with the government regarding rules, regulations, legislation and other such matters that concern the historic vehicle movement and hobby. Furthermore, national federations like FHVI clubbed together to form FIVA and, as of today, eighty national members from sixty-seven countries and five continents, representing over 1.5 million enthusiasts worldwide, are part of FIVA.

Apart from these national-level federations, several of the major automobile manufacturers, such as the BMW Group, Fiat Chrysler Automobiles, Jaguar Land Rover, Mercedes-Benz, Volkswagen and many others, as well as component makers, such as tyre company Pirelli, lubricant company Motul, paint specialists Glasurit, etc. are also members of FIVA. Thus FIVA is the worldwide organization dedicated to the preservation, protection and promotion of historic vehicles, their related culture and their safe use.

Since April 2017, FIVA has been a non-governmental partner of the United Nations Educational, Scientific and Cultural Organization (UNESCO), and continues to pursue its successful

FIVA World Motoring Heritage Year programme. We hope that eventually UNESCO will recognize historic vehicles as one of the world's cultural heritages.

At FIVA, I have been the vice president for communications and external relations since 2015, and was perhaps the first non-European/American member on the board.

Q. Moving on to the future of cars. We are now seeing self-driving cars enter the market. Do you see a future wherein they will completely replace human-driven cars on the roads?

Today the industry is at an inflection point in terms of technology, how cars will be used and how they are going to look. Due to all the issues concerning fossil fuels, automobiles powered by them will surely disappear, but that will take some time. In the meantime, we will see more and more hybrids, which will be powered by both fossil fuels as well as zero-emission energy forms such as electricity. My estimate is that it will take the better part of two decades for fossil-fuel-powered cars to completely disappear.

The most important change, though, will be in the way automobiles are used. About a decade ago, some 97 per cent of the vehicles on the road were privately owned and barely 3 per cent were for public transport (buses, taxis, etc.).

This proportion is going to change drastically. More and more people will give up owning a car, and the ones who still do will use them less and less. Concepts like car-share programmes, carpools, dedicated bus routes and several similar schemes and systems will become increasingly widespread. Thus the requirements of fuel and emission efficiencies, as well as the design and aesthetic standards, could be very different for these public-owned vehicles, compared to the ones owned by individuals and families. This has already started to happen in Europe as more and more people are giving up cars and have 'converted' to using the public transport system more often than ever before. Such trends will take time to reach countries like India and China, but it will surely happen.

Regarding driverless cars and vehicles, they are already a reality. A relatively new French start-up called Navya has been manufacturing and selling the world's first driverless vehicles since 2015. Some 200-odd vehicles—fifteen-seater minibuses and six-seater shared taxis—have already been manufactured, and they are operating in selective places and streets across the globe, in cities such as Paris, Lyon, Los Angeles and Perth. In all likelihood, this will also enter the sphere of public transport, wherein we will see the first popular use of driverless vehicles, followed by the sector of fleet taxis and ride-sharing services such as Uber and Ola. Once technology has developed to the point where every aspect works seamlessly, driverless vehicles will be much safer and a significantly more efficient alternative to vehicles driven by human beings, as most accidents happen thanks to human error.

The metro systems in several cities are good examples of how autonomous subway lines are much more efficient and safe than the ones operated by drivers. Although the very first driverless metro was launched in 1981, the shift to driverless systems has taken several decades, with the Delhi Metro's first driverless route, the Magenta Line, becoming operational only recently, in 2017. Yet there is no denying that the day is not very far when one will be travelling in a car with no steering wheel or driver.

 # NOTE TO PARENTS

The automobile sector has been one of the most booming industries to have a career in for almost a century now. At a basic level of understanding, it may seem that one should pursue a career in mechanical engineering to be part of this sector. However, the future may be very different.

With the rising trend of electrical, hybrid and self-driven cars, this sector will see an influx of electrical and electronic engineering know-how in a huge way. It will also see the need for computer engineers who can design artificial intelligence to drive these new cars.

A youngster can pursue a career in the automobile sector even without an engineering degree. With the need to constantly come up with newer, sleeker and aesthetically superior models, there is always room for product designers and artistic minds in the sector.

The automobile sector is not just a domain of large manufacturers—it provides plenty of room to innovate and enterprise. None of the major manufacturers make all their parts in-house. Instead they rely on a network of smaller companies to supply them with almost 80–90 per cent of the material that goes into the ready-to-drive car. Hence automobile innovation is a wonderful opportunity for today's youth.

A career in the automobile industry can also be chalked out from a management background. Several managers are needed to work in operation management to keep the automobile plants running smoothly. Other managers are also deployed on the sales side and in marketing the cars (and other vehicles) to the consumer.

 **EXERCISE**

Label the parts of an electric car. You can take the help of the box below.

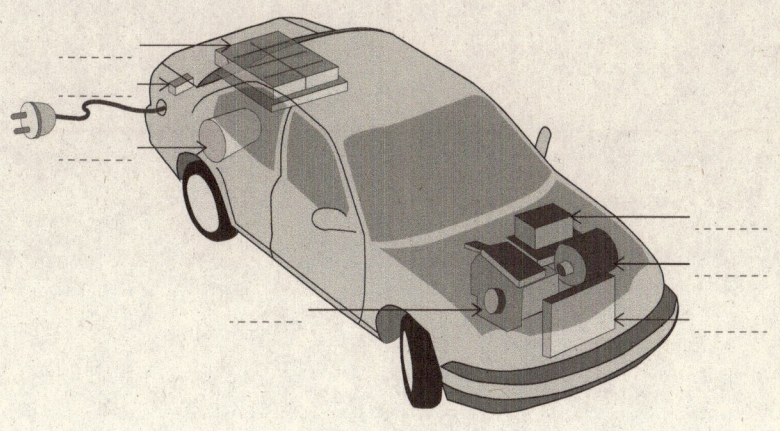

Engine	Power electronics
Radiator	Fuel storage
Electric motor	Battery
	Charger

CHAPTER 2

ENVIRONMENTAL SCIENCE

Before we talk about the environment, let's take a detour to talk about something pertinent to our home planet, Earth.

How old is Earth?

This single question has long racked the human brain. In the absence of scientific methods up until about 400 years ago, religion took the first guess at the answer. Biblical references determine the age of Earth to be 6000 years.[*] Islamic literature, while being ambiguous on the exact age, more or less points towards the 6000-year mark too. Zoroastrian, or Parsi, culture goes slightly further, estimating Earth's age as being anywhere between 6000 and 9000 years. Most of these numbers have been derived through processes of predictions based on the

_____
[*] This was calculated by James Ussher, an archbishop in seventeenth-century Ireland.

observable world of those times. And nobody back then could have imagined giant lizards walking on a planet dating back 25,00,00,000 years. Hence man's frame of analysis was limited.

But there is one outstanding civilization that ventured beyond the obvious predictions of the time. The most interesting estimate of Earth's age was proposed in India itself, captured in early Vedic texts, especially the Rig Veda, which is part of the sacred Hindu canon. It is in these texts that we see the hypothesis of day and night that span twenty-four hours, all attributed to Lord Brahma, the Creator, one among the Trinity. This Brahma day cycle was projected to extend to about 8.64 billion Earth years—about twice the actual age of the planet and roughly half the age of the universe as we know it today. Imagining such immense time spans was a work of genius. Of course, the measurement did not end there, as there are bigger units—such as a Brahma century, which spans trillions of years.

Derivations in science, too, have been a struggle since the seventeenth century. The goal is to unravel this one big puzzle: how old is our home, our Earth? Today we know that the universe is 13.8 billion (1380 crore) years old and that Earth is 4.54 billion (454 crore) years old. We've reached this far with the help of a variety of methods, ranging from observing the cooling of the planet from a hot ball of fire to the modern radioactive dating of rocks. The age of Earth as seen from the eyes of scientific inquiry goes much further back than what the realms of culture, religion and predictions could ever imagine.

Now I want to tell you a story of a man who set about unravelling the age of the planet and, on his quest, changed the course of the human race. His actions also went on to become the first major pushback against the pollution caused by burning fossil fuels.

• • •

In the year 1947 lived a man who was highly curious to find out the true age of Earth, and so he started researching the issue. He excavated the oldest rocks and did research on how old they actually were. Eventually, he found out that Earth is around 4.54 billion years old. The man who discovered the age of our planet was an American scientist named Clair Patterson. This ultimate revelation brought him immense popularity in the scientific world.

But Patterson's research life wasn't easy. He spent many years in college, studying to become a chemist. In 1950, he graduated with the highest college degree, a PhD in chemistry, from the University of Chicago. His research to determine the age of Earth was conducted at the University of Chicago and then at the California Institute of Technology (Caltech). Throughout his research life, Patterson was strapped for resources. To further add to his troubles, dating the planet back to billions of years ago was a very expensive process. He used lead measurement[†] in his research

---

[†] Lead (Pb) is a heavy yet malleable metal that is denser than most materials. It has a relatively low melting point. Lead is often used in bullets, batteries and radiation shields, besides its many uses in the construction industry

for a specific purpose—to determine the age of our planet. He had to work in old, dirty buildings, where he had to measure tiny amounts of lead that came from decaying heavier elements like uranium. During his research, Patterson also had to get rid of potentially every single stray atom of the element lead from his lab (as that could have interfered with the lead reading of the samples) before he could continue his measurements for determining the planet's age. He had to distil all the chemicals shipped to him and acid-clean all his apparatus every single day. This was also the beginning of what we know to be the state-of-the-art 'clean' lab. The Patterson lab and his new procedures for using clean samples led the way for future studies on the environment.

So why did Patterson choose lead for his research? Lead is a very heavy metal. A lead block is four times heavier than a block of iron of the same size. Interesting, right? This heaviness of the metal keeps it from decaying completely over a long period of time. So Patterson wanted to find really old samples of lead in order to gauge the age of Earth. This search for ancient and yet well-preserved samples of lead took Patterson on a wild hunt across the planet, literally from the North Pole to the South Pole. He also measured lead in samples taken from the oceans and found a startling result, which would trigger a paramount change in the industrial world of the mid-twentieth century.

In the samples Patterson drew from the oceans, he found that the lead concentration in shallow waters was several times higher than the lead found in deeper waters. As we know, it takes many decades for shallow waters to mix with the deep waters of the ocean—so it was evident that this additional lead in the upper layers of the oceans had been recently introduced into the waters. Now Patterson took his research further, right up to Antarctica. He dug holes in the ice and drew out 300-year-old samples of snow that were buried and preserved deep in the ice. Once again he found that the lead content in these old samples was significantly lower than that found in the atmosphere of the 1950s. Patterson did not rest; now he wanted to find out what was causing this spike in lead concentration. Armed with this agenda, he went from being a geologist to an environmental scientist.

Patterson and his team collecting ice samples from Antarctica to measure their lead content

Let me hold on to this story for a while and address something else. Many would be curious to know about the harm lead concentration can cause.

Well, lead is a known neurotoxin; it is a poison that affects the brain. It is especially harmful to children as their brains are still in the growth phase and put up less resistance. Exposure to lead causes slower, or retarded, brain growth and severe hallucinations too. Workers who were exposed to lead in factories often complained of imagining swarms of insects. They called the factory a 'house of butterflies'. Many even lost control of their minds and jumped to their deaths.

And then there was an industrial challenge. Lead is easy to melt and cast, and hence used in various applications since time immemorial. The Romans used lead in their water transport system, which were called aqueducts. Some believe it was lead that contaminated the water used by the Romans, and was partly responsible for their failing health, their irrational and violent tendencies that led to their decline and, eventually, the end of the Roman Empire. It wasn't until the dawn of the twentieth century that lead was employed on a wide scale again. It was the dawn of petrol cars. It was found that if a small amount of lead was mixed in the petrol, it would fix the problem of the 'knocking' of the engine, facilitating a smoother drive. Thus, during the 1920s, lead came back to haunt humanity, this time in the petrol of our cars. Tailpipes of this increasingly popular commodity became the renewed source of lead in the air. Over the next three decades, few people noticed the increasing lead concentration in the air—and those who saw it were quickly bought out and silenced by the big industries. Lead-mixed petrol had become critical to the three biggest industry groups: the petroleum companies that found it a cheap means of enhancing the fuel; the automobile industry that found better engine performance with leaded petrol; and, finally, the chemical industry that started making lead itself. By the 1950s, lead had become the first major pollutant that was threatening the very existence of humankind.

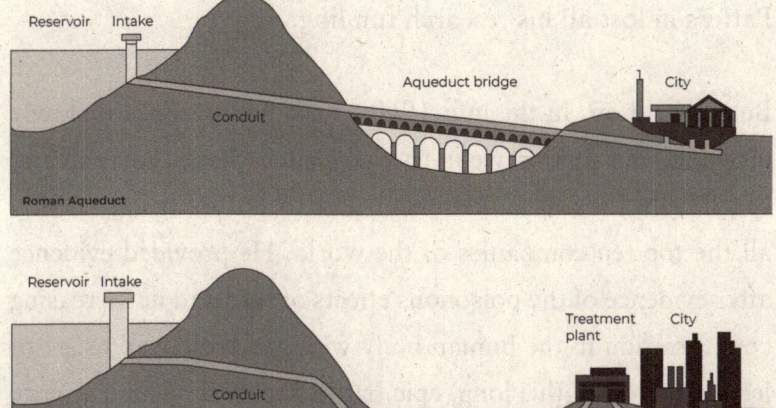

The Roman aqueduct vs the modern aqueduct

Now, let us come back to Clair Patterson who, by the 1950s, had discovered the global spike in lead concentration—in the air, in the water and in the human body itself. Patterson was perhaps the first scientist to observe the increase in lead content from the 1900s to the 1950s. He openly published the results and, like a true scientist, stated the truth: leaded petrol in cars was the reason for the lead spike. His findings about the neurotoxin being injected into the system alarmed the public. Ironically, till this point, Patterson's research was funded by the American Petroleum Institute. His words against leaded petrol did not go down well with the institute. First, they tried to offer him a handsome research grant, provided he changed his topic of research from lead to virtually anything else. When they could not buy out Patterson's science, they decided to strangle it. Overnight, Patterson lost all his research funding.

But he held on. In the mid-1960s, with public concern slowly growing, the matter went to the United States government, specifically its senate. Patterson had to go up against nearly all the top ten companies of the world. He provided evidence after evidence of the poisonous effects of lead and its increasing concentration in the human body with the prolonged usage of leaded petrol. In this long, epic battle, the truth behind science triumphed over the might of money.

By 1975, the US government asked automobile companies to use catalytic converters to control the emission of lead. By 1986, leaded petrol was almost completely out of circulation in the US. Other countries followed suit and, by

2000, nearly all nations, including India, eliminated the use of leaded petrol. Of course, this step, taken to prevent the deadly pollution caused by lead, cost the industries billions of dollars.

Patterson's scientific contribution to the environment was critical. In the US alone, the rate of violence went down between the 1970s and the 1990s. Studies were done to find out the reason for this decline. One suspect was lead. As you know by now, children's brains are especially susceptible to chronic lead poisoning. So, was it possible that kids who didn't breathe in leaded petrol fumes grew up to commit less violent crimes? The answer is: yes. The 56 per cent drop in crimes in the US from the 1970s to the 1990s was due to this simple fact. Patterson's efforts had caused vehicles to switch to unleaded petrol. No lead in the immediate environment meant better mental health, which, in turn, meant less crime. Similar results were derived when studies were conducted on the removal of lead pipes and the subsequent lowering of suicide rates.

Today, Patterson may not be as popular as other scientific figures, like Einstein or Newton. He did not even get a Nobel Prize, but his research was nothing short of brilliant. The scientist who started his life trying to find the age of Earth ended up saving its environment. He almost single-handedly pulled the world away from a high-speed crash into toxic lead contamination. Patterson died in 1995. By the time of his death, lead content in the average human being had decreased to a mere one-fifth of what it used to be in the 1970s.

● ● ●

It is now a globally accepted fact that our environment is altering, and it is largely the result of human activity since the industrial age, beginning in the mid-1800s. The world population has risen from just about 1 billion in 1900 to over 7.7 billion today, and is expected to peak at about 10 billion by 2040. This increase in population was also compounded with increasing per capita wealth, about six times in 2015 what it used to be in 1900. More wealth means more consumption, and more consumption often leads to more ecological damage. This surge in waste, in consumption and in pollution has pushed life to the very edge. Today, environmental scientists estimate that 150–200 species of plants, insects, birds and mammals become extinct every twenty-four hours! That's a single day!

However, extinctions are not uncommon in nature. Old species die out and give way to newer, and usually more evolved, species. But that is a natural process, something called the background rate of extinction. Rarely does this rate of extinction accelerate manifold over a short period of time, leading to something called mass extinction, wherein thousands of species are wiped out very quickly. In the past, there have been five waves of mass extinction:[1]

The **first mass extinction** happened about 444 million (44.4 crore) years ago. This happened due to the rise of the Appalachian Mountains in the US and eastern Canada, which led to ice formation, which, in turn, lowered the sea level. In this old world, all life existed in oceans. New silicate rocks that emerged from under the lowered water levels reacted with the carbon dioxide in the air, removing it from the atmosphere and causing freezing temperatures. Eighty-six per cent of the species that existed then were killed in this mass extinction.

Sixty-nine million years passed. The **second mass extinction** happened 375 million years ago. By this time, land life had started to emerge on the planet. Plants started evolving on land for the first time; they grew up to 30 metres tall. There were no land animals yet to check their growth, so these land plants covered the planet. Their branches fell and clogged the rivers and shallow oceans, covering the ocean surface. Algae bloomed in oceans, feeding on these decomposing plants, and consumed all the oxygen in the water in the process. Below them, the bulk of marine life choked. The petroleum reserves of today are often the dead life forms and algae from this extinction that wiped out 75 per cent of all living species.

The five waves of mass extinction and their impact on living beings and dominant (now extinct) species

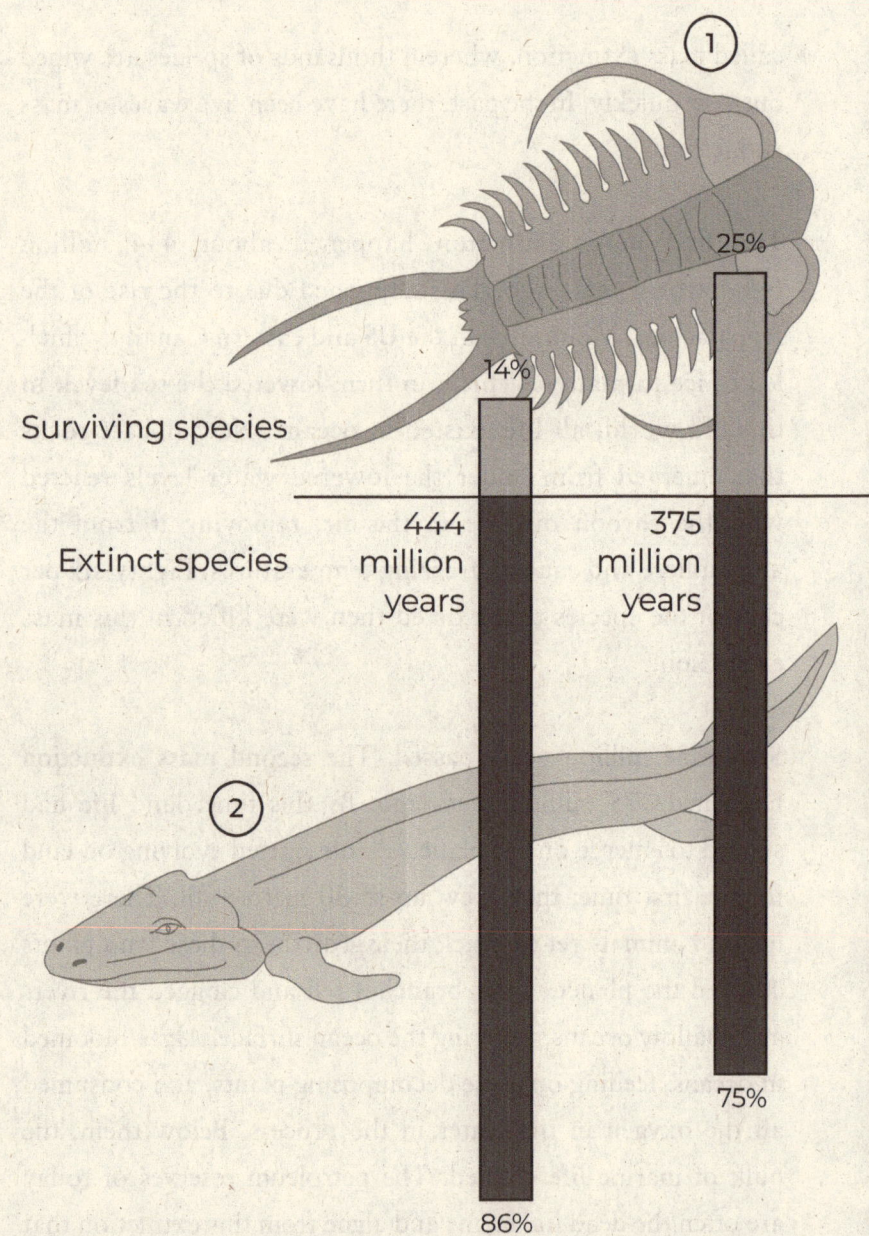

Surviving species

Extinct species

① 25%

14%

444 million years

375 million years

② 86%

75%

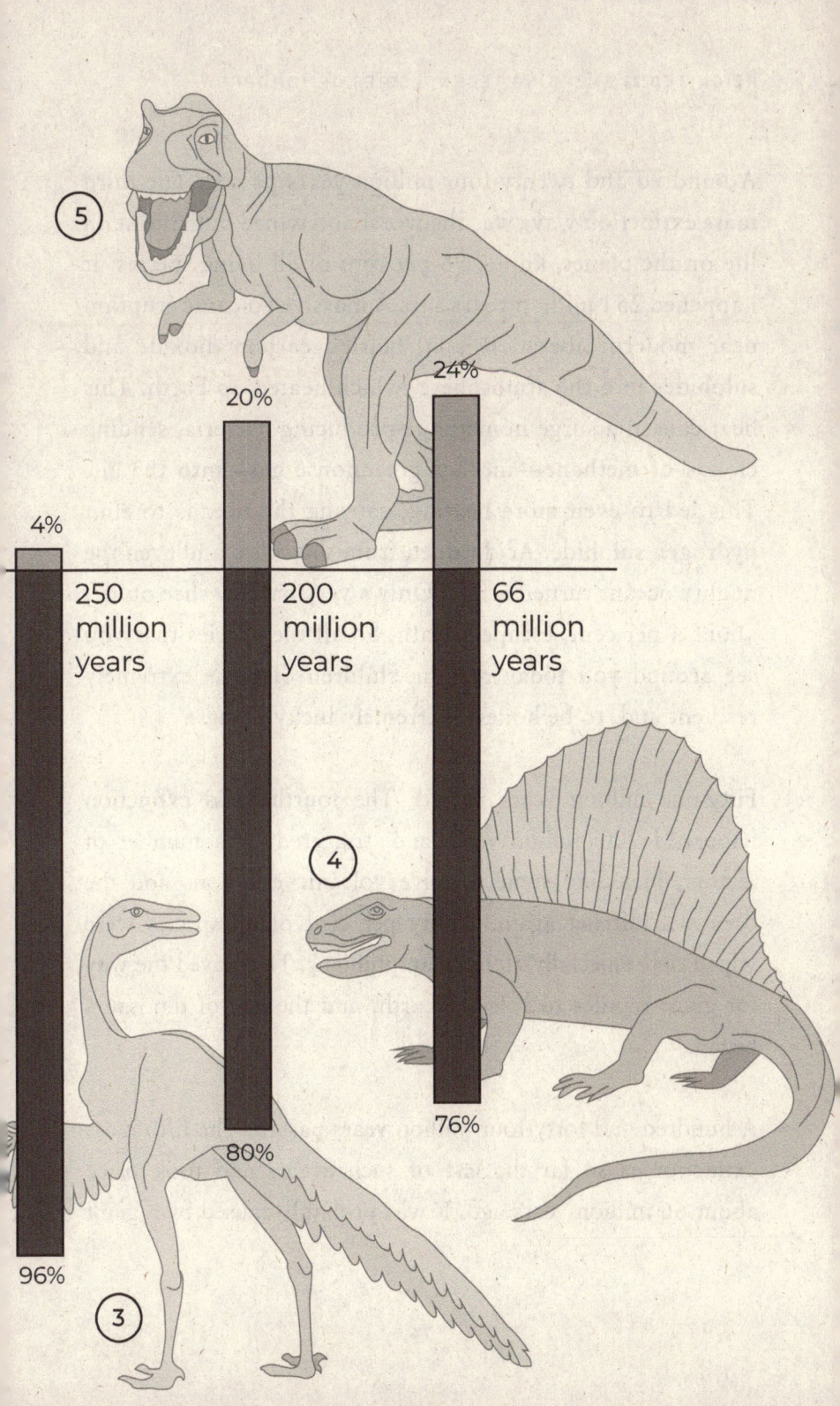

⑤

24%

20%

4%

250
million
years

200
million
years

66
million
years

④

96%

80%

76%

③

A hundred and twenty-four million years passed. The **third mass extinction** wave was the worst and wiped out almost all life on the planet, killing 96 per cent of all living species. It happened 251 million years ago. A massive volcanic eruption near modern Siberia, Russia, blasted carbon dioxide and sulphides into the atmosphere, which heated up Earth. This heat caused a surge in methane-producing bacteria, sending clouds of methane—another greenhouse gas—into the air. This led to even more heating, causing the oceans to emit hydrogen sulphide. Acid rained from the skies, and even the mighty oceans turned acidic. Only a very narrow slice of life, about 4 per cent, escaped death. So all the species that you see around you today are the children of these extremely resilient and, to be honest, extremely lucky beings.

Fifty-one million years passed. The **fourth mass extinction** happened 200 million years ago, triggered by a number of factors, including some massive volcanic eruptions and the oceans acidifying again. Eighty per cent of all species were wiped out, especially all large amphibians. This paved the way for giant reptiles to rule the earth, and the age of dinosaurs began.

A hundred and forty-four million years passed. The **fifth mass extinction** is so far the last of such events and took place about 66 million years ago. It was probably caused by a giant asteroid striking Earth at what is now the Chicxulub crater in modern Mexico. This sent shock waves across the planet and dust covered the skies, blocking the sunlight and creating a prolonged severe winter, with the average temperature dropping to 7 degrees Celsius. The sulphur rising with the dust caused acid rain, killing the plants. With the plants gone, the herbivores died, and with the herbivores dying, the carnivores starved. Seventy-six per cent of all species perished. This spelled the end for giant reptiles; dinosaurs went extinct and the age of mammals began.

The future of environmental science

So the obvious question to ask as a future environmental scientist is: how close are we to the sixth extinction event? In the last section, we talked about the background rate of extinction. Well, today the rate of extinction of species is 1000 times that of the natural or background rate, and so it is greater than anything the world has experienced since the vanishing of the dinosaurs in the fifth wave of mass extinction. Nearly all of this accelerated extinction is either due to climate change, global warming or overhunting and overfishing.

On the next page is a list of the ten hottest years of the last millennium.[2]

RANK	YEAR	AVERAGE TEMPERATURE OF THE EARTH ABOVE NORMAL BY . . . (IN DEGREE CELSIUS)
1	2016	0.94
2	2015	0.90
3	2017	0.84
4	2014	0.74
5	2010	0.70
6	2013	0.66
7	2005	0.65
8	2009	0.64
9	1998	0.63
10	2012	0.62

There is no denying the fact that we are nearing the sixth wave of mass extinction. There is also clear evidence that the burning of fossil fuels and the chemicals released by industries have made the planet considerably hotter. We have been recording global temperatures since 1880, and the projections we have are for over 1000 years. Of this data we have today, the ten hottest years are between 1998 and today. In fact, the five hottest years of the last millennium are all within this decade. In the past 1000 years, nothing has caused the global climate to heat up like we have.

● ● ●

Ecology rests on a very fine and delicate balance, and humans have developed the might to disturb it—a change that is mostly irreversible. Everyday human activities can impact this balance, which eventually comes back to affect human population. Take the case of what happens when we use air conditioners (ACs) and refrigerators. We use them to make the atmosphere cool, to prevent food from decaying and to keep the air clean and free of small insects.

However, the use of ACs and fridges releases a by-product called chlorofluorocarbon, or CFC. CFCs move up to the layers of the atmosphere and have a tendency to destroy oxygen bonds; in the case of our planet, they destroy ozone. Ozone is a layer of air that protects Earth's surface from receiving ultraviolet B, or UVB, rays. However, due to human activity, the ozone layer has developed a deadly hole. Today the hole in the ozone layer has grown roughly seven times the size of India. And while humans can protect themselves from UVB rays by staying indoors, amphibians and birds cannot. Among the worst affected are their eggs, which have lost the ability to produce new life due to the radiation of UVB. For instance, frog eggs rarely hatch to produce tadpoles. The frog population is therefore dwindling at the alarming rate of 4 per cent every year. In urban areas, they are already almost extinct. One doesn't hear the frog's croak these days!

With frogs out of the picture, mosquitoes and their larvae have a happy season. There are no tadpoles or frogs to feed on them. The food cycle has been interrupted; hence mosquitoes and other pests are growing in large numbers. They enter your home, making it dirty and unhygienic, and contaminate your food. To counteract this, we rely more heavily on ACs (with new features, such as air controls and filters) and refrigerators to keep our home and food clean. And so more CFCs are released, and the cycle continues.

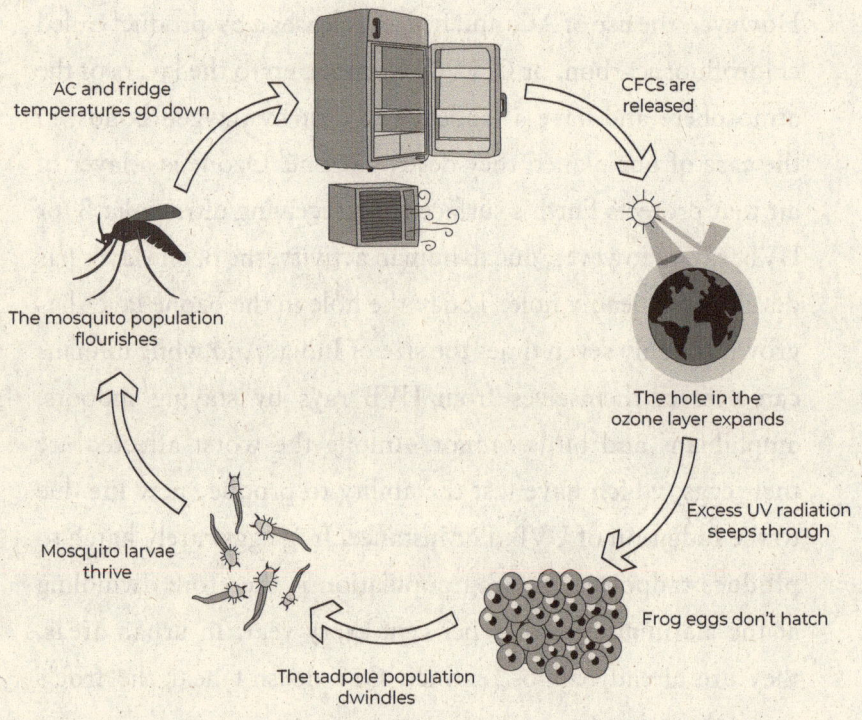

The CFC cycle

Let me revisit the mass extinction story. We, and all that is alive today—including plants, dogs, cats, fish, trees, insects and even reptiles—are immensely and, almost ridiculously, lucky to be alive. Just imagine how easily millions of other species could have been in our place—alive, still existing. If you like maths, you can crunch the numbers: We emerged from the 14 per cent of species that survived the first mass extinction and managed to grow to 25 per cent, which lasted through the second wave and yet somehow became the mere 4 per cent that escaped the third extinction. We then grew into the 20 per cent that survived the fourth mass extinction and then finally became the 24 per cent to have made it through the fifth mass extinction. We are among the rugged, hard-working, tenacious and extremely lucky species that roam our planet today.

Now let's look at it in another way. If 15,000 living species started out 450 million years ago, before the first mass extinction, only *one* would have survived today, after the five mass extinction events. Your future job, as an environmental scientist, will not only involve protecting humans from climate change but also endeavouring to protect every one of these unique and vivid species that fill the spectrum of life, each coloured in its own unique tale of triumphs and struggles.

What should I do to become an environmental scientist?

Environmental science offers you a wide array of fields to work in, such as global warming, pollution of air, water quality, soil quality. It is a diverse career; you can take up a specialized course for your bachelor's degree itself or do a bachelor's in physics, chemistry, geography, botany or engineering and then pursue a specialized master's degree in environmental science.

There are several universities, both in India and abroad, that teach environmental science as a subject. Most Indian Institutes of Technology (IITs), National Institutes of Technology (NITs) and other national institutions have environmental science as a well-developed subject. Globally, the University of California, Berkeley (UCB), Stanford University and the Massachusetts Institute of Technology (MIT) are the best-known colleges in this area.

Studying environmental science would mean working with large data samples and then deriving results from it. Hence technology, or IT, skills and mathematical abilities are very important. So learn about them in school to become a successful environmental scientist. Also, keenly follow geography and read about issues related to the environment on the Internet and in libraries. Publications like *National Geographic*, *The Green Guide* and *The Environmentalist* should be available in your library, so always go through these. Nearly every major international news website has a section on the environment, which is available for free!

Keep reading and learning, and perhaps you can be the one to shape the environment of other planets, where we may choose to live in the future.

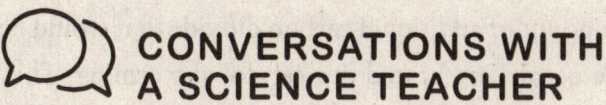

CONVERSATIONS WITH A SCIENCE TEACHER

Where on the planet is carbon dioxide stored?

There are several natural storehouses, or sinks, of carbon dioxide on Earth. The most obvious place is the carbon dioxide diffused in the air around us. The atmosphere carries about 3000 billion tons of carbon dioxide in it.[3] But there are several other such sinks. Trees also store carbon dioxide by converting it to carbon, which makes up their trunks and branches. In this way, all foliage together stores about 4500 billion tons of carbon dioxide. That is why it is so important to plant more and more trees. By contrast, the carbon dioxide locked in the remaining oil and coal reserves of the world is about 2400 billion tons. That is why it is important to minimize the consumption of fossil fuels. But the real source or hidden champion of carbon dioxide is something entirely different . . .

What is this source or the hidden champion among the sinks of carbon dioxide?

These are the oceans and seas. Water has a unique property— to dissolve gases. All the waterbodies put together store over 1,50,000 billion tons of carbon dioxide. You would probably know that heating water makes it slowly lose its gaseous components. That is why bubbles form when water is boiled.

Imagine the amount of additional carbon dioxide that would be released if the oceans are heated due to global warming. This, in turn, will heat up Earth and the oceans even more—leading to an endless, uncontrolled cycle called runaway.

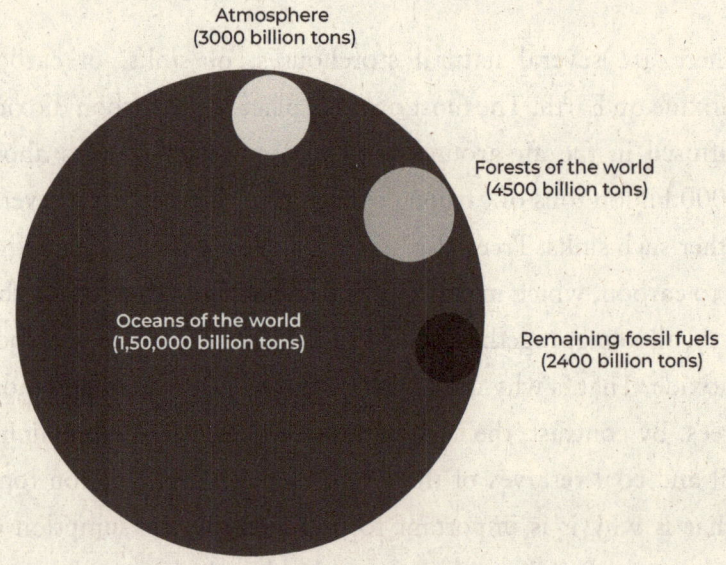

Carbon dioxide sinks and their proportions

These runaway cycles of temperature increase seem worrisome. Has it ever happened in the past?

Not on this planet, else we would not have been here at all. But there is a clear warning from our nearest planet—Venus.

So oceans are important for the storage of carbon dioxide, but do sea plants also produce oxygen—to balance it out?

Yes, they do! In fact, it is believed that up to 70 per cent of Earth's oxygen is produced by phytoplankton.[4] Phytoplankton are photosynthesizing microscopic organisms that live in the upper sunlit layer of almost all oceans and bodies of fresh water.

Why are oxygen-rich planets so rare? Why has life been possible only on Earth?

Oxygen is one of the most reactive elements found naturally in the environment. It reacts with any and almost every metal and forms oxides. If you find oxygen in pure form—without it having bonded with any other element on any planet—it is 100 per cent guaranteed that there is some form of life on that planet, which is actively producing pure oxygen.

The only reason we do find oxygen on our planet is because it has plants and trees. Trees produce oxygen that is readily available for life through the process of photosynthesis. So as much as we cannot find life on any other planet except Earth in our solar system, scientists suspect that some planets like Venus or Mars might have had life in the past—but only for a narrow window of time.

How were fossils formed? Why is it a limited resource now?

Fossils were formed when trees were uprooted and were unable to decompose. Due to their cell walls, bacteria were unable to

REIGNITED 2: EMERGING TECHNOLOGIES OF TOMORROW

feed on them. So the carbon in them was preserved for hundreds and thousands of years. This turned to fossil fuel, namely coal. Those that were preserved in the oceans were specifically called petroleum.

With time, the bacterial species adapted and evolved. They were able to decompose the dead trees and animals now. This meant that fossils could no longer be produced. That is why you must have heard that fossil fuels are a declining and very limited resource now.

If there were only animals on Earth and no trees, the planet would not have been able to sustain itself. Is that true vice versa too? Would Planet Earth continue to survive if there were only trees and no animals?

Animals need oxygen to survive, which plants provide through the process of photosynthesis. Similarly, plants also need carbon dioxide to survive, and animals are its major source. Technically, if there were no animals and only plants left, the absence of carbon dioxide and the excess of oxygen would kill the plants too. This is the irony. If there were only plants, there would have been no plants.

Carbon dioxide is a greenhouse gas. It creates a shelter or layer around Earth, and this shelter, in turn, helps keep Earth warm. It doesn't let the Sun's heat escape from the environment. Even though an excess of CO_2 makes our environment toxic, the absence of CO_2 would lead us to the ice ages, with no heat being trapped in Earth's atmosphere. This is another reason why plants wouldn't be able to survive. Either way, we do need a balance of both oxygen and carbon dioxide for all species to survive.

How much carbon dioxide is added to the environment by everyday activities?

As a future environmental scientist, it is a good idea to know about the emissions that we are all responsible for while going about our daily life. Here is a table that you can use to calculate your carbon footprint:

ACTIVITY	CO_2 EMISSION
Burning 1 kg coal	2.87 kg
Burning 1 litre diesel	2.70 kg
Travelling 10 km by car	2.10 kg
Travelling 10 km by two-wheeler	0.70 kg
Consuming 1 kWh power	1.27 kg

 **MEET THE EXPERT: COLONEL N. RAMACHANDRAN**

Colonel N. Ramachandran is our expert for this section. He is currently serving as the vice chancellor of Sandip University, Maharashtra. He was former vice chancellor of Periyar Maniammai University (PMU), Tamil Nadu, and is also the creator of the Periyar PURA (Providing Urban Amenities to Rural Areas)—a dream project of President A.P.J. Abdul Kalam.[5]

Q. What are the career opportunities in the next decade and beyond for scientists and experts in the environment sector?

The total world waste is estimated to be about 27 billion tons per year by 2050. And out of this, about one-third, i.e. about 9 billion tons, is expected to be produced by Asia—essentially India and China. So if we assume India bears 50 per cent responsibility for this figure, then the amount of waste attributed to us is about 5 billion tons. Just imagine the havoc this waste is going to wreak! This is no longer going to be a question of mere pollution as, finally, it is going to affect the lives of commoners too.

These predictions are for 2050, and we still have thirty-one years left. If we start working on this now, by the time we reach 2050, a complete generation will have passed. So if people need to live peacefully on this planet even after thirty years, the responsibility of all environmental scientists, environmental technocrats and environmental managers will be to overcome the issues pertaining to environmental degradation.

This is the need of the hour because already many are suffering from the after-effects of air pollution, with diseases like asthma, bronchitis and cancer. Every monsoon, due to the public intake of contaminated water, hospitals are flooded with patients suffering from diarrhoea. Due to the consumption of fruit and vegetables grown in soil with excess chemicals, our health is worsening. These things need to be studied, recorded, analysed and mapped. Apart from these, a problem that needs to be addressed is awareness. The younger generations need to be the torchbearers of spreading awareness and must take proper steps to mitigate and resolve these issues. And this is where the career opportunities lie.

Q. You have worked on various projects related to the environment. Can you tell us about some of them?

As vice chancellor of Periyar Maniammai University, I was associated with various projects related to the environment, which led us to establish what is known as a zero-carbon campus. Through various green practices, by 2030, the campus will be carbon-neutral. We have planted bamboo across about 10 acres of the land under the National Bamboo Mission, as bamboo releases one of the highest amounts of oxygen. Every acre's plantation can produce 62 tons of oxygen per year and absorb 88 tons of carbon dioxide. Apart from bamboo, we've also planted more than 70,000 trees on campus and introduced micro-irrigation at all levels to conserve water. We have also initiated the planting of more than 30 lakh trees in the Thanjavur district of Tamil Nadu. We have replaced all traditional lamps and bulbs with LEDs and are using solar-powered appliances like solar heaters, solar refrigerators, solar fans, etc.

Moreover, we have also created a unique waste-disposal mechanism for liquid and organic waste in the form of a bio-methanization plant that has a 500-cubic-metre capacity. The plant reduces about 292 tons of carbon emission per year. Additionally, all the greenhouse gases, including carbon dioxide, captured by this plant are used to generate 100 kW of power, which is used to electrify the campus; the leftover sludge that is released is converted to vermicompost. This compost is then used by local farmers (who have been given prior training by us).

We have also installed a biomass-gasifier with a capacity of 200 kW. It is an alternative source that produces energy from abundantly available agricultural waste. By doing this, we are reducing about 253 tons of carbon emission per year.

Another unique project—of making hollow bricks or stabilized mud blocks from waste—has been initiated by us at the university. So far, we have produced about 2 million such blocks, which were used to construct a 9 km long wall. If the same wall had been built with regular bricks, it would have used up about 37 tons of wood, which would have led to the erosion of about 45,000 tons of fertile topsoil. So this technology has prevented both deforestation and soil erosion, thereby reducing about 9400 tons of carbon emission.

Q. You have also worked with A.P.J. Abdul Kalam on ground-level implementation of a sustainable rural development system called PURA.[6] Please tell us about it.

This is a very interesting and, at the same time, emotional subject for me. Providing Urban Amenities to Rural Areas, or PURA, has now been renamed by the Government of India as the Shyama Prasad Mukherji Rurban Mission. Both the vision and the project are one and the same; the only difference is that now funding is also available to implement such projects.

In 1996, based on the ideas of a great social reformer and our mentor, Thanthai Periyar—who believed that villagers should get the same amenities as enjoyed by people living in cities and towns—PMU launched a rural development programme. When A.P.J. Abdul Kalam became the President of India and advocated the concept of PURA, we realized that the programme of rural development adopted by us in 1996 at PMU bore a strong resemblance to the PURA concept. During his visit in 2003, President Kalam inaugurated the PURA scheme and affectionately named it Periyar PURA.

PMU has adopted about sixty-five villages in the Thanjavur district of Tamil Nadu for their economic upliftment and for the implementation of sustainable development projects.

The implementation of developmental activities in line with the PURA concept has resulted in significant impact on empowering and accelerating rural development. It has helped the areas of agriculture, employment, education, etc. and in addressing issues like the migration of people to towns and cities.

On the educational front, Periyar PURA worked from elementary school to the college level. Activities such as vocational training, virtual classrooms, e-tuitions, awareness creation and skill and leadership development were conducted among schoolchildren. These efforts led to a 9 per cent increase in the literacy rate. Skill development training on agro-based activities was given to about 2700 women. Small structures like water-harvesting units and ponds were made, and some existing ones were renovated so that farmers have access to water all year round. This resulted in an increase in the cultivable area for different crops—from 32,384 acres to 35,702 acres. Apart from this, about 30,000 rural women were engaged in many income-generating activities, as they were also given training in vermicompost production, nursery techniques, tailoring, embroidery, bakery, hollow-block making and carpentry. In fact, some of the services at PMU, like catering, cafeteria service, laundry, printing and tailoring, are run by these trained women. This arrangement, besides being a sustainable income source for these women, also ensures quality service to the end users.

 **NOTE TO PARENTS**

The environment has become a matter of great concern, and so in the future there will be an exponential rise in the demand for environmental scientists. It is a multidisciplinary career, and students can approach it via several streams, including maths (analytics), physics, chemistry, botany, geology and even agriculture.

Environmental science is truly a global topic and nearly all countries in the world have a great demand for experts in this domain. With global warming on the rise and weather change very apparent, environmental scientists are crucial assets to any nation's economy and growth.

All major companies recruit environmental scientists for a variety of roles, including audits, and also for making strategies to minimize the environmental impact of the companies themselves. Environmental scientists are also required in non-governmental organizations (NGOs) for research work in the field of conservation and environment protection. There is plenty of funding granted to environmental researchers in case your child decides to go into the field of academics related to the environment.

EXERCISE

1. As a future environmental scientist, you should be aware that vehicular exhaust from automobiles releases carbon dioxide, which is ultimately causing global warming.

Earlier in this chapter, you found out how much CO_2 is generated by various modes of transportation and fuel consumption. Using that data, calculate the amount of carbon dioxide that is added to the environment by your family every month.

(Hint: You might want to compute the consumption of petrol/diesel by your car/two-wheeler and your generator, if you use one. Of course, you also consume fuel when taking public transport, but let us ignore that for this problem. You will have to go through your electricity bill to determine the exact number of units used every month.)

2. Let's look at this problem from the perspective of the impact of aircraft travel on the environment. Imagine that you're on a trip from New Delhi to New York. The flight distance is roughly 12,000 kilometres (which is completed in about eighteen hours of flight time in a Boeing 777 aircraft). A typical Boeing 777 jet consumes about 7500 kilogrammes of fuel, or 10,500 litres, per hour. You already know that every litre of fuel burnt generates about 2.3 kilogrammes of carbon dioxide.

Using these figures, can you estimate the tons of CO_2 generated in a single flight from New Delhi to New York?

(Hint: 1 ton of CO_2 = 1000 kg of CO_2)

The answer is _____ tons of CO_2.

CHAPTER 3

In 2011, President A.P.J. Abdul Kalam and I visited the famous Harvard University in the United States of America.[1] Located in the north-eastern part of the USA, it was established way back in 1636. Harvard boasts 158 Nobel laureates and eight US Presidents, including former US President Barack Obama. President Kalam and I spent about two weeks at this university, meeting some of the world's most famous scientists, understanding their work and imagining a future when their research would come into action.

One of the professors we met there was Hongkun Park, a professor of chemistry and physics, and his work interested us greatly. A man with a ready smile and round glasses, Park is from South Korea. The professor was doing pioneering work in a new area of human imagination—nanotechnology, which is the science of working with particles that are way too small to be visually inspected.

Let me explain this better. Nanotechnology is the science of working with matter that is in the range of 10^{-9} metres in dimension. Let's look at the smallest measurement on your ruler—it is a millimetre. A human hair is about 1/10th of a millimetre. Now, take this single strand of hair. Slice it along its width (not its length) into 100 equal parts. Of course, this cannot be done with any ordinary blade or knife, so just imagine the process. Each of these 100 parts would be about 1 micrometre thick. Red blood cells, several bacteria, most animal and plant cells are in this range of size. Now it gets harder. Take any one of these 100 parts and imagine slicing it into 1000 equal parts along its width. The thickness of each of these 1000 parts is a single nanometre (nm)! Hence a nanometre is a one-billionth part of a single millimetre. Viruses are in this range of size. If you want to be a nanoscientist, you need to work with particles in this range of size. Of course, this would need special equipment and a really, really powerful microscope.

Let us come back to Harvard nanoscientist Hongkun Park. What Professor Park showed us was almost beyond the realm of present-day human imagination. Park is the inventor of nanoneedles, needle-like structures made of silicon or boron nitride that can pierce and deliver content into individual targeted cells. Now there are about 37.2 trillion cells in the human body. Imagine this nanoneedle to be an injection that pierces right through a single pinpointed cell from this array of cells that make up your body. This is how the science of nanoparticles

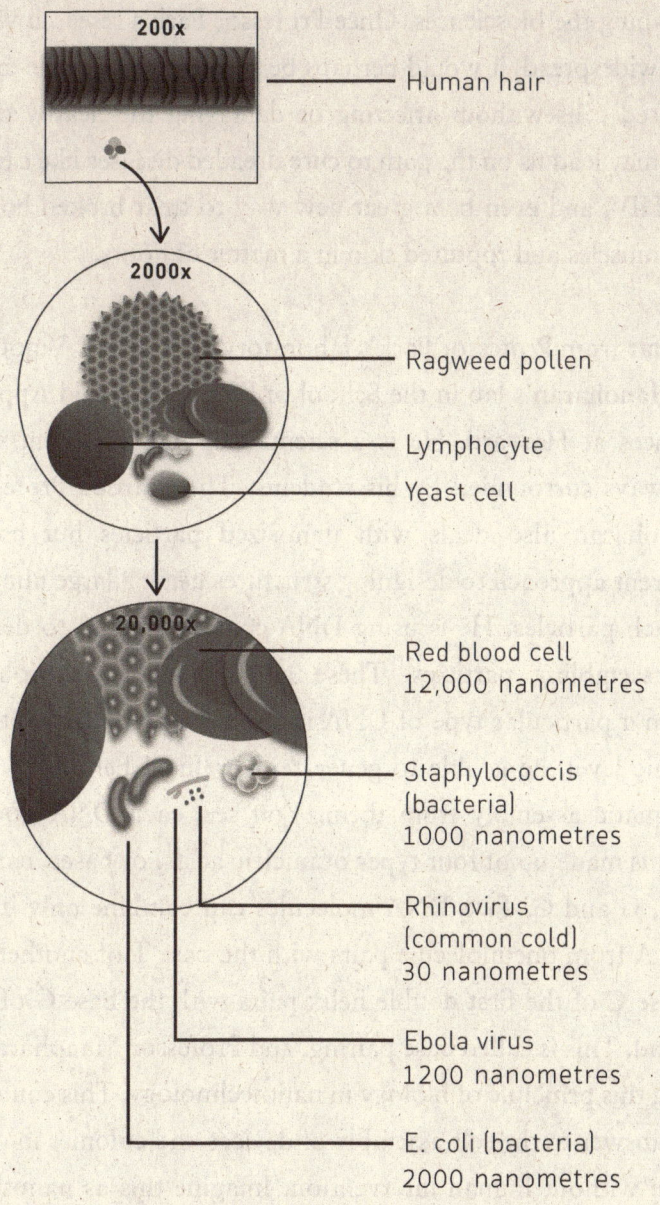

200x — Human hair

2000x
— Ragweed pollen
— Lymphocyte
— Yeast cell

20,000x
— Red blood cell
  12,000 nanometres
— Staphylococcis
  (bacteria)
  1000 nanometres
— Rhinovirus
  (common cold)
  30 nanometres
— Ebola virus
  1200 nanometres
— E. coli (bacteria)
  2000 nanometres

Microscopic living beings on the nanoscale

is shaping the biosciences. Once Professor Park's research work goes widespread, it would perhaps be possible to treat the exact diseased cells without affecting or damaging the nearby cells. This may lead us on the path to cure dreaded diseases like cancer and HIV, and even be a great new way to treat broken bones, torn muscles and ruptured skin in a matter of hours.

Not far from Professor Park's laboratory is Professor Vinothan N. Manoharan's lab in the School of Engineering and Applied Sciences at Harvard. He is a scientist of Indian origin, who is always surrounded by his students. The bearded Professor Manoharan also deals with nanosized particles but has a different approach to designing structures using a large number of such particles. He is using DNA-coated material to design self-assembling particles. These are bio-based nanorobots. When a particular type of DNA is applied on a particle at the atomic level, he is able to generate a prefixed behaviour and automatic assembly from them. You see, each DNA double helix is made up of four types of nucleic acids, or bases, named A, T, G and C. Two DNA molecules can combine only if the base A from one molecule pairs with the base T of another, or if base C of the first double helix pairs with the base G of the second. This is called base pairing, and Professor Manoharan is using this principle of biology in nanotechnology. This could be our answer to the self-assembly of devices and colonies in deep space without human intervention. Imagine this as nanosized dust particles being thrown on a planet pre-programmed to assemble themselves into useful structures. This is how nanorobots would work.

I am sure you know of the Marvel hero Wolverine from the film series X-Men, the one who can release strong claws from the back of his hands. While Wolverine's claws can slice through metal, he has an even more important superpower—the ability to heal himself rapidly, within a matter of minutes. Time and again, he takes big falls, punches and even bullets. But all he does is lie still for a while before the wounds rapidly heal and eventually disappear.

Of course, he's a character from a comic book, but even in reality we may come close to the possibility of rapid healing powers with the help of nanotechnology, more specifically nanorobots. In the future, nanorobots like the one President Kalam and I saw at Harvard can be injected (or ingested) into the body, where they will travel along the blood stream and reach the exact cells that need to be repaired. They will then assemble themselves and go about the task of healing the cells— by adding proteins to them or binding the lose cells back to the tissue and removing the dead cells to remove any clogging. After this they will be digested into the body like any normal food. Such nanorobots can be equally effective in fighting off cancerous cells and severe infections.

• • •

In 2011, President Kalam and I went on a teaching assignment to the University of Kentucky in the United States of America.[2] It was a relatively long assignment, stretching almost three weeks. About fifty students were working with us on some very unique projects that focused on bringing sustainability to the world. Students would often come in groups or individually with their questions, and we would spend hours thinking with them. One such student was Stephanie. She was a science teacher in a primary school and was on a study break. One day, she asked President Kalam, 'Sir, I have a personal question for you. Of all the things you have achieved in your life, which is the one that has given you the greatest joy?'

It was an unexpected question but an interesting one nevertheless. We all awaited the answer. I wondered whether the answer would be being the Missile Man or the President or a space scientist, or whether it would be the nuclear empowerment of his nation.

President Kalam replied, 'My moment of bliss came when I was working on the missile development programme.'

'So that is the answer. Missiles made him happy,' I thought. But my conclusion was premature.

President Kalam continued. 'So when I was working in the missile development sector, we made a unique product. It was a carbon-carbon nanomaterial that was exceptionally strong.

We used it to make the missile's nose cone—the part that experiences the maximum heat and stress.' He explained the missile's workings, but evidently something else was about to come and we all waited.

'While I was in the Defence Research and Development Organisation (DRDO) in the 1980s, I went to meet a doctor friend of mine who worked at the Nizam's Institute of Medical Sciences in Hyderabad. He introduced me to the children who had been severely affected by polio.'*

President Kalam continued. 'There were dozens of these children. Each of them had a metallic caliper to support their feet. But the caliper itself used to weigh over 4 kilogrammes in each leg. Seeing this, my friend asked me if there was something we, missile scientists, could do about this. My mind lit up, and an idea came to me. We went back to our material lab and worked on the carbon-carbon composite nanomaterial. It was strong and weighed as per the needs of the missile. But the need of the missile was also the need of these polio-affected children. So we at the Agni missile team went back to the drawing board. We used the same nanomaterial of the carbon-carbon composite to design shapes that would fit

---

* Back in those days, polio was a major ailment that permanently damaged the nervous system and weakened the muscles. Today, thanks to advances in medical science, we have zero cases of polio in the nation.

the legs of the little children. To our amazement, these new calipers were not only low-cost and strong, but also weighed less than 400 grams in each leg. We could not wait to see the polio-affected children wear them.'

His eyes sparkled as he paused for a moment and recalled the incident. He looked around the room and fixed his gaze on something, as if to connect to the time gone by; he was clearly picturizing his Agni days.

'The day eventually arrived. About thirty children were selected. We removed their heavy iron calipers. They were all curious about what was going to happen next. Then we installed the newly developed carbon-carbon calipers on their legs. We were very hopeful that they would work, though it was the first time such an attempt was being made. Once the children were fitted with these calipers, we asked them to walk. To our surprise, they not only started walking but also running! Their new calipers, built using nanomaterial, weighed less than one-tenth of their metal calipers. Now they could even cycle!

'A little child from the group walked up to me and said, "Sir! My dream was to play football, can I do it now?" We nodded. His mother, behind us, had tears in her eyes.' President Kalam looked at Stephanie, who by now also had tears in her eyes. 'This was my happiest moment.'

Smart application of nanoscience is now becoming the hallmark of medical advances and will continue to be so in the future.

The future of nanoscience

Nanotechnology is a science that is just about to take off, and when it does, it will transform virtually every sphere of our daily lives. If all goes at the correct pace with continued government and private support, in about fifteen years nanotechnology can be our solution to almost every problem we face today, be it pollution, disease, superstrong structures and energy. Can you imagine this future? Can you imagine the year 2034?

• • •

One fine summer evening in the year 2034, twenty-five-year-old Rakesh is jogging in Lodhi Gardens, New Delhi. When nanotechnology started shaping medical science in about 2025, Rakesh got himself a special vaccination of nanosensors. These extremely small particles, billions in number, were injected in his body. The nanosensors—now in his blood, muscles and organs—transmit data about temperature, flow, movement and foreign particles at regular intervals. This data also flashes on his watch, which enables him to effectively see what exercising, such as jogging, is doing to his body at the very cellular level. Moreover, with these sensors, even the slightest variation in temperature or the presence of a virus is detected easily and Rakesh is alerted.

Thus diseases are combated at the very start. And so during any emergency, when the doctor needs to diagnose him, this critical data is available for him to prescribe the exact treatment.

So Rakesh is happy with his jog, and after about an hour, he goes home and his mom offers him a glass of water. Rakesh does not need to worry about whether the water is pure or not, something that was a concern about a decade ago. In 2034, using advanced nanofiltration technology, all taps have been fitted with low-cost nano-purifiers. Unlike the previously used RO water systems, there is no wastage here, and the device is much cheaper and lasts several years.

After finishing his breakfast, Rakesh heads out for work. He approaches his self-driven car. The online circuit of this car has been designed using nanorobots, which can make circuits of small dimensions that control cars quite accurately. In fact, the car itself has been built using nanomaterial, which reduces flaws. Even small internal dents are able to heal automatically before they become larger problems. Rakesh is proud of having such a car whose parts are built from nanocomposite materials. These parts are stronger, lighter and more chemically resistant than metal. The car is also corrosion-resistant and has better fuel efficiency. It also has better gas mileage as nanoparticles prevent any airborne particle from reaching the combustion chamber. Rakesh is happy; he is helping nature by reducing his carbon footprint.

As he drives past, he looks back at his house. The roof is laid with decorative solar panels. These are not the panels of 2019, which converted 14 per cent of the energy they received and wasted most of it. Nanotechnology-based panels are multilayered, increasing the surface area and reception of sunlight, thereby converting more than 90 per cent of the solar energy from the mighty Sun. The 800-square-foot rooftop solar panels in his home could produce 250 kWh of energy a day. This is well above what his house needs, so Rakesh sells this excess power to the grid, where it powers heavier industries.

Fifteen years ago, in 2019, without nanotechnology, the same area of rooftop panels would have produced barely 40 kWh of energy—not enough for a single house. Nanotechnology has enabled solar power to completely replace all fossil-fuel-based energy generation. In 2019, power plants were generating 10 billion tons of carbon dioxide every year, one-third of the overall emissions. In 2034, this is zero, which is helping the planet heal and cool. Global warming has been stemmed, thanks to nanotechnology.

Let us come back to Rakesh. Professionally, Rakesh is a civil engineer. He is part of the team that builds and maintains the bridges of the city. As he visits a site the next day, he checks the nanosensors placed at every joint of the bridge. He also checks the detailed data acquired from the sensors. Through one of these reports, he comes to know about hairline cracks in the construction of the bridge, but he is not that worried as preventive measures have already been taken. In fact, many preventive measures were taken during the manufacturing of the parts, when some nanomaterials were injected into them. Hence all Rakesh needs to do is monitor everything as the nanoparticles rapidly fill the minor cracks and stop them from deepening. While monitoring this, Rakesh smiles, satisfied; bridges and structures that are nano-enabled are expected to last for at least 200–300 years.

In the evening when Rakesh gets home, he finds that his mom has developed an allergy due to the UV rays from the Sun. The hole in the ozone layer, which was stopped from expanding only about a decade ago, has still not healed completely. He rushes to the pharmacy and buys sunscreen lotion. However, this isn't the sunblock used in 2019—these are made from nanoparticles. These nanoparticles absorb sunlight, including the dangerous ultraviolet ones.

Later at night, after looking at reports of the bridge's repairs on his computer, Rakesh decides to check its batteries. The computers now are faster, smaller and more power-efficient, with long-lasting batteries. He doesn't need to worry. These powerful batteries are fitted with carbon-nanotube-based transistors.

The next day, as Rakesh prepares to head to work, he gets a call from the hospital. His grandmother has slipped in the bathroom and probably broken a bone. He immediately decides to head to the emergency room with his mother. The doctor performs two procedures on his grandmother. First, he takes readings from her implanted nanosensors to determine where exactly her bone has cracked. They detect cracks in four places. Now, in 2019, this would have been serious; but in 2034, things are treated differently.

The doctor injects a 10 ml solution of nanorobots in her blood stream. They are programed to be controlled by an external computer. The computer guides them through the veins and to the exact location of the cracks. Once they reach the spot, the nanorobots immediately 'stitch' the broken tissue and bone together. Other nanorobots fuse the crack by completely covering it like glue. Within five minutes, Rakesh's grandmother feels the pain going away and senses strength returning to her leg. While she is plastered as a precaution, she is told to remove it the very next morning; her four fractures will have healed by then.

In 2034, with great advancements in nanotechnology, fast and more accurate medical diagnostic equipment is being made. Technologies like lab-on-a-chip are small, low-cost implantable or wearable diagnostic tools, which can test the parameters of any human being, thereby lowering the risk of diseases spreading before being detected. Most children born after 2030 are injected with these implants—0.5-millimetre chips—at the time of vaccination, and the data is shared on the cloud for their doctors—often AI-based tools—to monitor and address anomalies, if any.

Medical devices, like implants, with nanomaterial bodies are more durable and resistant to infection. In pharmaceutical products, the use of nanoparticles not only improves their absorption within the body but also makes them easier to reach the specific target. Even the delivery of chemotherapy drugs targeted at specific cells, such as cancer cells, is achievable using nanoparticles.

For young Rakesh, who barely remembers his early childhood in the late 2010s, a life without nanoscience is impossible to imagine. The story of Rakesh and his world in 2034 is the future of nanoscience and how it will change everything around us. Can you imagine some other aspects of life wherein such nanoparticles can make life simpler, cleaner and better?

What should I do to pursue a career in nanotechnology?

Nanoscience has a wide career path as it touches on several different dimensions of application, such as medical science, construction, the space sector, botany, agriculture, the environment, to name a few. At the same time, it is a relatively new and evolving branch of science, with a limited number of experts. In India, various IITs have departments dedicated to the field of nanoscience, which are all developing rapidly. The Indian Institute of Science, Bengaluru, also offers several programmes in nanoscience.

Globally, the race to be the best institution in nanoscience is between the world's best universities. It is widely regarded that the Massachusetts Institute of Technology, Stanford University and Harvard University—all in the USA—and the University of Cambridge in the United Kingdom are the world's best places to study this field. Closer to India, even Singapore and South Korea are engaged in remarkable work in nanoscience.

If you want to pursue a career in this field, you will need to put in some extra effort as the sector is very agile and continuously changing. As a nanoscience expert, you can expect to be sought-after by almost all the major companies of the world, from cars to jets, from medical science to space technology firms.

Merely reading traditional books will not help as you need to constantly update yourself using sources on the Internet as well as scientific journals. You must also keep following the experts in the area. It is a cutting-edge field of science and needs mastery over both physics and chemistry. A good expert in nanoscience is able to think laterally, see the problems around us and deploy their knowledge to solve it. This solution-centric, innovative approach is the hallmark of nanoscientists. You will need to start cultivating it right away.

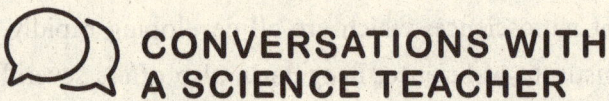 ## CONVERSATIONS WITH A SCIENCE TEACHER

How can a consumer tell if a product contains nanomaterials?

Consumers cannot identify the presence of nanomaterials in a product with the naked eye. To reliably assess the nanomaterial component in consumer products, they have to rely on a declaration that is not yet mandatory for companies or industries; but this is set to change in the coming years. In 2012, the European Food Safety Authority (EFSA), while addressing the issue of nanotechnology in food, made the marking and labelling of food containing nanomaterials mandatory and also extended it to cosmetics in 2013.

The development of techniques and methods for the reliable detection of nanomaterials in various products is in process and being evaluated by the authorities. Currently we have no technology to check whether products actually contain nanoparticles or other nanomaterials, as claimed by their manufacturers in advertisements. Marking and labelling is the only option; however, it has been observed that participants are complying with the marking and labelling obligation.

What were the earliest products made using nanoscience?

This is an interesting question. The conceptual understanding of nano is only about sixty years old and dates back to when Nobel Prize–winning American physicist Richard Feynman explained its usage as a science in a 1959 lecture. But that does not mean humankind did not unknowingly apply nanoscience in manufacturing products before that.

In fact, nanoscience-based products originated in India, more specifically southern India. During the era of the Chera kings, way back in the sixth century BCE, Indian metallurgists manufactured something called Seric iron (or wootz steel), which was regarded as the finest steel in the world. This was exported to the Romans, the Egyptians, the Chinese and the Arabs. This steel was manufactured by way of a very complicated process, often using special plants and even deploying specific monsoon winds. Wootz steel is known to have carbon nanotube structures in them and bonds of carbon and iron. Of course, the makers had no knowledge of nanoscience back then, but, through several rounds of trials and improvements, they achieved perhaps the world's first nanoscience-based product.

Wootz steel was widely used throughout the world to make weapons, especially in the Middle East. A sign of its strength is apparent in a Persian phrase—'to give an Indian answer' in Persian

A wootz steel factory in Tamil Nadu, sixth century BCE

means to give a sharp and fitting reply, just like Indian Wootz steel. Wootz steel was manufactured for years and years until, in 1866, the British forcibly banned its trade and the art was lost.

Are there any specific health risks of using nano-products?

Ideally not. The novel properties of nanomaterials should not have negative effects on human beings. However, health risks cannot be ruled out completely as the released particles can enter the body, distribute themselves in ultra-fine quantities and accumulate in various organs. Therefore, health risks of using nano-products can be present, especially if the materials remain in the body for a long time and have the opportunity to build up.

In general, metallic nanoparticles, nanotubes and nanofibres could lead to greater health risks because of their small structure, high mobility and higher degree of reactivity. Unbound nanoparticles, which are free to move around, could enter the human body via three paths—the respiratory tract, the skin and the intestinal tract—and have a toxic impact. Scientists believe that the inhalation of nanoparticles poses the greatest risk, though the materials in themselves are not very toxic. They could be harmful if they are inhaled as they may get deposited in the lungs and the respiratory tract. The possibility of nanoparticles penetrating healthy human skin has been ruled out by the latest scientific findings, while the risks involved in the intake of nanoparticles via the gastrointestinal tract are not yet known.

How are nanomaterials classified on the basis of their dimensions? What are zero-, one- and two-dimensional nanomaterials?

The classification of materials in the nanoscale regime is based on the number of dimensions of a material that are outside the nanoscale range (which are dimensions above 100 nanometres).

Accordingly, zero-dimensional (0D) nanomaterials have nano-dimensions in all the three directions—length, breadth and height. This means that no dimension along any of the three axes is greater than 100 nm. Metallic nanoparticles, including gold and silver nanoparticles, belong to this class. Imagine them to be very fine, like grains of sand, only in nano-dimensions.

In one-dimensional (1D) nanomaterials, one dimension of the structure is outside the nanoscale. Nanotubes, nanorods and nanowires are some examples of this class. Imagine them like long but very thin wires.

In two-dimensional (2D) nanomaterials, two dimensions of the structure are outside the nanoscale. This class includes different kinds of nano-films, nano-sheets and nano-walls. Imagine these like very thin sheets of paper, with their thickness in nanometres.

How does the nanoscience manufacturing process promise both—extreme precision in structure and environmental cleanliness—at the same time?

Traditional manufacturing processes operate in a top-down fashion, taking a chunk of material and removing small parts of it—for example, by crushing or by reacting with chemicals—until the final product (part) is achieved.

However, nanoscience builds products in a bottom-up fashion. It starts with single molecules and joins them together to form a product wherein every atom is in its precisely designated location. In comparison to the other approach, this method has potentially much less material waste as leftovers and hence greatly reduces pollution.

How is nanotechnology different from biotechnology?

The nature of the materials in both is the basic difference between biotechnology and nanotechnology. The living (or dead) biomolecules and organisms are the consideration in biotech. They typically range from 3 nm in size up to large organisms of several metres. Nanotech (or nanoscience) typically only deals with living, dead or non-living (including man-made) particles that are smaller than 100 nanometres.

MEET THE EXPERT: V. RAMGOPAL RAO

Professor V. Ramgopal Rao is currently the director of IIT Delhi. Prior to this, he was the P.K. Kelkar Chair professor in the department of electrical engineering, IIT Bombay. He has over 450 research publications in the area of nanoscale devices and nano-electronics to his name, and he is the inventor of forty-three patents and patent applications, which include fifteen US patents.

Q. Nanotechnology is said to be the science of small sizes. But what is so special about nanoparticles that we need a completely new field to study them?

Fundamentally, nanotechnology deals with very, very, small dimensions. It is called nanoscale and is in the order of 10 nanometres. But nanotechnology isn't merely about size. You see, what happens is that when certain materials are brought to nanoscale, they start to show new and unique properties, which are different from the properties that they show in bulk form. This is what interests a nanotechnologist.

For instance, take the case of gold. We all know that gold is shiny yellow. But it looks yellow because of its bulk properties. If you were to start reducing gold to nanoparticle levels, then it would no longer be yellow! In fact, the colour of gold nanoparticles is known to change with alterations in its size. This is because when we reach the nanoscale, the optical properties of the material also change with its size.

Take another example, of silicon dioxide, which is considered one of the best electrical insulators in the world. If you take a 1-micrometre-thick layer of silicon dioxide and apply a potential of 100 V across it, no current will flow. However, instead of 1 micrometre, if you take a layer of 1 nanometre, the observation will be surprising. The same material, which was an insulator at 1 micrometre, now becomes a great conductor.

So these are the type of changes you see in a material's properties when you switch to nanoscale. This happens mainly due to the quantum mechanical effects as the particle–particle interactions tend to be very different when you go down to very small sizes. This is how nanotechnology started finding tremendous application, because these new properties—which we get by just reducing the particle size—could be used for a variety of purposes. This excited the scientists and engineers, and they started to explore this field further. So while chemists and material scientists started synthesizing these materials in nanoscale form and then studied their properties, engineers started work on applying these new properties to improve existing products, either in terms of performance or economics.

Q. Why are microprocessors in computers not considered a product of nanotechnology despite the fact that their size is of the order of 10 nm?

The microprocessors available in the market today are using sub-10 nm as the minimum feature size in many of their transistors. A typical current-generation Intel processor has over 7 billion transistors packed in an area of about 450 square millimetres.[†] All the integrated circuits (ICs) available today have about 10–15 nm as the critical dimension in an electronic device. But this is not nanotechnology because even though the dimensions have come down to accommodate more devices, there is no real change in the properties that are attributed to quantum mechanical effects. Many of the quantum mechanical

---

[†] For example, the twenty-two-core Broadwell (Xeon E5) by Intel.

effects that set in are unfortunately degrading the performance of conventional devices used in microprocessors. Efforts to build tunnelling transistors are also ongoing, which can benefit from the nanoscale phenomenon, but so far they have not seen industry applications.

As I told you, nanotechnology is not only about change in dimension but also a resulting change in property that can be exploited for application. While in the case of the modern microprocessor it is just the application of Moore's law—which states that 'the number of transistors in an IC doubles every two years'—this is not nanotechnology, because the change in dimension is not driving any real change. Also, nanotechnology, is traditionally associated with bottom-up processes, while semiconductor industries use top-down processes involving lithography. But these are all matters of definition, and one need not bother about it.

Q. You studied electrical engineering. How did you develop an interest in nanotechnology?

My interest in nanotechnology grew because of some questions, such as this one: instead of just depending on Moore's law, can we create something like a tunnel transistor?

Tunnelling is a quantum mechanical process based on the properties of an electron's movement. It becomes very prominent at nanoscale. So can we invent and innovate a new device that behaves differently with higher levels of performance?

My field of study has always been ICs, and since these devices are already in the 10 nm domain, my objective has been to make use of some nano-effects and build an application that is otherwise not possible—instead of just depending on Moore's law. I also use many nanotechnology concepts to improve the sensitivity of sensing platforms for applications in health and environmental domains.

Q. How are advances in nanotechnology impacting our daily lives?

Nanotechnology-based products are already in the market.

Let's take the example of nano-paints. There is an Indian company called I-CanNano Paints, which deals in nano-paints that aim to improve the strength and longevity of traditional paints used on walls. There are also material science specialists who are selling nano-based materials for a variety of applications. Most of such materials are used for coating applications. For example, using nano-coating on tools can strengthen them exponentially, which, in turn, would increase their reliability and longevity. So nano-based materials in the form of coatings are widely available in the market. A nano-based silver coating developed at IIT Delhi is also widely applied to textiles all over the world.

But the devices that make use of nano-effects are still mostly under development. So even though you might be using a 10 nm device, it is still not nano because it doesn't use any nano-effect. The devices that could use such effects are not in the market yet.

In medicine, targeted drug-delivery systems also use nanotechnology. Many such drugs are already available in the market and many others are under field trials. Targeted drug delivery for cancer treatment is a competitive area right now as drugs for this treatment have already hit the market.

In textiles, nano-based alternatives are also already in the market. These are interesting products; if you spill coffee on your shirt, you don't need to worry about the stain as the shirt is already coated with a nanomaterial that will not allow the coffee to stick to it, similar to the lotus effect. You just need to wipe the coffee off, and you won't have a stain on your shirt. Textiles reinforced with antibacterial coating are already appearing in the market. Even automobiles are beginning to use nanomaterial-based coatings that have high scratch resistance.

Coming to agriculture, studies about dispensing fertilizers and pesticides in nano-form are already underway. It has been observed that plants tend to absorb them better when the chemicals are given in nano-form, and this way the prescribed dosage is reduced, which ultimately helps in protecting the environment.

Therefore, the applications of nanotechnology cover everything from healthcare to textiles to agriculture.

Q. What is the course of study one should undertake to pursue a career in nanotechnology?

The study of nanotechnology starts much later in the traditional education curriculum. This is one thing that many institutions in India have overlooked. When nano became very prominent and people wanted to explore it, they started Bachelor of Technology, or BTech, programmes in nanotechnology—but it doesn't work that way. For me (as I am an electrical engineer), the study of nano came after I had sound knowledge of electronic devices. Because it is only then that I became aware of these materials that have these properties. Only then did I start playing within the nanoscale in order to improve the performance of existing devices.

So here is my advice. The ideal way is that you first become an electrical engineer, textile engineer, automobile engineer, mechanical engineer or agriculture scientist, etc. and then start applying the principles of nano in your particular field. Therefore, there is little merit in courses like a BTech in nanotechnology. In fact, even master's-level programmes in nanotech are too early an introduction. Enough courses related to nano must, however, be introduced at the undergraduate and postgraduate levels. In a nutshell, you should study traditional disciplines and gain exposure to nanotech through various courses or minor degree programmes. Nanotechnology can be thoroughly explored at the PhD level.

 **NOTE TO PARENTS**

Nanoscience is the frontier technology of our species. It is as revolutionary as the discovery of microorganisms more than a century ago by Louis Pasteur. Like Pasteur's discovery opened up an entirely new space of technology and medical industry, nanoscience is destined to do the same. Everything that exists around us, from commodities and food to jets, stands a great chance of being completely transformed by the nano revolution.

A career in this field is destined to be marked by long years of academic research—longer than usual. It's absolutely necessary to pursue a master's degree to enter this field, potentially leading to a PhD. However, it has long-term benefits too. The opportunities in this sector are rapidly expanding, both in terms of employment and entrepreneurship. In the future, traditional companies will have to employ nanoscience experts to help them develop existing products into flawless, precise ones using nanoscience.

 **EXERCISE**

The year is 2050. You are the head of a new division under the United Nations, created to explore new planets for settlements. This is called the Interplanetary Strike for Elevating Alternative Regions, popularly INTERSTELLAR, named after a movie made on this topic about forty years ago.

INTERSTELLAR has been told about two likely planets in nearby solar systems, located far off but still within a five-year travel period from our planet. Considering how large the universe is, this is just a stone's throw away! Two probes have already been sent to these planets, and the reports are promising. The gravity and heat are suitable for human habitation, and the people of Planet Earth are excited about the possibilities.

However, as head of INTERSTELLAR, you know that there will be significant problems in the coming days. Humans are very sensitive to the environment and need a certain suitable mix of gases and water to survive. Moreover, the crust of the planet needs to bear soil in order for plants to grow, and hence produce necessary food. Thankfully, you have the Indian Institute of Nanotechnology (IIN) in New Delhi for help. They have promised to design nanorobots that can be sent to any planet in order to conduct the necessary chemical reactions to produce any necessary elements and compounds such as oxygen and water. However, you need to programme them for a particular reaction.

1. The first planet, called Xeter, poses a serious challenge—scarcity of water. Barely 1 per cent of its surface is water, and your INTERSTELLAR team tells you that you need it to have at least 50 per cent water for humans to survive on it. Probes have, however, shown one interesting finding. The planet is filled with sodium acetate, a white powder spread all over its surface. You are wondering if this can be converted into water. IIN's nanorobots are capable of carrying chemical packets to start any reaction. INTERSTELLAR needs you to determine what gas they should carry to make water from the available sodium acetate powder. Can you find out and give the instructions?

2. The second planet is called Krypto, and it contains water in abundance but in solid form, i.e. ice. It also lacks a critical component of human life—oxygen. Initially INTERSTELLAR thought it would electrolyse the water into oxygen, but that proved to be a costly process in terms of energy and so the plan was abandoned. Then the latest probe highlighted something that excited everyone. The planet is filled with sodium percarbonate. INTERSTELLAR wants you to determine how it can use this sodium percarbonate to generate oxygen. What process should the IIN nanorobots carry out on planet Krypto?

CHAPTER 4

Have you watched the 2015 science fiction movie *The Martian*? This award-winning film, based on the novel by Andy Weir, was even screened for astronauts who were in space at the International Space Station (ISS)! The movie tells the incredible story of a group of astronauts who land on the red planet, Mars, as part of the Ares III crew. However, on this mission, just as they are about to leave for Earth, a massive Martian dust storm strikes, resulting in one astronaut named Mark Whatney getting stranded on the planet. Alone on the Martian surface, with no means of communicating with his crew on Earth or Ares III, Whatney's only chance at survival is to meet the crew of the next mission to Mars, Ares IV, scheduled to land after four long years. With limited food and oxygen at hand, the astronaut, who is an expert in agriculture with a background of botany, decides to take matters into his own hands. To survive, he becomes the first Martian farmer: he repurposes Martian soil by recycling human dung, makes water from hydrogen with leftover fuel and then grows his own potatoes. This becomes his means of survival, and, of course, with several other innovations on Mars and on Earth, he is able to sustain himself on the red planet till he is rescued. Of course, he encounters several difficulties on Mars—which you can find out by watching the movie yourself. But, getting to the point: he is able to survive largely due to his knowledge of agricultural science!

• • •

Acquiring the ability to grow plants for food and rear animals was a turning point in human history. Before we became farmers and animal rearers, we were hunters and foragers. This meant we were running behind animals to hunt them for meat or scouring for fruit-bearing plants. But there were two fundamental problems with each of these food-gathering tasks. First, there was no guarantee of a successful hunt. Even when equipped with rudimentary spears, stones and clubs, humans were not as fast as some of the other animals of prey, like wolves and tigers. Unlike animals, man doesn't have claws or sharp teeth with which to attack predators, or sharp eyes to see in the dark, or strong legs to outrun them. The only fundamental advantage early man had was fire. But while fire was a good defence and scared large predators away, it was a poor weapon when it came to hunting. Often the disorganized hordes of humans went into the jungles and grasslands and came back empty-handed and with an empty stomach.

Second, foraging, or searching for fruit and other edible plants and roots, was filled with more dangers. The forests were brimming with numerous trees, but most of the fruit was poisonous. For instance, even today only about 10 per cent of white wild berries are edible; the rest are toxic to humans.[1] Hence selecting the right fruit based on colour and smell alone was a difficult task and prone to errors. There was no medical science back then, and so, quite literally, one bite into the wrong apple was a one-way ticket to heaven.

Agriculture allowed us to steer clear of both of these problems. It allowed us to grow food in a fixed area, near rivers, where humans could settle, and thus it laid the foundation for larger communities and civilizations to evolve. It also allowed us to cultivate and eat only specific plants—the ones that suited us best.

So who started agriculture?

This question has no clear answers. Different crops were grown and different animals were domesticated in different parts of the world and, with migration and trade, they started learning from each other. In fact, the dates vary from crop to crop and from animal to animal. From what we know till now, the earliest known grain collectors are at least 22,000 years old. However, one cannot be sure whether humans actually grew these grains or merely collected and ate the naturally fallen grains.

Here is a summary of what we know about the history of agriculture.[2] Can you mark the items mentioned below that you use in your daily life?

CROP/ANIMAL	HOW LONG AGO CULTIVATION/ REARING/ DOMESTICATION BEGAN (IN YEARS)	LOCATION
Dog[3]	15,000	Europe
Pig[4]	13,000	Mesopotamia (modern-day Iraq)
Sheep	12,000	Not known
Wheat, barley, lentils, pea, chickpea, flax	11,500	Levant (Modern Syria and Iraq)
Cow[5]	10,500	India, Pakistan, Turkey
Sugar cane[6]	10,000	South East Asia (New Guinea)
Potato, sweet potato[7]	9000	South America
Rice[8]	8200	China
Coca[9]	8000	South America
Banana	8000	South East Asia
Moong, soya	7500	Not known
Maize	6000	Not known
Cotton	5500	India, Peru
Camel	5000	Not known

Notice that the Old World (Asia, Africa and Europe) and the New World (North and South America) grew completely different crops. This went on till the late fifteenth century—which was only about 500 years ago—when Columbus, who was actually looking for India, accidentally discovered America.

It was only around 300 years ago, in the sixteenth century, that the Old World learnt of vegetables like the potato and the sweet potato. Today, India and China grow almost 40 per cent of the world's potatoes. In India, we use the potato in nearly every food preparation, but no more than three centuries ago, the farmers of India would have found the potato an alien crop. Similarly, the people in the Americas would never have seen a dog, sheep, pig, a sheaf of corn or even a cow.

The job of the earliest agricultural scientist, especially those dealing in crops, was crucial. From finding fertile lands with access to water in order to sow seeds, to nurturing the plants and ensuring they remained disease-free—they had to ensure it all. Of course, scientific knowledge grew at a very slow rate back then, with individuals mostly working with trial-and-error methods. It was only in the last 200 years that we started understanding *what* makes a plant grow and *how*.

Plants essentially need nutrients, much like us humans. They need carbon, oxygen, hydrogen, nitrogen, phosphorus, potassium and several other elements in smaller quantities. The first three in the list can be obtained from atmospheric air and water. Nitrogen, on the other hand, is a different case altogether. Nitrogen is critical as it is a component of chlorophyll. It is, therefore, essential for photosynthesis, the process that produces food for the plant and, in turn, for us. Almost three quarters of the gases in the atmosphere is nitrogen. But there

A timeline of the domestication of different animals and crops

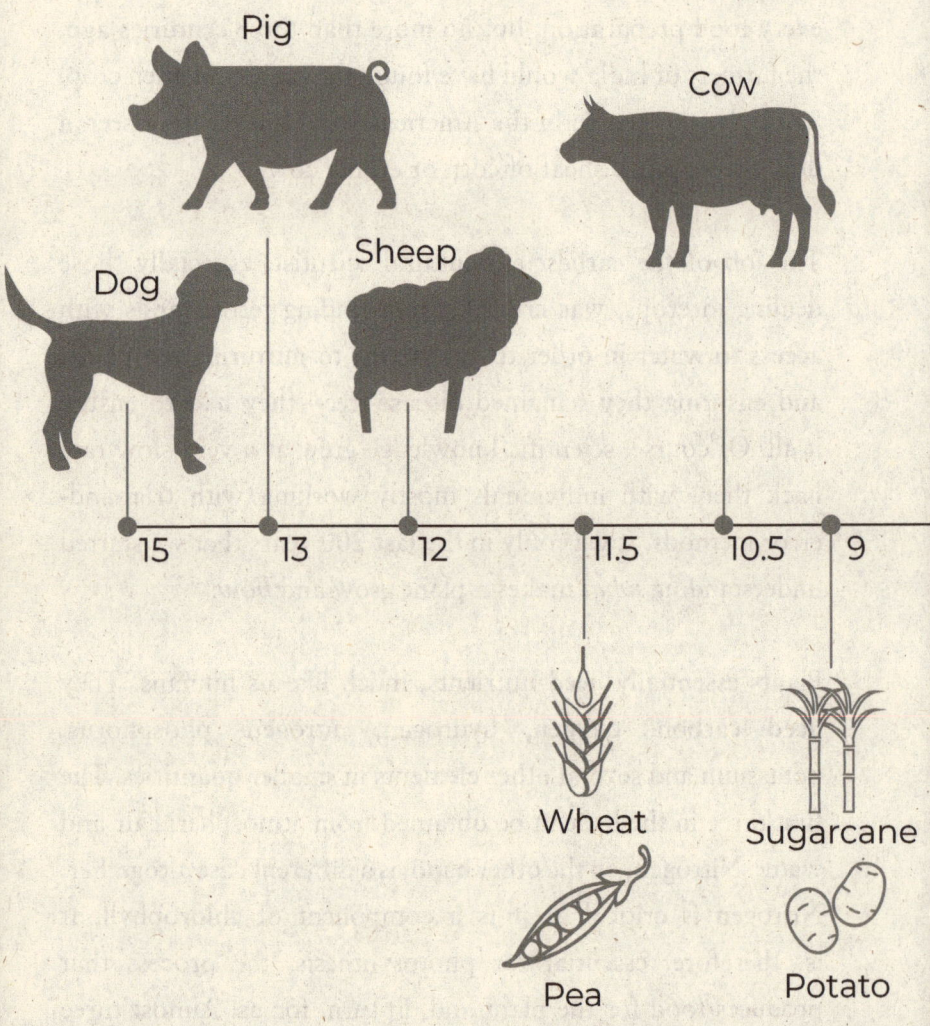

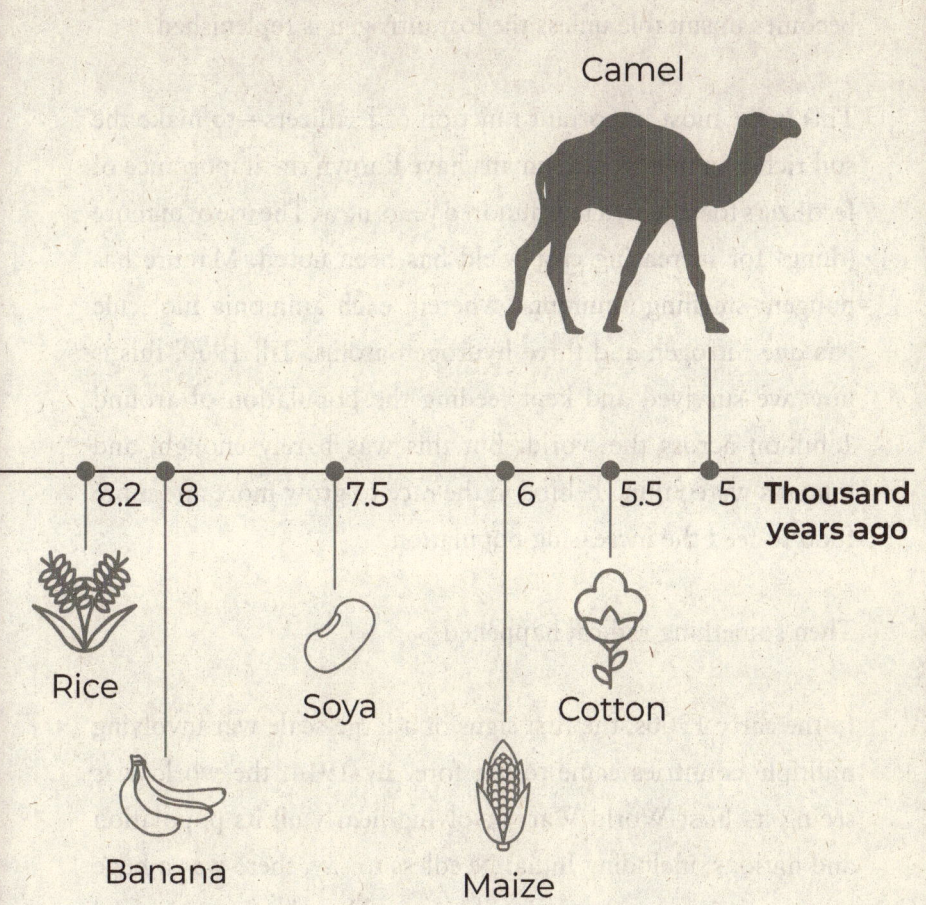

Camel

8.2   8   7.5   6   5.5   5   **Thousand years ago**

Rice

Soya

Cotton

Banana

Maize

is a problem. Plants do not know how to use it directly from the air. Instead they rely on getting the nutrient from the soil, where it is sparsely present. The soil loses its nutrients, especially nitrogen, when plants are grown in the same piece of land over and over again for human consumption. Over time, the soil becomes unsuitable unless the lost nitrogen is replenished.

This is the most important function of fertilizers—to make the soil richer in nitrogen. Humans have known the importance of fertilizers for at least a few hundred years now. The use of manure (dung) for increasing crop yield has been noted. Manure has pungent-smelling ammonia, wherein each ammonia molecule has one nitrogen and three hydrogen atoms. Till 1900, this is how we survived and kept feeding the population of around 1 billion across the world. But this was barely enough, and humans were falling behind in the race to grow more and more food to feed the increasing population.

Then something radical happened.

In the early 1900s, the first signs of a large-scale war involving multiple countries came to the fore. By 1914, the world was seeing its First World War, involving nearly all its population and nations, including India. Needless to say, there was a huge demand for explosives during this time. Thus the first industrial effort to make nitrogen compounds began because explosives needed nitrates (compounds of nitrogen).

It was in 1909 that a German chemist named Fritz Haber developed a process to synthesize ammonia from nitrogen in the air (he would go on to win the Nobel Prize in Chemistry). Soon factories emerged all over the world and speedily produced nitrates. But these were set up not to grow plants but to make bombs. These nitrate factories made rising profits as the world was plunged into the bloodshed of the First World War (1914–1918) and then the Second World War (1939–1945).

Fritz Haber

In 1945, after the Second World War was over, the United Nations was formed to maintain peace in the world. Though global conflicts seemed to dwindle in number, the focus of the military changed to nuclear weapons, and so the need for traditional explosives, too, dwindled. In the rather desperate times of reduced demand in the military sector, these nitrate factories around the world discovered a new market—agriculture. During this period, large amounts of nitrate compounds were made, converting nitrogen from the air to powder form. This was sold as fertilizers to farmers. It revolutionized the farms. Scientists had found a relatively cheaper and sure-shot way of fixing nitrogen from the air and into the soil. Now the era of urea fertilizers dominated the global agriculture scene, starting with the USA in the 1950s and spreading to almost the entire world. The factories that made the bombs of yesterday were now researching growing the plants of tomorrow. The global nitrogen fertilizer production grew from about 15 million tons per annum in 1960 to almost 120 million tons today—an eightfold increase.

The future of agricultural science

The Martian's hero, Mark Whatney, growing crops on Mars is, of course, just a story, but it is not far from what can be a reality—as you will read in the chapter on astrobiology. We are planning to send humans to Mars by the mid-2030s. Hence in the future we will need the ability and the science to grow plants and engage in agriculture on other planets too.

Whether cultivating on Earth or on Mars, multiple challenges await us:

1. **Reducing the dependency on water:** Agriculture consumes more than half of the total fresh water of Planet Earth. Therefore it will be critical to invent crops that need far less water to grow. Of course, on other planets, the shortage of water may be far more severe, and we must be prepared.
2. **Reducing the dependency on land:** With cities growing rapidly, more crops will need to be grown in smaller areas of land. We will also need to stop clearing the indispensable forest cover, which is currently being destroyed to make room for farms. We will have to come up with a solution to this—wherein forests are not destroyed for farming purposes.
3. **Removing the dependency on weather:** Most crops are dependent on weather conditions. Extreme hot and cold cycles kill crops. So do floods and droughts. All plants are dependent on the sunlight they receive, and hence crops grown in some areas of the world cannot be grown in others.

The future of crops lies in ridding agricultural processes of these dependencies.

Agricultural scientists are working extensively to solve these challenges, and two of the most promising solutions have been aeroponic and vertical farming. In aeroponic farming, soil is not needed to grow plants as nutrient-laden mist is directed at the roots. Plants here receive photons not from the Sun but from special LED lights, and hence can be grown day or night. Since they are grown in an environment where the climate is controlled, these plants yield produce throughout the year. It is truly a 365 x 24 farming industry. And because scientists are constantly checking and sensing the health of the plants, there is no risk of disease or wastage. Controlled nutrients directed at the plants means better nutritional value of the grain or the fruit—several times higher than what we get from traditional methods, and that too without the use of any pesticide. The biggest advantage, however, is in terms of water use, as aeroponic farming uses less than 10 per cent of the water used in traditional cropping. This can be a huge advantage to countries like India, which is now water-stressed.

Now imagine a vertical farm, which is a building that's 100 metres in width, 100 metres in length and twenty-five storeys high. This is similar to the dimensions of a large corporate office. With the use of aeroponic-friendly plants and a controlled climate, this building will be able to produce as much of a harvest—vegetable or fruit—that is produced by a traditional farm of 600 hectares (6 square kilometres). So imagine a building like this producing what a 6 km long farm can yield!

To comprehend the true potential of this, we must think in larger figures. Suppose we were given the difficult challenge of replacing every single farmland in India with vertical farms. That means replacing every single plantation of wheat, rice, lentils, fruit, vegetables, tea, maize, sugar cane and every other foodgrain you can eat, grown across the 6,50,000 villages of India. This is a mammoth task, which would also be a certain challenge on the next planet we inhabit. But can we do it? What is the answer to this question? Let us work it out together. It would not be a bad idea to grab a pencil and a sheet of paper to figure this out with me.

India has about 90 million hectares, or 9,00,000 square kilometres, of farmland. Each thirty-storey vertical farm of 100 metres by 100 metres can replace a 6-square-kilometre farm. Hence, to replace every single farm in India and grow an equivalent amount of food in vertical farms, we would need about 1,50,000 vertical farms. These farms would occupy a land area of 1,50,000 x 0.01 = 1500 square kilometres. In other words, 1,50,000 vertical farms put together in an area spanning the entire city of, say, Delhi would be enough to replace *all* the farms of India. As a result, almost a million square kilometres of land would be released from existing farms, roughly the combined area of the three largest states of India—Rajasthan, Madhya Pradesh and Maharashtra—or about one-third the land area of India. We can grow forests in these lands and restore our oxygen balance.

But, wait—there is more. What about conserving water?

As I said before, India is a water-stressed nation. A nation is considered water-deficient if it has less than 17,00,000 litres of water per person per year. In the case of India, this figure is 14,00,000 litres of water, which is well below the stress mark.[10] Eighty-six per cent of water is used in the irrigation of farms, and the remaining in industries, power generation and household usage. Hence when we have the scientific ability to follow a completely vertical farming model, we will be saving about 80 per cent of India's total water resources. This would mean that the per capita water availability would be almost four times that which is now, mitigating the water deficit of the nation.

Of course, we are at least a few years, if not a couple of decades, away from this. But what you should keep in mind is the possibility of an agricultural revolution. The method of cultivating crops was invented 12,000 years ago when a resourceful human being sowed seeds of wheat in porous soil by the river. This may reach an entirely different level when agricultural scientists establish a vertical farm on the next planet, perhaps Mars, where the seeds from Earth germinate into life in an entirely different world. Will *you* be this agricultural scientist?

What should I do to become an agricultural scientist?

Agricultural science is a multidimensional field. Typically these scientists study plants and animals, and they may work with soils and farming practices. Modern vertical farms also deploy an array of agricultural data scientists who have the knowledge of computers and mathematics. Those agricultural scientists who work in the field of producing fertilizers are also well equipped with the knowledge of chemistry.

To become an agricultural scientist, you can pursue a variety of subjects. Of course, the easiest route is to study courses in agricultural science, which are available at the bachelor's and master's levels. Such courses often deal with geology, chemistry, food sciences and biosciences. To become a successful agricultural scientist you need to develop a keen understanding of biology, both botany and zoology. The knowledge of chemistry is also very important. Geography will give you the tools to study weather patterns, which is also an important factor in agriculture. Above all, you need to have a keen interest in reading about farms, farming and food technology. India, being a largely agrarian society, prominently focuses on developing the curriculum for agricultural academies. Some of the major institutions are Indian Agricultural Research Institute (IARI), National Dairy Research Institute (NDRI) and Punjab Agricultural University (PAU), among others. You can also find many such courses outside India, including those in the USA and Australia—two of the leading nations in agricultural research.

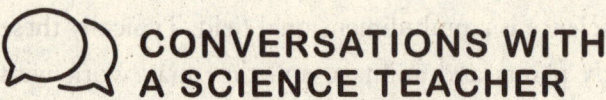

CONVERSATIONS WITH A SCIENCE TEACHER

How much water do crops typically consume?

Quite a lot. All plants need to be irrigated by large amounts of water. Plants process water in two different ways—transpiration and evaporation. The plant roots go deep into the ground and extract water from the soil. This water moves up the stem and into the leaves, from where it then escapes into the atmosphere. This process is called transpiration, and it happens mainly during the daytime. Then, as you probably know, water on any open surface, be it water over soil or on any part of the plant, undergoes the process of evaporation from the surface. Both transpiration and evaporation depend on the exposure of the area, the temperature, the wind speed and also the time taken by the plant to grow.

India is a relatively warmer country and uses traditional methods of cultivation that are more water-intensive. That is, it fares worse in terms of the amount of water used for agriculture. So it fares badly than the global average of water usage per kilogramme of crop. For instance, while globally one kilogramme of rice consumes about 2500 litres of water, in the case of India that number is around 4000 litres.

Let us discuss the water needs of other crops. Can you guess which is the most water-intensive food on the planet? Chocolate! One kilogramme of chocolate needs over 17,000 litres of water to grow.

Here is a list of some popular food and other items we consume on a daily basis and the water resources needed to grow them:[11]

ITEM	QUANTITY	WATER NEEDED (IN LITRES)
Goat	1 kg	10,412
Cotton	1 kg	9980
Pork	1 kg	5988
Butter	1 kg	5553
Chicken	1 kg	4325
Cheese	1 kg	3178
Olive	1 kg	3025
Rice	1 kg	2497
Sugar	1 kg	2000
Pasta	1 kg	1849
Bread	1 kg	1608
Pizza	1 unit	1239
Milk	1 litre	1020
Wheat	1 kg	1000
Apple	1 kg	822
Banana	1 kg	790
Potato	1 kg	287
Cabbage	1 kg	237
Tomato	1 kg	214
Egg	1 unit	196

How much have we transformed the plants and animals of the planet by way of agriculture?

The domestication of plants and animals, which began 15,000 years ago, starting with wheat and the dog, has come a long way. Seven thousand years ago, in 5000 BCE, when we became farmers, the global population was about 20 lakh (2 million). Two thousand years, in 1 CE, the population became 2 crore (200 million).[12] Somewhere in the late 1800s, the population crossed 100 crore and since then has grown rapidly to over 750 crore (7.5 billion) today. This very rapid growth in the population of human beings has completely transformed the animal kingdom.

To understand this impact, we will choose two years—1900 and, a century later, 2000. Study the table below, which shows the total weight of particular species (biomass) down the years.[13] All figures are in billion kilogrammes of weight.

YEAR	HUMANS	WILD ANIMALS	ELEPHANTS	DOMESTICATED ANIMALS	CATTLE
10,000 BCE (12,000 years ago)	1 (0.01 per cent)	200 (99.9 per cent)	Unknown	0	0

YEAR	HUMANS	WILD ANIMALS	ELEPHANTS	DOMESTICATED ANIMALS	CATTLE
1900	65 (23 per cent)	50 (17 per cent)	15	175 (60 per cent)	115
2000	275 (30 per cent)	25 (3 per cent)	1.5	600 (67 per cent)	400

Here is what you should have noticed in the table above. The population of wild animals halved between 1900 and 2000—and their total share became less than 3 per cent. Today, for every biomass of wild animals, human mass is eleven times more and a whopping twenty-four times that of domesticated animal mass. Remember, when we started agriculture 15,000 years ago—a mere second on the Earth's clock—there was no domesticated animal mass at all.

What are GM crops? Are they harmful?

Genetically modified crops, or GM crops, are plants whose DNA has been artificially altered to modify their characteristics. Scientists hand-pick and extract specific genes from a plant and inject them into others using genetic engineering. Thus the process creates a new species with an improved set of characteristics, which is otherwise not found in nature.

Percentage change in the relative mass of wild animals, domesticated animals and human beings

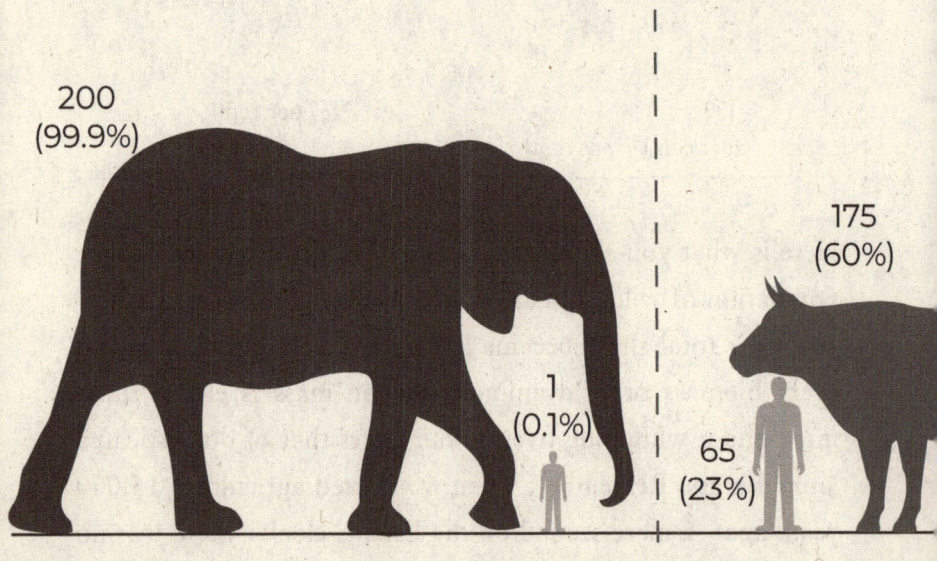

200
(99.9%)

1
(0.1%)

175
(60%)

65
(23%)

10,000 BCE
(12000 years ago)

1900 CE
(100 years ago)

 Mass of all
wild animals

 Mass of all
human beings

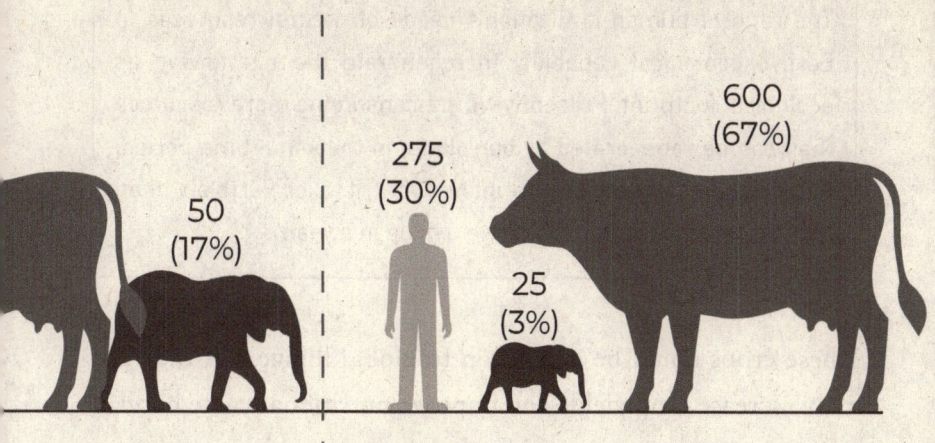

50
(17%)

275
(30%)

25
(3%)

600
(67%)

2000 CE
(Today)

Mass of all
domesticated
animals

All figures are in
billion kilogrammes

This technique is widely used in agriculture. GM crops don't require as much water, land or pesticides as traditional crops, hence they not only lower production costs but also shrink our ecological footprint.

> The ratio of human civilization's usage of natural resources to Earth's ecological capability to regenerate them is known as ecological footprint. Presently we are consuming more resources than can be regenerated by our planet in the same time period. According to the Global Footprint Network, it takes Earth eighteen months to produce that which we use up in a year.

These crops could be a solution to global hunger, as they not only increase crop yields and improve nutritional value but can even be grown on marginal land and inhospitable conditions.

Despite these benefits, there are definitely some cons of GM crops as well. First, they make us more prone to allergies. Studies have shown that you can be allergic to the GM version of a food even if you have no such complaint against the non-GM version. Second, GM crops could lead to undesirable consequences for human health. Many GM crops possess antibiotic-resistant genes, and consuming them could lead to a dramatic decrease in the effectiveness of antibiotics. Additionally, some studies conducted on animals have raised concerns of disturbance in the digestive system after the intake of GM crops. It's hard to define the full extent of the damage they could do to our bodies because the required research is incomplete.

What is organic farming?

Organic farming is a method that avoids or largely excludes the use of synthetic inputs, such as fertilizers, pesticides, hormones, etc. This method is not new to India; rather, it has been followed since ancient times. The primary aim of this farming technique is to cultivate the land and raise crops in a way that keeps the soil alive and in good health. This is ensured by the use of crop leftovers (which are composted to be used as manure), animal manure and other biological materials. Also, the use of genetically modified crops is not permitted in this kind of farming. This method not only increases farm productivity but also repairs decades of environmental damage caused by the use of synthetic compounds.

Which countries lead the global agricultural production?

Although food is a fundamental economic product, only a handful of countries have actually excelled at its production. The world's leading food-producing countries also top the list of countries with the highest geographic area since most agricultural commodities require a lot of land.

Agricultural produce is highly dependent on geographical conditions. This is the reason that the production of some crops is widely spaced out while others are highly concentrated. Climate and its corresponding types of vegetation also play a role in the level of agricultural production.

Let's look at a report from the UN's Food and Agriculture Organization (FAO) that lists the leading producers of some crops in 2015–2016. It can be found in their statistical database, called the Food and Agriculture Organization Corporate Statistical Database (FAOSTAT).

CROP	FIRST	SECOND	THIRD
Wheat	China	India	Russia
Rice	China	India	Indonesia
Maize	USA	China	Brazil
Sugar cane	Brazil	India	China
Potato	China	India	Russia
Tomato	China	India	USA
Apple	China	USA	Poland
Chickpea	India	Australia	Myanmar
Banana	India	China	Indonesia

Despite being one the largest producers of most of the agricultural crops, India's yield rates (tons produced per hectare, or t/ha) are lower than even its BRICS counterparts.[*] Currently, for rice, India is at the twenty-seventh place out of forty-seven countries as its yield rate is 2.4 tons per hectare, while that of China is 4.7 t/ha and Brazil's is 3.6 t/ha. In the case of wheat, India has a higher yield rate than that of rice, but it still lags behind many countries. With a yield rate of 3.15 tons per hectare, India is ranked nineteenth out of forty-one countries. Here we fare better than Brazil's yield rate of 2.73 t/ha but still lag behind China, which has a yield rate of 4.9 t/ha.

MEET THE EXPERT: ADAM WOLF

Adam Wolf is the founder and chief scientist of Arable Labs, Inc. He holds a PhD in biology from Stanford University. He has also taught at the famed Princeton University. In his scientific career, he has lived and researched in many locations, such as Russia, Africa, Europe and East Asia, bringing a global perspective to the application of data in solving real-world problems.

---

[*] BRICS is the association of five emerging economies, which are Brazil, Russia, India, China and South Africa.

Q. You have worked in the field of agricultural science for several years. What made you choose this field as a career? What were your motivations?

I always wanted to know how things work, which I now understand to be the purpose of an engineer. For instance, in high school, I was teaching myself how to make beer. This process involved getting the right grains and the yeast, and working on the fermentation. It also required all sorts of equipment. So I went to college and literally studied beer making, or fermentation science, as the major was called. And what I found was that behind this small glass of beer was nothing but the vast realm of agriculture. I realized that studying agriculture was the ultimate pursuit for understanding how things work. Here, we are not only understanding the engineering but also the genetics and the biology behind the diversity of crops, their domestication and their breeding. We are also studying politics and war, because issues such as land, its distribution and who owns it are very much decided by a patriarchal society. It is difficult to understand any civilization without understanding land and agriculture. So I kind of figured that agriculture is a lens through which one can study almost anything in society.

Q. What role has cooked food played in our leap from apes to humans?

The first thing that differentiated us (*Homo sapiens*) from the apes (Australopithecus) was that we started to cook food. That meant that we didn't need to spend nearly as much time and energy chewing. The great apes chew for more than ten hours a day! With this high-density food, we could then fit and power a larger brain in a relatively smaller body cavity. So cooked food ensured our leap to humans from apes.

As soon as we started cooking food, we started domesticating, picking and choosing food. For instance, we chose grains on the basis of taste and energy content. So this agricultural intensification reinforced the formation of society.

Q. One of the critical problems that we are facing today, especially in India, is the shortage of fresh water. Agriculture consumes over 80 per cent of the world's fresh water and there is an urgent need to make agriculture water-efficient. What is being done by technology, especially Arable Labs, to realize this goal?

The water issue is complex. A lot of water is used for the crops that are exported, and so there is a virtual water trade going on. For example, if you are growing nuts and these nuts are being sent overseas, you are basically shipping water (which was used to grow these nuts) from your country to some other country. Also, the choices that people make about the kind of food they are eating dictate what farmers produce. So I am careful to not place the blame on farmers.

To think about what drives decision-making, let's look at an example: Recently there has been a lot of news about the widespread adoption of smartphones in India because the price of data plans has dropped dramatically. When the price of data was high, people optimized how they used the phone to keep the usage low. So what I am trying to say here is that when the price is high, people try to find ways to be efficient, and when the prices are low or when something is for free, nobody cares. Farmers are no different from other people and are making decisions based on the prices they pay. So as long as the water is free, there is no motivation to use it efficiently. This is one aspect of the water problem that is related to economic value.

Now, there is the question of how to achieve efficiency. There are a couple of aspects we need to look at. The first is fundamentally measuring the water used, which is not achieved. Just imagine a country full of doctors, among whom none have weighing scales in their hospitals and clinics to weigh anyone. Or imagine they have no means to measure the patient's blood pressure. Without these, the doctors can only guess. Now, a doctor is a smart person but here they are doing guesswork. This is the state of water management in agriculture. Since there are no means of measurement, there is no way to be rigorous about the water that is required nor the water that has actually been supplied to the crop.

Between these two problems, we at Arable Labs measure both— the water that is required and the water that is applied. To measure the former, we use a process called evapotranspiration. It is a method by which the water that plants are taking in from the soil is given back to the atmosphere. Here it is possible to measure the demand for water by a plant by using a radiation budget. For example, imagine you have a lake, and to calculate how much of the Sun's radiation is falling on the lake, you study the rate of evaporation of the lake. In addition to this, we have a device called the spectrometer, which measures the light that is absorbed by the plant as well as the light that is reflected by the plant. So we can assess the canopy cover, which determines the potential evaporation required for a particular crop.

Calculating what a crop requires enables farmers to be more proactive in managing resources, rather than being reactive. We have also developed a rain gauge that uses microphones to measure the character and intensity of the rainfall. Here, a microphone is covered with a dome-like structure that essentially acts like a drumhead. When rain falls on it, the microphone catches the frequency that the drumhead resonates with. So all together, the device is quantifying the whole water budget and the crop's reaction to its excess or deficit.

Q. **Most farmers in the developing world, like those in India, are at the mercy of the weather. Every year we hear stories of how unpredictable weather has destroyed farms. What are the different technologies that can be used to lower these unprecedented risks?**

This falls under the category of decision support. Here we are still talking about science; however, the focus is now more on behavioural psychology than on weather prediction or engineering. People often make planting decisions based on the calendar, following some rules. For example, they plant crops every year on a certain day because that is the way their father or grandfather did it. And moving away from the established rules carries risks for them. One of the biggest risks is regret, as people feel worse if they receive bad results following someone else's advice than if they'd got the same bad result by ignoring that piece of advice. So how do we build trust—make them believe that the information you are giving them is better than what they have been doing for years? What they are doing may not be ideal, but they are still making a living from it.

So here come the most sophisticated digital technologies that have a feedback loop, wherein you invest a little trust in the technology and it gives you back something that rewards that trust. For example, if I visit Delhi and need to go somewhere, I open Google Maps and check how much time it is going to take me to reach. Suppose Google Maps says that, with Delhi's traffic conditions, it will take thirty-five minutes. So I think that it might take me thirty-five or perhaps even forty-five minutes, given the traffic. With these technologies there is this reinforcement or supporting loop that lets us build additional trust. Due to the constant use of this technology, I have started trusting it. I still have faith that, even though I have never been to Delhi, when I visit and use that application, it is going to give me an accurate answer. And this trust is what farmers need to develop towards technology. This is why I called this behavioural psychology—because it has a lot more to do with understanding people's mental models than accurate weather prediction. The forecasting tools are more advanced than people's faith in them.

Q. Do you think that vertical farming is the future of agriculture? Will vertical farms replace conventional farms in the future?

Replace? Never.

Let's divide crops into two categories: calories and nutrients. Wheat, rice, corn, pulses, etc. go under the calories category, while lettuce, apple, mango, banana, papaya, etc. are categorized under nutrients. The calorific crops are grown extensively and their farmers make no money. They are often subsidized by the government to maintain stability in the economy. However, when we come to the nutritious crops, we see that they are high-valued and often perishable; it is also very difficult to ship them from one place to another without significant loss of the yield. Now, the consumers of nutrient-rich crops, who are often in cities, want them to be fresh and flavourful. So in the years to come, you will probably see vertical farms of these nutritious crops on the periphery of cities.

Q. How do you think we can achieve the dream of cultivating crops on other planets? Do you think we can do it on Mars?

There is no water on Mars, and water is one of the most critical ingredients for plant growth. This is what makes Earth special—that we are the only known planet with fresh water. There are other places in our solar system that have water either in vapour form or in the form of ice but not in liquid form. On Mars, you have sunlight, so you can construct greenhouses and get the temperature right; but without fresh water, it won't be possible.

Q. What is your message to the youth who wish to become agricultural scientists in the future?

That the problems in this domain are challenging, interesting and numerous. That agriculture may seem like a sleepy corner of the economy, but it's actually very complex and sophisticated. You can make one of the greatest contributions to humankind if you revolutionize this field, because it touches everything. You will see the fruits of your labour in every grocery store you visit and in every meal you eat. There is no greater satisfaction.

NOTE TO PARENTS

We are 7 billion people today. By 2050, we will almost touch the 10-billion population mark. By 2060, we will definitely be on course to establish settlement beyond Planet Earth. How will we feed so many humans? How will we create farms without destroying jungles? How will we grow crops in space, on the Moon and, above all, on the red planet—Mars? These questions are more critical to the continuity and happiness of human civilization than perhaps any other. And these questions will be answered by the agricultural scientists of tomorrow.

Somehow agricultural science is not considered among the nation's priorities in the present context. But this view is very narrow and quite flawed. Even today, agricultural scientists are finding the best of jobs, both in the government and the private sector. This holds truer outside India. In places such as Australia, the Gulf nations, Europe and the USA, agricultural scientists are paid on a par with the highest-paid professionals, such as lawyers and doctors. Moreover, the career keeps one closer to nature and often away from pollution-filled cities.

The best part, however, is the sense of contribution to humankind. An agricultural scientist can witness, from the very early days of their career, the progress and the impact of their research. Jobs for agricultural scientists are available after all degrees, even diploma courses, and hence students tend to become independent early in their careers, and can choose to alternate between jobs and higher education.

 **EXERCISE**

Calculate the water footprint of your kitchen. For this, you need to follow certain steps:

1. First, go to your kitchen and prepare a list of items used to cook lunch, and their quantities.

2. Corresponding to the items, note down the quantity of water used to grow them, with the help of the table we had discussed earlier in this chapter. Do not worry if some items are not on the list; you can make an approximation for them or look their values up on the Internet.

3. Do not forget to add items you might be ordering in, like pizza, or the bread, butter and cheese in your refrigerator.

4. Calculate the total amount of agricultural water consumed during one meal.

5. Divide this number by the number of people that are going to eat that food. This will give you the water footprint of your kitchen for each person.

Encourage your friends to do the same and compare your results!

You may also use the link http://righttowater.in/watercalc/index.php, which will help you calculate these numbers quickly.

Total water footprint of my kitchen: _____ litres
Total water footprint per person: _____ litres/person

CHAPTER 5

DEFENCE & WEAPONS

10 September 1780

Near the historic city of Conjeevaram (Kanchipuram), in the southern Indian state of Tamil Nadu, were the plain lands of Pollilur (Perambakam). On this day, a new chapter of military history was about to be written. Under the clear skies, two armies stood facing each other: the British, led by Lieutenant Colonel William Baillie, and the Indian army, led by Tipu Sultan of Mysore (now Mysuru).

In the past twenty-three years leading up to this day in 1780, the East India Company had successfully established their dominance over most of India. By then, the Mughals, under Shah Alam II, had been reduced to a shadow of their former glory, confined to the areas around Delhi. The British had already defeated the rich Awadh, or Oudh, rulers as well as the powerful Bengal rulers, first in the Battle of Plassey (1757) and then again in the Battle of Buxar (1764). By this time, it was clear that the British armies could not be defeated by the Indians. They had superior arms and better training, and, of course, the Indian kingdoms were way too busy fighting among themselves to present a united front to the British.

So, with this confidence, when the day broke, Baillie ordered his men to march towards the Indian army in formation. They had rehearsed wars and done military exercises for years, fought campaigns and always emerged the winners. For Baillie, victory was certain. The armies drew closer— they could see each other clearly as they were only about 3 kilometres apart. Baillie noticed a thin line of soldiers up ahead, which suggested that Tipu had very few soldiers on the battlefield.

He smiled.

Then, suddenly, from the distant horizon, arrow-like objects sprang into the sky. These things were on fire and moving rapidly towards Baillie's army. At first there were only a dozen or so, but then, in a matter of a few seconds, hundreds of these 'flying arrows' took off from the Indian side, filling the skies.

'Mysore rockets! Take cover! Mysore rockets!' yelled the soldiers behind him.

Baillie could not believe his eyes—Tipu had fired his new weapon from almost 2000 metres away!

'Will these even cover this range?' he asked himself.

In another few seconds, his doubts were dispelled. To the horror of the British army, these rockets, each a metre and a half in length, ripped through their ranks.

Tipu's Mysore rockets against the British army, 1780

They now noticed that the rockets were made of iron pipes instead of the usual bamboo sticks. Each had an attached double-edged sword in place of a wooden guiding stick. This was the world's first military rocket: a short-range missile. Iron pipes allowed for more gunpowder in them, hence the much longer range. The rockets were, of course, not as stable as modern missiles—they would wobble towards the last leg of their journey. However, Tipu used even this to his advantage—by attaching a metal sword to it. So each rocket blasted through the British formation and later turned into a spinning sword, causing great panic among soldiers and horses alike. Tipu arranged for batteries of such rockets—up to five rockets in a single rocket battery—which were operated by a new rank of soldiers, the Mysore rocketeers.

Within an hour, even before Baillie's army could reach Tipu's small army only 3 kilometres away, the rockets destroyed them. Of the 7000 British men who fought in the Battle of Pollilur, about 3000—nearly half—were fatally wounded and had to surrender, with no way to dodge the rockets on open ground. Baillie was captured, and he lived in a dungeon for the rest of his life.

This defeat was the worst that the British had faced in any conflict against Indian forces until that time. The rocket technology helped Tipu hold out against a much more powerful enemy till 1799, when he was finally defeated and killed by a much larger British force led by Major General David Baird of Scotland (part of the British homeland). Two days before his final defeat, Tipu's rocket storage had been accidently hit by a stray British shot, destroying much of the stored rocket ammunition.

Tipu's Mysore rockets were an astounding leap in the science of rocketry. The British were smart enough to pick up the used rocket shells and copy the design. Even then, it took them twenty-four years to come up with their own Congreve rocket in September 1804. Its inventor, Sir William Congreve, took out a patent for the rockets, making a name as well as money for himself across Europe in the field of warfare. However, later, science would balance itself out: history now remembers the Congreve rocket as only a copy of the Mysore rocket invented by Indians.

These British copies of the Mysore rockets were used by them against their arch-rival Napoleon Bonaparte of France in the Napoleonic Wars that lasted from 1803 to 1815, including the famous Battle of Waterloo, in which Napoleon was decisively defeated.

The Mysore rocket provided inspiration for another creation. In 1812–15, war broke out in the continent of North America between the United States of America and the United Kingdom. Remember, back then, the United States was a newborn nation with only a fledgling army. Here, too, the United

Kingdom successfully deployed the Mysore rockets against the Americans in the Battle of Bladensburg in 1814. Thirty-five-year-old lawyer and amateur poet Francis Scott Key was watching these rockets explode during a fort bombardment. He was inspired to see a large American flag flying above the fort under the sparks of these Mysore rockets. Witnessing this scene, he wrote a poem for his motherland, titled 'The Star-Spangled Banner'. This was later adopted as the national anthem of the United States of America. The song begins (notice the last line):

O say can you see, by the dawn's early light,
What so proudly we hailed at the twilight's last gleaming?
Whose broad stripes and bright stars through the perilous fight,
O'er the ramparts we watched, were so gallantly streaming?
And the rockets' red glare, the bombs bursting in air . . .

Few people know that the fifth line of the national anthem of the United States is inspired by an Indian technology invented in Mysore, halfway around the world. Of course, modern missiles, like the Agni, that are technically categorized as intercontinental ballistic missiles took another 200 years to make an appearance.

The Mysore rocket is the technology that, almost two centuries later, formed the basis of mankind's quest to move beyond the confines of its home planet. Based on the principles of an iron-pipe-and-sword-guided rocket in the Battle of Pollilur, we made rockets that could take us to the Moon and Mars, and perhaps beyond. In the field of warfare, it evolved into modern missiles that can now travel up to a staggering 16,000 kilometres.

India's role in the global rocket technology is internationally recognized today. In 2011, President A.P.J. Abdul Kalam and I visited the world's most renowned museum for aerospace—the National Air and Space Museum of the Smithsonian Institution in Washington DC, which is the capital of the United States.[1] This breathtaking museum spans several floors and showcases a variety of things, from dust from the Moon to parts of the earliest rockets we sent into space and to the Moon. But the section that was the most interesting to us was the one dedicated to the evolution of rocketry. This section opens with a model of the Congreve rocket, and rightly credits the earliest military rockets of England to the original Indian rocket used by the prince of Mysore, Tipu Sultan. The largest aerospace museum in the world traces the roots of all modern rockets and missiles back to India, and credits Indian scientists working more than 200 years ago for their ingenuity in building the world's first metal-cased military rocket.

Now, to end this section, let me take you back to the man who finally managed to overpower Tipu Sultan—

Major General David Baird of Scotland. In 2017, I visited the famous Edinburgh Castle. This magnificent castle—situated on a volcanic hill called Castle Rock, in the capital of Scotland, Edinburgh—was built in the twelfth century. It has several galleries devoted to the nation's war heroes. One of the prime attractions here is the Scottish people's military operations against India while fighting for the British Empire. The first display is of David Baird. Under his portrait, his achievement is listed as: '. . . He defeated perhaps the fiercest enemy of the British in India, the tiger of Mysore . . . Tipu Sultan.' The glass case contains few items owned by Baird, and is filled mostly with swords and artefacts that belonged to Tipu Sultan and his father, Hyder Ali. Set up by those who eventually defeated and killed Tipu Sultan, this grand castle does not fail to mention that the earliest rockets, which wreaked havoc on the British military with an iron pipe filled with gunpowder and a spinning sword, came from the mind of an Indian military genius who still inspires today.

• • •

Human conflict is an inconvenient truth. It is a dark blot on the history of human civilization. Most experts agree that war is defined as 'an active conflict that has claimed more than 1000 lives'.[2] By this definition, of the past 3400 years of recorded history, humans have not engaged in war only for about 268 years—less than 8 per cent of our existence.[3] Since the time of our inception as a species, wars have claimed almost 1 billion lives! And wars and weapons are expensive. Collectively, countries across the world spend more than 1700 billion dollars annually to maintain their militaries. That's about Rs 11,90,00,00,00,00,000, which is about Rs 38 lakh per second! You are right in thinking that is a lot of money, mostly spent just to defend against each other. You are also right in thinking this money can be better invested in other ventures. NASA has estimated that the cost of sending the first four humans to the planet Mars would be about 6 billion dollars. Let me put this into perspective for you. This means that if all the military spending of the world was diverted to Mission Mars from the noon of any Monday to 10 p.m. of the following Tuesday—just for thirty-two hours— we would have enough resources to send our first four Mars walkers to the red planet!

Then why do we need militaries and military scientists?

In 2013, President Kalam was once asked this question by a young girl in Ahmedabad.[4] 'Missiles can destroy lives and material. Then why did you make them?' she asked innocently. There was stunned silence in the hall. I was sitting behind President Kalam and even I was thinking what a suitable answer to this deep question would be. President Kalam then replied,

'Because strength respects strength. If India wants the strongest nations to respect us, our progress—then we need to be strong ourselves.'

The world is far from achieving a state of perfect peace. There will always be humans around us who, like bullies, may have a tendency to harm our peace for their narrow gains. To ensure the safety of our harmony and progress as a nation, we need to have strength on our side. It is a necessity that we must bear. Better weapons mean putting fewer lives at risk, by neutralizing only those who are criminals and those that attack us first, without harming anyone who is innocent.

The global military industry has another contribution—towards human scientific progress. Engineering and technology meant for military use have given us some of the finest consumer goods we see around us today—from ships and aircraft that can avoid collisions, to radios, duct tape, cameras, the Global Positioning System (GPS) and even the Internet. All these products of civilian usage were first created for the military. If you are interested to know more, here is a table of some of the everyday items that have originated from the military. See how many you can spot around you every day:

MILITARY INVENTION AND YEAR	DEVELOPED BY	USED IN THE MILITARY	DERIVED CONSUMER PRODUCT
Sonar (sound navigation and ranging)[5] 1910s	British and US armies	To detect German submarines during the First World War	Sonar is used by modern ships and for deep-sea explorations to detect objects and prevent collisions.
Sanitary napkin 1920s	British and French armies	To stem the bleeding of wounded soldiers; cellulose was wrapped in bandages	Modern sanitary napkins
Walkie-talkie 1930s	Canadian and US armies	By commanders to communicate with their soldiers, and vice versa; a two-way device	Used for portable radio communications
Duct tape 1942	US army	To seal ammunition boxes	Used as sealing and packaging material

MILITARY INVENTION AND YEAR	DEVELOPED BY	USED IN THE MILITARY	DERIVED CONSUMER PRODUCT
Microwave 1945	US army	It was accidentally discovered that radar transmitters used in the US army could release heat.	Microwave ovens
Nuclear technology 1940s	US army	For nuclear weapons. The first nuclear bomb was dropped on Hiroshima, Japan, in 1945.	Used in nuclear power plants and radiation-based medical treatment
Jet engine 1940s	Germany	To build faster fighter aircraft; invented towards the end of the Second World War	All large and medium passenger aircraft

MILITARY INVENTION AND YEAR	DEVELOPED BY	USED IN THE MILITARY	DERIVED CONSUMER PRODUCT
Digital photography 1960s	Russian (USSR) and US armies	On spy satellites, so that there was no need to recover the film reels that were stored in canisters and thrown from satellites orbiting in space	Modern cameras, including camera smartphones
The Internet 1960s	US army	To network computers and share data between different units of the military	The World Wide Web (WWW)
Satellite navigation 1970s	US and Russian armies	To train nuclear weapons on specific targets in order to maximize destruction	The Global Positioning System (GPS), which aids navigation. Today, taxi-booking services like Uber use this technology.

This close coordination between military and civilian applications is a continuing process, and more and more products will continue to jump from the military domain to our kitchens, drawing rooms and everyday life.

The future of defence technology

Future wars will change in three ways.

First, weapons in the future need to be more precise as there will be a larger share of low-intensity conflicts, such as terrorism. These will not be defined by heavily armed adversaries but by those who blend in in with civilians and innocents. The greatest challenge for security and defence forces will be to successfully identify these adversaries without harming innocents in the process.

The second trend will be cyberwar, wherein the Internet will become a battleground, and computers and other networks will become targets. In a connected world, everything from railways, airways and power lines to security systems and the water supply will be hampered if the networks supporting them are under cyberattack. Crucial military data could be stolen or altered, and missiles, ships, fighters and submarines could be completely overpowered if the computers controlling them go haywire. To combat cybercrime, future weapons scientists need to design robust weapons.

The third will be the trend wherein weapons are unmanned and there are more machines than men on battlefields. To meet this development, future weapons will need to be intelligent. Today, the US army conducts more missions using drones, with their pilots sitting in remote buildings halfway around the world, than actual piloted fighter jets. Robot soldiers are under development and will soon be inducted into armies, and machine-based surveillance is already replacing regular policing on the streets.

So the key aspects of future weapons will be precision, robustness and intelligence. Let me take you through some of the weapons that we will encounter in the future and that you, as a weapons scientist, will need to develop. Some of these have already appeared in the movies of yesterday and are well on course to becoming the weapons of tomorrow.

Laser guns: If you have watched any of the Star Wars movies, you will have certainly come across heroes and villains carrying small pistols that shoot not bullets but glowing laser lights. These guns seem to have almost endless ammunition and can incapacitate the target in a single strike. Well, this imaginary weapon is about to turn real, at least partially. The United States of America successfully tested the world's first Laser Weapons System (LaWS) in July 2017, which is now mounted on a warship. It is a 3-foot-tall device that looks like a telescope and is able to focus a massive number of energy-carrying photons on a pinpoint object. It works at the speed of light and can strike fast, moving missiles, planes and drones. Interestingly, each laser strike costs less than Rs 70 but can burn multi-crore war equipment in a matter of seconds.

Dragon Skin: *Iron Man*, the Marvel comic-turned-movie, shows the hero, billionaire scientist Tony Stark, developing a wearable suit that is immune to rifle shots and bombs. The Iron Man's suit protects him from his enemies, even the heavily armed ones, while he goes about saving the world. How close are defence scientists to actually realizing such a super-suit? Quite close, actually. Next-generation bulletproof suits like Dragon Skin, which was used by the US army, have shown the ability to stop multiple rifle fires. In a test, almost 120 bullets were fired at one from multiple assault rifles and then a grenade was exploded next to it, but the Dragon Skin armour still managed to survive without any of the shots or bomb fragments piercing it. Anyone inside it would have survived too, despite the heavy firing.

What should I do to become a weapons scientist?

In times of war, it is the quality of weaponry that leads to triumph or a bloody defeat. The professionals responsible for designing, developing and testing a country's military hardware and weapons systems (including lifecycle management) are called weapons engineers.

Weapons science or weapons engineering is a very specific domain, hence no college or university is currently offering a bachelor's degree in this field. After graduating in traditional engineering disciplines, such as mechanical engineering, electrical engineering, mechatronics, electro-optics, aerospace engineering, materials engineering and chemical engineering, you can pursue a master's degree in courses of defence and security, which are offered by various colleges and military academies. There are several universities both in India and abroad that teach weapons science as a subject, such as the Defence Institute of Advanced Technology, the Institute of Armament Technology and College of Military Engineering, all three in Pune. Abroad, the University of Leeds in the UK, Taylor's University in Malaysia and the American Military University, Naval Postgraduate School and the United States Military Academy in the US are good colleges to pursue master's degrees in the weapons domain.

Weapons range from small arms like assault rifles to heavy weapons like tanks, cruise missiles, fighter aircraft and submarines. Basically, this field is an amalgam of a number of branches of engineering. Furthermore, civilian applications of these technologies for everyday use have made life easier.

You will usually find a weapons engineer spending most of their time in military workshops or research and development labs, where they use computers and other systems to conceptualize and design new weapons. And during manufacturing processes, you'll find them on production floors.

A master's degree in security studies, armament engineering, microwave and radar engineering or engineering in combat vehicles will enhance your chances of securing a career in the field of weapons engineering. In addition to this education, you must possess the ability to think critically and have strong analytical skills to become a weapons scientist.

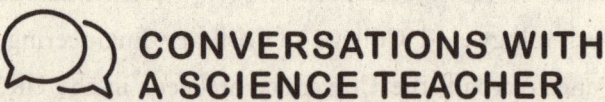 **CONVERSATIONS WITH A SCIENCE TEACHER**

Which are the most powerful militaries in the history of the world?

The crown for the strongest military power has changed heads over time. Nations have risen and fallen, not just due to war but due to natural calamities, disease, new technologies and civil unrest. It is an interesting study to list the most powerful armies in the history of humankind. Let us look at the timeline below:

YEAR	COUNTRY/CIVILIZATION/DYNASTY WITH THE STRONGEST MILITARY
1500 BCE	Egypt
700 BCE	Mesopotamia
300 BCE	Greeks under Alexander
200 BCE	Mauryan army, India
50 BCE	Han dynasty, China
100 CE	Romans, Italy
450 CE	Gupta dynasty, India
600 CE	Chinese army under the Sui dynasty
800 CE	Caliphate army, Saudi Arabia
1000 CE	Song dynasty, China; Cholas, southern India
1250 CE	Mongol army under Genghis Khan (one of the largest in world history)
1500 CE	Spanish army
1700 CE	Qing dynasty, China; Mughals, India
1800 CE	French army under Napoleon, followed by British army
1900 CE	British Empire
1920 CE (after the First World War)	US army, followed by British army
1940 CE	German army (called Wehrmacht)
1945 CE (after the Second World War)	US army; army of the USSR
1980 CE onwards	US army

Notice that India and China dominate the list of historic armies until 1900 CE, after which they came under colonial rule and the better-equipped British army, which took advantage of the countries' infighting.

Which are the most powerful armies in the world today? And how many soldiers do they have in active service at this point in time?

Here is a list of countries ranked according to their active military deployment:[6]

RANK	COUNTRY	ACTIVE MILITARY
1	China	20,35,000
2	India	13,95,100
3	United States	13,48,400
4	North Korea	12,80,000
5	Russia	9,00,000
6	Pakistan	6,53,800
7	South Korea	6,25,000
8	Iran	5,23,000

But do not assume that a large army is a more powerful army!

About a century ago, armies were as strong as the number of soldiers who served in them. But now, with machines fighting closely with humans, the headcount of soldiers is less significant. Today, the strength of an army is determined by its technological advancements, arms and ammunition, degree of training and the acumen of its defence scientists. Armies are a combination of the air force, the land force and the navy, and a healthy mix of all three is necessary to win any battle.

If you go purely by numbers, China has the largest army in the world, with over 20 lakh active and armed soldiers, followed by India, with about 14 lakh soldiers. The United States stands third in this list. Interestingly, a much smaller nation, North Korea, is number four, above Russia. However, this list does even take into consideration the type of weapons a country possesses, hence powerful armies like that of the UK, France, Germany and Japan do not even feature on it. However, to calculate the strongest army, one must take these factors under consideration too. For example, in any situation of war, it is likely that the US or Russia will, in just a matter of days, wipe out the North Korean army without much challenge.

A more complete army strength score is calculated in the Global Firepower Index, which analyses the strength of a nation's army on fifty different parameters, including the type of weapons, number of soldiers, training received, industrial strength, resources, technology and many other factors. According to this list, the top fifteen countries are as ranked below:

1. The USA
2. Russia
3. China

4. India
5. France
6. The United Kingdom
7. South Korea
8. Japan
9. Turkey
10. Germany
11. Italy
12. Egypt
13. Iran
14. Brazil
15. Indonesia

How do bullets work?

The modern bullet was invented as early as 1826, with minor alterations taking place over time. However, the word 'bullet' is often incorrectly used in everyday speech to refer to a cartridge. A bullet is not a cartridge but rather a component of it. The cartridge consists of the following:

- **The bullet,** the projectile: This is the top portion of the cartridge, which fires out of a gun.
- **The case,** which holds all the parts together: This is the part of the cartridge that falls off when the bullet fires out of the gun.
- **The propellant,** such as black gunpowder: This burns to produce gases, which expand and push the bullet outwards.

- **The primer,** which ignites the propellant: This is where the hammer of the gun strikes, which starts the reaction to burn the propellant.

There are different mechanisms employed in different types of guns to strike the primer. Mostly, there is always a rounded metal object called the firing pin, which strikes the primer and initiates the process. For example, when you pull the trigger of a revolver, the hammer moves forward and the pin strikes the primer. This creates a spark, which ignites the propellant, which is generally a mixture of two compounds: fuel and an oxidizer. This reaction forms huge volumes of gases at very high speed, which then

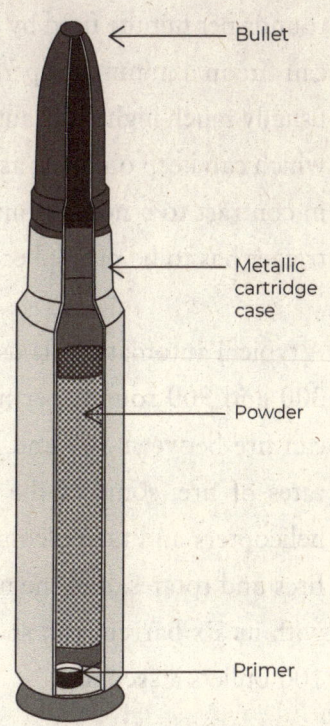

The parts of a cartridge

forces the bullet out of the gun at a very high speed. The extractor then gets hold of the rim and ejects the empty casing from the gun to make space for the next round. You will be surprised to know that nearly half of the total weight of any cartridge is the casing. Only about one-third of the weight is the bullet, and the remaining is the propellant.

How quickly can bullets be fired from a gun?

This is called the rate of fire in a gun. It is a measurement of the rounds per minute fired by a gun, or the number of bullets a gun can fire in a minute if operated continuously. The rate of fire is usually much higher for automatic weapons like a machine gun, which can keep on firing as long as you hold down the trigger—in contrast to a non-automatic weapon like a pistol, where the trigger has to be pressed each time a round is fired.

A typical automatic rifle used by modern military fires between 300 and 900 rounds per minute. Slightly larger machine guns can fire between 500 and 1000 bullets per minute. For higher rates of fire, some of the largest guns, such as those used in helicopters and tanks, come with multiple barrels. Each barrel fires and rotates, and the next barrel fires on. An M61 Vulcan, with its six barrels, can shoot up to 6000 rounds a minute, i.e. 100 bullets a second.

One of the biggest challenges of a higher rate of fire is the problem of extreme overheating of the gun mechanism, which may lead to jamming and even explosions, causing harm to the user. Hence guns are carefully designed, with a proper cooling mechanism in place—based on water, air or special gases. Guns used in aircraft and helicopters are able to fire at higher rates partly due the colder air around them as they are at a sufficient height.

Which are the world's best missiles?

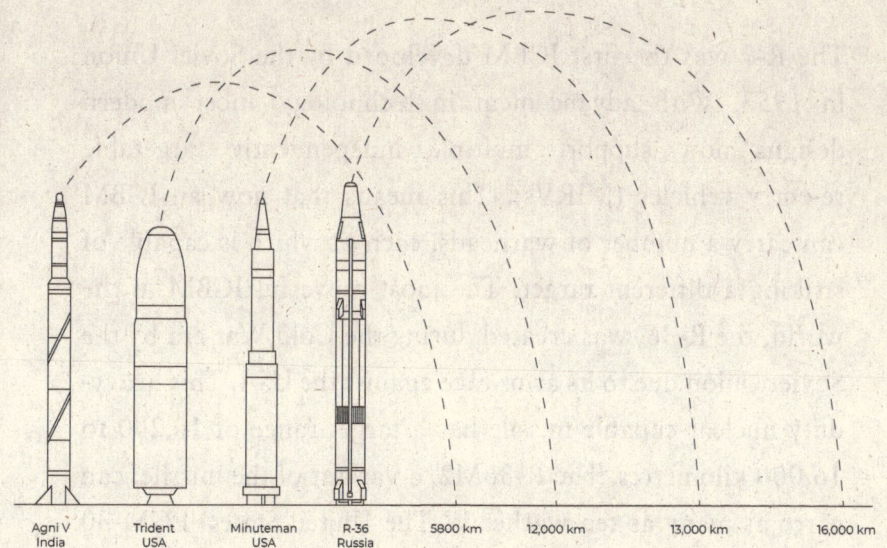

| Agni V India | Trident USA | Minuteman USA | R-36 Russia | 5800 km | 12,000 km | 13,000 km | 16,000 km |

Ranges of different ICBMs

We live in a time when powerful countries and terrorist organizations are contesting for world power. A common way in which this is attempted is through the attainment of nuclear arms and their delivery systems, such as intercontinental ballistic missiles (ICBMs). An ICBM can be launched like a rocket directly into the higher layers of Earth's atmosphere, up to 1200 kilometres high, where the warhead detaches and falls back to Earth at a speed of almost 30,000 kilometres per hour. These are guided ballistic missiles with a minimum range of about 5500 kilometres. They can be silo-based (ground-based missile station), rail-based or submarine-based, and are mobile on roads.

The R-7 was the first ICBM developed by the Soviet Union in 1953. With advancement in technology, most modern designs now support multiple independently targetable re-entry vehicles (MIRVs). This means that now an ICBM can carry a number of warheads, each of which is capable of striking a different target. The most powerful ICBM in the world, the R-36, was created during the Cold War era by the Soviet Union due to its arms race against the USA. This heavy-duty nuclear-capable missile has a target range of 10,200 to 16,000 kilometres. The R-36M2, a variant of the missile, can carry as many as ten warheads. The United States' LGM-30 Minuteman missile has a range of 13,000 kilometres and can span over half the planet. The USA also perfected submarine-launched ballistic missiles, or SLBMs, such as the Trident, which has a range of 12,000 kilometres and can be carried and launched underwater by a submarine.

India took a leap forward in missile technology in the 1980s under the leadership of A.P.J. Abdul Kalam, who is known as the Missile Man of India for his contribution to the technology.[7] India's most advanced nuclear-capable ICBM, the Agni V, has an approximate range of 5500–5800 kilometres and can carry a 1500 kg nuclear warhead. Indian researchers are now developing Agni VI, with a range up to 12,000 kilometres.

Which is the world's best fighter aircraft?

A fighter aircraft is basically designed for air-to-air combat against other aircraft. The parameters of a fighter plane are speed, manoeuvrability, weapon payload (the amount of explosive power it can contain), stealth and the ability to evade radar detection.

Before 1942, fighter jets had propellers, or large fans, revolving openly in front of them to give them power. The world's first operational jet-powered fighter aircraft, the Messerschmitt Me 262, was built by Nazi Germany in 1942. However, they came too late and too few in number for the German air force to win the war.

To understand fighter aircraft completely, one needs to understand the concept of aircraft generations. Fighter aircraft are extremely complicated machines and go through rigorous engineering and scientific evolution. With each major change, new features and powers are added. Each such major design change becomes part of a new generation. So far we have evolved to five generations, and sixth-generation fighters are at least ten years away—something you may be working on as a defence scientist.

Study the table on the next page to understand aircraft generations like an expert:

GENERATION	PERIOD	KEY FEATURES	EXAMPLE	APPROX. COST OF EACH AIRCRAFT IN RS*
1	1942–1950	• Jet engine	Me 262 (Germany), F80 (USA), P80 (USA)	1 crore
2	1950–1955	• Swept wings (wings were inclined backwards rather than perpendicular to the body of the fighter) • Infrared missiles for close distance air-to-air combat • Basic radar	MiG-15 (USSR), F86 (USA)	13 crore
3	1955–1970	• Supersonic (faster than sound) speeds • Medium-range missiles	MiG-21 (USSR), F4 (USA)	100 crore
4	1970–Still in service	• Long-range radar • Advanced bombing capability • High agility in air	F16 (USA), F15 (USA), MiG-29 (USSR), Mirage 2000 (France)	140 crore

* In case of multiple aircraft, the most low-cost aircraft's cost is listed.

GENERATION	PERIOD	KEY FEATURES	EXAMPLE	APPROX. COST OF EACH AIRCRAFT IN RS*
4+/4++	2000–Still in service	• Stealth technology to reduce radar detection • Extreme agility due to better structural design	Sukhoi Su-30 (USSR), F18 (USA), Rafale (France)	400 crore
5	2010–Still being improved	• All weapons are internal to maximize stealth • Better fuel utilization	F22 (USA), F35 (USA)	800 crore
6	Yet to be developed	• Extreme stealth • Morphing (ability to change the external shape based on the mission) • Smart skins to improve sensors • Energy weapons like laser guns	–	Around 2000 crore

The only operational fifth-generation aircraft in the world is the Lockheed Martin F-22 Raptor, which was inducted into the US air force in 2005. Along with being the most expensive fighter aircraft till date, it is also the most advanced. This aircraft stands as the king of fighter jets in the entire world for now, due to its advanced twin engines that provide it super manoeuvrability, amazing stealth abilities and advanced weapons systems. Currently, there are less than 200 such aircraft in the world.

In India, the HAL Tejas was the output of the light combat aircraft (LCA) programme initiated by HAL (Hindustan Aeronautics Limited) in 1983. The HAL Tejas was developed as a replacement aircraft for the Indian Air Force's (IAF) ageing MiG-21. It was officially inducted into IAF in 2015. Originally launched to serve as an air-superiority aircraft, it has become the smallest and lightest class of aircraft. This single-seat, single-engine, multirole light fighter costs about one-fifth of the F22. Of course, the HAL Tejas is a fourth-generation fighter aircraft.

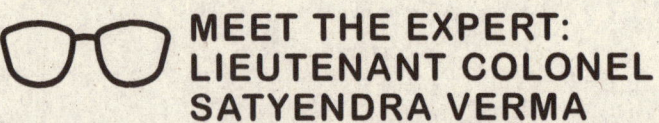

MEET THE EXPERT: LIEUTENANT COLONEL SATYENDRA VERMA

Now retired, Lieutenant Colonel Satyendra Verma was an officer of the Corps of Signals of the Indian Army. He is a seasoned skydiver, who has performed over 1200 skydives across the world, including in countries like the US, Switzerland, Russia, Malaysia and, of course, India. He also has a patent to his name for developing a software system to build flexible sand models using GIS (Geographic Information System) data.

Q. In your career in the Indian Army, you are sure to have handled several weapons. Which was your favourite?

The fun thing about serving in the army is that, irrespective of your role, they expose you to each and every part of it. Even the basic officers' training at the Indian Military Academy (IMA) in Dehradun involves learning the role and duties of an infantry solider (those who battle on foot). So recruits are physically and mentally trained to experience the life of an infantry soldier, including handling their weapons, so that when we are ready to work with them, they know what it really feels like. As we move into the second and third terms, the training progresses to that of section level, then to platoon level, then to company level, and then, finally, when you become an officer, you are given charge of a department. In my case, it was the Corps of Signals, which is responsible for the (military) communications of the Indian Army during times of war as well as peace.

So even while being trained as a communicator, I was trained as an infantry solider. We got to see all kinds of weapons. Of them, my favourites were my rifle and my radio, and I used both these weapons in the most effective manner in combat.

The rifle I am talking about is the INSAS AR (an abbreviation of Indian Small Arms System Assault Rifle), which I used during my initial training. It used to be in my hands at all times, even when I was running long distances for combat training. On all my runs—stretching 10–40 kilometres—I had its barrel in my hand and part of its weight on my shoulder. After such rigorous training, a weapon almost becomes part of your body. Even today, I can close my eyes and feel its shape on my shoulder! It can fire thirty rounds in one go, which is the capacity of its magazine. The rifle has a range of 400 metres. The smaller the weapon, the shorter the range, and any soldier who has seen action on the battlefield usually prefers a gun that has a longer range.

Now, let's come back to my other favourite—the radio, which was my main weapon as a communicator. It is fascinating being equipped with technology alongside a weapon, because as a member of the communications unit of a bigger fighting unit, even the most important plans had to be linked to feasibility of communication. For instance, during navigation of a terrain, I had to constantly communicate with the team to let them know where our commander needed them to stop so that they could remain within communication range at all times. It was my job to communicate with the entire formation. This made us an integral part of the main decision-making body, and we were exposed to the complex and demanding workings of ground-level action.

Q. How is the radio used by the army different from the conventional radio that we use in our civilian lives?

The radio used in the military is very different from the one we use in our day-to-day lives. For you, the radio is a one-way device. This means that there is a station that is transmitting waves that your device is receiving. So what we use in our everyday lives is basically a radio receiver, whereas what we use in the army is both a radio receiver as well as a transmitter. You have a radio at one end and there is a radio at the other end as well; using this, soldiers can communicate with each other. You cannot communicate both ways with the radio we use at home. The military radio works the same way as the mobile phone of today; the only difference is that mobiles use multiple towers to communicate and the military radio is used to connect directly to the person one wants to talk to. There are three kinds of radios, with varying frequency ranges: UHF (ultra high frequency), VHF (very high frequency) and HF (high frequency). So depending on the kind of communication we want to undertake, we make a communication plan and then move the radio detachments to different locations in order to communicate.

Q. How will new-age wars be fought, and how will they differ from the ones in the past and the ones being fought now?

Crystal-gazing into the future of wars and warfare, I feel it will not involve humans. However, it is going to take a long, long time before the human element is completely removed. In the next ten to twenty years, the technology of AI will be embedded in most of our weapons systems. That will assist humans greatly.

The cyber angle, too, is equally important, and I am sure that in the next thirty years, cyberwars are going to peak. This is because cyber-offensive technology is growing and advancing, whereas the defensive capability of nations, including our own, is lagging behind. However, hopefully we will soon catch up. With quantum computing coming to the fore and drones taking over, I think it is going to be a very different scenario, and the army is not going to look like the one I joined, served and retired from.

Q. Which countries lead the race in terms of contesting cyberwars?

In case of cyberwars, if a particular country is definitively doing well, it actually means that the country is not doing well. This is the rule, because secrecy of power is a critical element in cyberwar strength. Coming back to the question, cyberwars upturn the whole context of power of numbers, power of weapons and power of nuclear weapons. Here, all you need are experts in this field and you don't have to move on the battlefield. These smart people, while just sitting in one place, can wreak havoc on big, powerful countries. This creates a unique asymmetry in the power structure that is not based on the number or type of lethal weapons but on human expertise in offensive cybercrime.

The last ten years have seen a number of such attacks happening secretly, but by now they are in the open; everybody knows who's behind them. Russia, Israel, the US and China have been involved in various incidents against other countries, and more recently North Korea and Iran have also joined the group.

The parameters are different in cyberwar. For example, if a small cybercrime group in North Korea hacks into the workings of Warner Bros. Pictures, then the President of the United States will need to issue a statement, since the company is based there. So, here, even though the army is not involved and no physical act of aggression has taken place, the infiltration is still viewed as a threat. Thus in cyberwarfare, the focus will not remain confined to the military but will extend far beyond. And so it is very important for every country to understand these focus points and prepare for them. Then there are the nationless cyber-groups, such as Anonymous. But here it should be noted that these groups don't cause much havoc; most of the chaos is caused by state-backed groups, which are controlled and trained by states like China, the US, Russia and Israel.

Coming to India, we have pockets of excellence in this field, and as a nation we are in the process of consolidating them and creating an integrated cyber-command. Once that happens, I am sure civilian experts will be allowed lateral entry into the army so that talented young cyber experts can join the forces and contribute in whatever manner they can.

Q. What kind of hierarchy is followed by the fighting forces of the Indian Army?

Rule of thumb: one is to three. Here, the lowest form or group is one section that has ten soldiers. This section can be further broken down into three bunkers, with three people each under one leader, who is a non-commissioned officer (NCO). Then three such sections make one platoon, which is commanded by a junior commissioned officer (JCO).

Now, three such platoons would make one company, which is commanded by a major. And three such companies make one battalion, which is the main fighting unit commanded by a colonel.

Further, three such battalions usually form one brigade, which is commanded by a major general, and three such brigades form one division, which is commanded by a general officer. And three such divisions form a corp.

Hence the rule: one is to three.

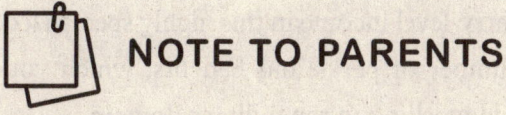

NOTE TO PARENTS

The weapons sector has become a matter of great concern, importance and security for any country. Weapons science is a truly global topic, and nearly all countries in the world now have a great demand for experts in this domain. Hence, in the future, there will be an exponential rise in the number of weapons scientists. Given the tension among nations to become superpowers in the world, and due to the fight over resources, weapons scientists will be extremely important assets to any nation.

While the military handles the operation of weapons, a weapons engineer handles the thinking, planning and designing of these weapons. Hence the military is the only employer of weapons engineering graduates. However, to meet the demands of more and more sophisticated weapons of warfare, the scope of employment for weapons specialists has increased in recent years, though their employment still remains confined to the military only.

As a weapons specialist, which one can become after some years of experience, your job will be to oversee the research and development of new weapons according to the needs of the army within the given time frame and budget. One can expect to have an excellent entry-level income in this highly specialized field, along with a number of perks and benefits, which you will be entitled to while working in the military domain.

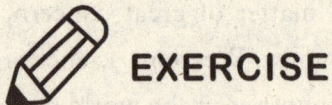 **EXERCISE**

Rearrange the following missiles in ascending order of their range:

1. Akash (India)
2. Ghauri II (Pakistan)
3. Nag (India)
4. Prithvi-III (India)
5. DF-31 (China)
6. Agni V (India)
7. UGM-133 Trident II (USA)
8. Shaheen-III (Pakistan)
9. M51 (France)
10. Dhanush (India)
11. K-15 (India)
12. LGM-30 Minuteman III (USA)
13. Shaurya (India)
14. Hwasong-15 (North Korea)
15. BrahMos (India)
16. R-36 (SS-18) (Russia)
17. DF-5A (China)

CHAPTER 6

In 2017, *Life*, a famous science fiction movie was released. It tells the story of a six-member crew aboard the International Space Station, which is on the brink of one of mankind's greatest discoveries: the first evidence of extraterrestrial life on Mars.

The movie opens with the return of the unmanned spaceship Pilgrim 7 from Mars to International Space Station, with soil samples potentially containing evidence of extraterrestrial life on the red planet. Hugh Derry, an astrobiologist who is paralysed from the waist down, gets a dormant spore from the sample. A spore is like a seed, and many bacteria, fungi and plants are known to convert to spores in adverse climatic conditions. This helps them survive during difficult times. When favourable conditions return, the spores turn back into living organisms.

This cell, still a spore, is named Calvin by popular vote conducted among American schoolchildren. When Calvin receives favourable air and moisture in the space station, to everyone's amazement, it grows several cells and becomes a multicellular being. This organism from Mars keeps growing rapidly but remains under control.

Then, due to a lab accident, Calvin becomes inactive. As Hugh attempts to revive him with electric shocks, Calvin becomes hostile and manages to escape from the contained laboratory through the air-conditioning ducts and goes missing somewhere in the space station.

It is now that the crew realizes Calvin is an intelligent being, who is now also hostile. Calvin grows in size by devouring a lab rat and a fellow crew member. He later breaches ISS's cooling system, severing its communication with Earth. Surviving crew members David and Miranda reach the conclusion that the only way to get rid of Calvin is to return it to outer space. Finally it is decided that both will take a one-person pod in opposite directions: Miranda towards Earth to live and tell the world about the deaths of her fellow crew members by an alien, and David into deep space to die with Calvin.

I won't go into the details, as this movie is a treat for all sci-fi fans, but let me tell you that in the end, Calvin—who is aboard a pod with a crew member—reaches Planet Earth! What happens next is not depicted in the movie, so I leave it to your imagination.

Now we come to the gist of the tale: contact with any form of alien species, however small, would be a monumental event in human history. It would be a moment of joy, celebration and caution too. Scientists who work on this mission in real life—of finding life beyond Earth and planting life from Earth on other planets—are called astrobiologists.

• • •

Are we alone in the universe?

This is an age-old question that has puzzled philosophers, seers and, most importantly, scientists. The branch of science that deals with life in the universe is called astrobiology. It can also be described as the biology of space.

Humankind's first serious attempt to communicate with beings beyond the planet came as late as 1946. Just after the Second World War, Project Diana was successfully tested by the United States Army Signals Corps. They set up a powerful transmitter, a receiver and an antenna array (multiple connected antennae) in New Jersey and sent a radio wave towards the Moon, our nearest celestial body. A large part of this cone of radio waves passed right across the Moon without hitting it. But a tiny fraction hit it and bounced back, and a smaller fraction of this bouncing wave was caught by the receivers on Earth. This completed a 'ping' from the Moon. It took 2.5 seconds for radio waves to travel to the Moon and return to Earth, covering a journey of almost 7,68,000 kilometres. This happened at the speed of light on 10 January 1946.

Of course, we now know that there was nobody on the Moon to hear our radio signals. The Moon is devoid of air, has no water and hence no life. But let's forget about the radio waves that bounced back from the Moon, and think of that much larger spectrum of radio waves that missed it and were released randomly into space in 1946. The farthest of these radio waves would have now travelled seventy-two light years in all directions, i.e. roughly 7 billion kilometres.

They would have hit Venus, our nearest planet, in a little over two minutes. The likelihood of life there is relatively low as the average temperature of Venus is about 462 degrees Celsius, enough to melt tin and lead. And in an atmosphere that is more than 90 per cent carbon dioxide, the chances of life are low.

Our first radio waves would have hit the red planet in exactly four minutes and twenty seconds from the time they were transmitted. Now, Mars is more promising. While quite cold for humanlike species, it is still within range for some of the life forms found on our planet. At its equator on a hot summer day, Mars can go up to 20 degrees Celsius. The trouble is that even a summer night would be minus 73 degrees Celsius—much colder than the minus 50 degrees in Oymyakon, Russia, the coldest inhabited place on Earth. Of course, the atmosphere is only 1 per cent as dense as Earth, and mostly made up of carbon dioxide. As of now, we have not been able to find evidence of life on Mars, but there may be a chance that the planet harboured life in the past, if not in the present. So did they hear our radio waves?

I have high hopes for Mars, and as possible future space-walkers, do not be disheartened by the carbon dioxide concentration on the planet, or for that matter on any planet. Scientists are working on something called MOXIE (Mars Oxygen In-Situ Resource Utilization Experiment). The aim of this experiment is to produce a small amount of pure oxygen from the Martian atmospheric carbon dioxide, which, in time, would lead to enough oxygen to support a small colony of humans.

Let us come back to 10 January 1946 and our first transmission into space.

In about thirty-two minutes from transmission, these waves would have hit the giant planet Jupiter, and then at the eightieth minute, the ringed planet, Saturn. Both planets are way too heavy, with way too much gravity, and are wreaked by violent storms, which would all make the chances of finding sustainable life near zero. However, there is a ray of hope—by way of the three bodies that are part of these two giants of the solar system:

The first is **Jupiter's moon Europa.** Our missions so far suggest that it may have a surface of silicates, similar to that of Earth, and oceans of liquid water too. The trouble is that temperatures here do not rise above minus 160 degrees Celsius. You may wonder how water is in its liquid form here. It is because of the very low pressure of the atmosphere. The biggest clue comes from the fact that Europa is now known to create ten times more oxygen than hydrogen, similar to Earth. The generation of oxygen is a very encouraging sign and indicates that some life form may already be present there. So in the future we could use this oxygen to generate heat for the planet to be warm enough for us to live on.

Our second hope is in the form of **Saturn's moon Titan,** the second-largest of all moons in our solar system. Titan's biggest drawback is that it lacks water, but there is ample liquid methane and ethane, and also frozen rocks on it. The biggest encouragement comes from the existence of organic compounds (made of carbon) in its atmosphere. Organic compounds are the building blocks of all life, both animal and plant. Therefore, the chances of unique forms of life that can survive without water are present.

Not far from Titan is another of Saturn's fifty-three named moons, the much smaller **Enceladus.** It is only about

500 kilometres across but we now know that it has several geysers of water vapour, along with organic compounds. The little moon has liquid oceans beneath a crust of ice, with hotspots (high-temperature places, similar to hot springs or volcanoes on Earth) that could sustain life, like the ones we observe in our polar oceans. These hotspots can be imagined as fountains of liquid gushing out of the icy crust of Enceladus. But how does a small moon so far away from the Sun keep its water from freezing? The answer lies in gravity. The tiny Enceladus experiences itself being pulled by gravity in many directions—from Saturn and several of its much larger fellow moons. This keeps its ocean churning and prevents them from freezing completely. This also means that, beneath the cold, icy crust, its ocean might be very violent—a subsurface tsunami moon.

Whether there is life on Europa, Titan or Enceladus remains a mystery and a hope, but the fact is that they haven't yet returned the radio ping from Earth sent in 1946. But then again, there is no guarantee that they were even listening to our feeble signals.

Let us come back to this radio wave that was sent in 1946.

After hitting Titan, about eighty minutes since its origin, our first communication into space would have continued its journey into eternity at the speed of light itself. In about four hours, they would have crossed the last planet in the solar system, Neptune. Beyond this, with the pull of the Sun weakening, there is only darkness and small chaotic bodies. Just before hitting the five-hour mark, our radio waves may have touched the famous Halley's comet in its farthest position, before continuing its journey towards the Sun.

Then the waves would have embarked on a long, long journey into the endless space beyond the solar system. It would have taken them another four years and two months to reach the nearest star—the Proxima Centauri. In roughly double that time, in about eight years, they would have reached the brightest star in the night sky, Sirius. This star is about twice the mass of the Sun. We know little about whether any of the planets around it are hospitable to life.

But there is one special planet that has caught everyone's attention. It is the Ross 128 b, and our radio waves would have reached it in about eleven years since their transmission (the planet is eleven light years away from us). Revolving around a red dwarf star called Ross 128, much smaller than the Sun, the planet Ross 128 b is quite close to its star and hence just about as warm as Earth. It seems to have a crust and oceans, and looks very similar to Earth. It is about 30 per cent heavier than our planet and, having an average temperature of 21 degrees Celsius, is perfect for life to flourish. Moreover, it is abundant in carbon, oxygen, aluminium, calcium and iron. So far, it looks very promising, and there is a chance that there is Earth-like life on Ross 128 b. But there is a problem too. Ross 128 b goes around its sun in a much smaller orbit, which it completes in about ten days. Hence one year on Ross 128 b is a little more than a week here. While creating new calendar systems is not a big problem, the real problem stems from another, linked phenomenon. In the language of space, Ross 128 b suffers from something called tidal locking. It means that at such close distance from its host star, one side of the planet always has daylight and the other is in darkness forever. Could you live on such a planet?

You might wonder—what if the first radio waves are heard by aliens? What would they hear? I almost forgot to tell you! The first ping we sent out contained the sound of a church bell. I am sure that even if aliens heard it, they would be able to make little sense of it and that it would be impossible for them to know where it came from. Maybe they are waiting for us to send some more information about us—our biosphere's signature and, of course, a return address. If you thought of this too, you are not alone. The great scientists of the 1970s pondered over this exact issue and then NASA sent out the Voyager 1 and Voyager 2 probes on deep space journeys.

Unlike radio waves, the Voyagers were hardware—800 kilogrammes of space equipment each. They were, of course, constrained in speed, travelling at about 55,000 kilometres per hour. But they carried cameras to photograph planets and study them. Launched in 1977, together they reached Jupiter, Saturn, Titan, Uranus and Neptune, before escaping beyond the solar system in 2012 (Voyager 1) and 2018 (Voyager 2)—thirty-five and forty-one years since being launched. Most of the images you see of Jupiter and the planets beyond it are available, thanks to the Voyagers. The Voyagers also have a special gift for any intelligent alien species they might encounter. Each vehicle contains a special message about us: a phonograph record, i.e. a 12-inch gold-plated copper disc containing carefully selected sounds and images that portray the Voyagers' journey and the vividness of life and culture on Earth, our world. This is the Golden Record. It contains greetings of peace said in fifty-five different languages, including ten from India—Hindi, Bengali, Urdu, Odia, Telugu, Gujarati, Marathi, Punjabi, Kannada and Rajasthani—higher than any other country's share. The Golden Record also contains 116 images, depicting not just human life but also insects, animals, birds and fish. It has the sounds of wind, water, oceans, volcanoes, mud pools, trains, planes and rocket lift-offs. It contains some of the best music from around the world and a special one-hour recording of human brainwaves. It has speeches from personalities, including former US President Jimmy Carter and former secretary-general of the United Nations Kurt Waldheim, as well as the footsteps and laughter of famous astrobiologist and cosmologist Carl Sagan.

The cover of the Golden Record divulges the address of our solar system in a special way—by a diagrammatic representation of the position of the fourteen known pulsar stars vis-à-vis the Sun. On top of the disc is written, 'The Sounds of Earth'.

Do you think aliens will ever be able to understand the contents of the disc? And if they do, which part of the Golden Record do you think would excite them the most?

Regardless, our radio waves are penetrating other solar systems, and our sounds and images are just crossing over beyond that into distant space, in the hope that they encounter other living beings on their way. Maybe in your lifetime the ping will return, or a disc full of information will come our way.

Till then, we wait.

The future of astrobiology

There will be two major quests for astrobiologists of the future: first, to continue the mission of searching for alien life, beyond Planet Earth; second, and perhaps more importantly, to discover and create extraterrestrial habitation for humankind and other life forms on new planets.

Why is the second quest more important?

In the chapter on the environment, we discussed how easily large fractions of living beings have been wiped off the face of the planet by mega calamities. These are the mass extinction events, and Earth has seen five such events, wherein anything between 75 and 95 per cent of the surviving species was killed in a short span of time. Today, we face the threat of another such event—whether it is because of asteroid strikes, volcano eruptions, solar flares, earthquakes or even pollution and mega viruses. Hence we need to protect life—and not just ours, but also of other animals, plants and birds—by spreading them across other planets. It is our insurance.

By 2020, NASA will roll out serious efforts to inhabit Mars by sending the first rover, targeted at kick-starting human landing. NASA is aiming to put the first human on an asteroid by 2025 and on the Martian surface by 2030. When we go to Mars, it will probably be for a few weeks, if not months, as the journey to Mars will be much longer and a lot more expensive than the one to the Moon. The Indian Space Research Organisation (ISRO) is also expected to play a role in the Mars missions of the future, as it was we who developed the most cost-efficient way to reach Mars with our Mars Orbiter Mission (MOM), or the Mangalyaan project. In 2014, ISRO successfully launched MOM to the red planet in just Rs 450 crore (around $64 million). A popular space fiction movie called *Gravity*, which released around the same time, cost Rs 700 crore ($100 million) to make. In 1997,

NASA's famous Pathfinder, a robot on Mars, had cost over Rs 1220 crore ($175 million).

• • •

Landing on Mars is one thing and living there entirely another. To live on any planet other than Earth, we would have to induce a controlled climate change there—perhaps in a limited area, to begin with. Multiple technologies will need to work in tandem to make this happen.

On our quest to live on the red planet, or any other planet, multiple new industries will need to flourish. These include the ones that deal with better solar-powered vehicles, water-generating devices, oxygen-production centres, waste-recycling centres, extraterrestrial clothing, traction and fuel development and, of course, low-oxygen and low-water food manufacturing technologies. Then we would need a complete overhaul of medical science. Diseases that are easy to handle on Earth may easily mutate in extraterrestrial climate and become more critical and much more dangerous to human life. Since we will take selected animals and plants from Earth, much like aboard Noah's ark, there is every chance that these species will grow in number beyond our calculation and imagination in the absence of natural predators that control their numbers on Earth. Hence botany and zoology will be critical sciences under the umbrella of astrobiology.

Knowledge of these disciplines will enable us to reach the next planets we aspire to inhabit.

What should I do to become an astrobiologist?

The Milky Way consists of over 200 billion stars and at least 100 billion planets. This is just one galaxy, and there are about 10 billion such galaxies in the observable universe. And the job of an astrobiologist is to search for extraterrestrial life in these galaxies. This is a relatively young yet exciting field that mainly focuses on exploring worlds in our solar system and beyond it for signs of past, present or precursors of life.

This interdisciplinary field requires an understanding of life and the environment that supports it, as well as planetary and cosmic phenomena. It encompasses knowledge and technique from many fields, including physics, chemistry, astronomy, biology, ecology, planetary science, geography, mechanics and geology. This is the reason there is no specific, defined course for you to study to become an astrobiologist.

However, you can enrol in massive open source online courses, or MOOCs, offered by several international universities to nurture your interests. Also, there are a number of websites that can keep you updated about recent advances.

Later in your educational career, you may choose a specific area of specialization, which may present itself at the master's level or even at the doctoral level. This kind of specialization is already available in universities across the world and, depending on the area you choose to work in, you will have options to explore.

With over fifty active space missions, of which many are primarily designed to explore extraterrestrial life, we will definitely be able to find traces of life beyond Earth in this universe in the next decade or two. These traces will not only pave the path for us to establish a colony there, but also help us understand our future better.

 **CONVERSATIONS WITH A SCIENCE TEACHER**

What are the most critical things needed for life to grow on any planet?

Since Earth is the only known planet to have life, we can conclude that the following things make it possible:

- Its temperature and gravity
- Its rocky surface
- The presence of atmosphere

- The presence of water and oxygen
- The presence of greenhouse gases, including carbon dioxide, which keep the planet warm
- The Moon, which holds the spinning Earth in position
- The ozone layer, which cuts off harmful radiation

But there is more to this.

We are assuming that the only way for life to exist is in Earth-like conditions. You may wonder if life could flourish in entirely different conditions as well. After all, even Earth has seen vast variations in climate, and every time a different kind of life has flourished. One billion years ago, Earth was an entirely different planet, about fourteen degrees hotter than it is today on an average. If you live in Delhi and have seen the hottest summer noon of 45 degrees Celsius, try to imagine those early ages when the highest temperature would have touched 60 degrees Celsius. Yet there were living beings on the planet even then.

What is the probability of finding life on other planets?

Let's assume that there are one trillion solar systems in total (there are actually many more than that!). The Sun is a medium-sized star; about one-third of all stars would be similar in size. So there must be about 3,00,00,00,00,000 (one-third of a trillion) solar systems whose sun is similar to ours.

Of these solar systems, each will have a third planet, some of which must be similar to Earth in size. Again, Earth is a medium-sized planet. Assume that about a quarter of all planets is like Earth. Thus there will be about 75,00,00,00,000 planets that are almost at the same distance from their stars as the Earth is from the Sun, and are Earth-sized too.

Of these, assume that about 33 per cent have rocky crusts and another 50 per cent have atmospheres. So about 12,50,00,00,000 planets will not only have the size and temperature of Earth, but also its shape. They will have mountains and air currents too.

Of the ones with atmospheres, we will have to look for those with the right balance of carbon dioxide and oxygen. While carbon dioxide is abundant in the atmosphere, oxygen is relatively rare. Let us assume that about 1 per cent of the remaining planets have them both. That still leaves us with 12,50,00,000 (1 per cent of 12.5 billion) planets with the necessary gaseous composition.

Of the remaining, about 1 per cent may have bodies of liquid water or similar life-giving liquid. That is about 12,50,000 planets with rocks, clouds and rivers—enough for plants and flowers to flourish.

To support the existence of higher-order animals, these Earth-like planets should also have a single moon, similar to ours, to determine the tides and, more importantly, to hold Earth straight on its axis. About 10 per cent of the shortlisted planets have a single large moon. Hence about 1,25,000 of the Earth-like planets in the universe would have a moon similar to ours.

Finally, Planet Earth also has certain other critical gases—namely the greenhouse gases besides carbon dioxide, such as methane, which captures heat energy. It also has the ozone layer, which protects us from the harmful ultraviolet rays of the Sun. Not more than 1 per cent of the selected planets would have an ozone layer, or a layer that could effectively reflect UV rays. This still leaves us with about 1250 planets almost identical to Earth in terms of land, water, their moon, temperature, gaseous composition and similarly protected from harmful rays. By this model of estimation, therefore, there are about 1250 likely Earths whose life forms are very similar to ours.

Some might even have humanlike animals with intelligence and the ability to communicate. Some of these planets might have dinosaur-like creatures, while others might only have plants and tiny insects. But one thing is almost certain: life does exist beyond Planet Earth and, some day, with advancing technologies to move into space, we may indeed shake hands with an alien life form!

What is the need to colonize other planets?

Broadly, there are two reasons for us to colonize other planets.

First is the long-term survival of human civilization. We could easily survive any case of a natural or man-made disaster by delocalizing ourselves from Earth. As predicted by the famous theoretical physicist and cosmologist Stephen Hawking, human civilization will become extinct in the next 1000 years if we do not establish colonies in space. Why did he say this? Because we are running out of space and resources due to overpopulation, and space colonization could help us establish a balance between the demand for and the supply of natural resources. Then there is always the danger of a comet going astray from its gravitational tug. It could head straight to our planet, or Earth's atmosphere could fail to burn up the large meteorite. In addition to this, we are vulnerable to any super virus mutating and engulfing human life entirely; and then there are mega volcanoes that can choke the air with dust and pose a threat to all forms of life. Basically, colonizing space is our backup plan in case of any sort of planetary or ecological catastrophe. Much like a backup of important data on a hard disc.

Second, both material and energy resources in space are limitless. According to different estimates, only our solar system has enough resources to support over a billion times the needs of human civilization today. Beyond our solar system, there are several hundred billions of stars that virtually offer an endless supply of resources, providing infinite growth potential. Utilizing these resources can lead to much economic development. For instance, take the thousands of little asteroids between Mars and Jupiter. These are all rich mines of uranium and thorium, which can give us energy. Every ton of asteroid material has about 100 grams of the platinum group metals (PGMs), and every ton of PGM has about 250 grams of uranium. A medium to large asteroid in the Mars–Jupiter space weighs about $20,000 \times 10^{12}$ tons. This means it can be mined for up to 5,00,000 tons of uranium. To add another perspective, one ton of uranium can generate 24 billion kWh of energy. The city of Mumbai consumes about 15,000 billion units of power a year. Hence a single asteroid has enough uranium to power the entire city of Mumbai for 800 years. Remember, there are thousands of such asteroids just between Mars and Jupiter.

How do we know that alien species will not attack us?

A huge spaceship full of aliens has landed on Earth! They are viciously attacking us. Some humans are being ruthlessly kidnapped, while others are falling victim to their powerful death rays!

Don't get too scared, these criminal aliens appear only in sci-fi novels and movies.

Let's assume that one such spaceship has indeed landed on Earth. Since they are the ones who have found 'extraterrestrial life', according to them, *we* are the aliens. Looking at their ability to travel across the galaxy, it would not be wrong to assume that they are more 'intelligent' than us. They would have travelled to our planet either to utilize resources or to make a colony here. In either case, there is no reason they wouldn't prove to be disastrous for us. But what if the situation were reversed? If we are the ones to find traces of intelligent life beyond our planet, then we would be technologically superior to that life form, and hence it can be assumed that they would not attack us.

 **MEET THE EXPERT: CHARLES COCKELL**

Professor Charles Cockell is an astrobiology professor in the School of Physics and Astronomy at the University of Edinburgh. He is also the director of the UK Centre for Astrobiology. Currently he is investigating life in extreme environments on Earth and the habitability of extraterrestrial environments, as well as studying the growth and behaviour of organisms in space, using the International Space Station.

Q. What is astrobiology?

It is a very broad field. It spans the origin of life and how life persisted on Earth over 3.5 billion years. One of its profound questions is: could there be life elsewhere in the universe? Astrobiology is the link between science and space—it is the study of life in the cosmic context.

Q. What does Mars actually look like?

Mars is a little smaller than Earth and, as a result, has a lower gravitational force. It has about three-eighths the gravity of Earth. It has also got a thinner atmosphere. So the atmospheric pressure is about 100 times lower than that on Earth, and is numerically about 600 pascal, very close to the triple point of water (the temperature and pressure at which all three forms of water, namely ice, water and vapour, coexist). This means that on the surface of Mars, liquid water is generally not stable. In most areas of the planet, the water either freezes into ice or vaporizes into gas and disappears into the atmosphere. That's why we don't see large lakes and rivers on the surface of Mars today. They existed in the past, when the atmospheric pressure was higher and it was possible for water to be stable on the surface of the planet.

So it's a very interesting planet because, in the past, it was a lot like Earth in some ways. But, at the same time, because of its extreme conditions today, it is a very alien planet compared to Earth. Many things are very different there, including its high radiation, its very low temperatures and its vast, dusty volcanic surface.

Q. What is the composition of the Martian atmosphere?

It is mainly composed of carbon dioxide, along with small amounts of nitrogen. It contains about 0.012 per cent oxygen, which is much less than what is required by humans for breathing.

Q. Can we live on Mars?

The long-term ambition of many space programmes is to go to Mars, and India has experience in sending space probes to the red planet. Eventually, of course, we would like to go there as human beings. It would be a difficult environment to live in, because it has no useful oxygen. So you'll need a spacesuit. The atmosphere is very thin and there is no magnetic field, so the radiation is much higher. From that point of view, it has a more dangerous environment than this planet. So there's no doubt that Mars will be quite a perilous place to live in, much more so than Earth. It's actually quite an unpleasant place too. But of all the planets in our solar system, it's the most Earth-like, with lots of water in the form of ice. At least there is some atmosphere, unlike the Moon, so you get some protection. And it inspires fascinating science questions: Was there life on Mars? What is the history of the planet? Thus there are many scientific reasons for humans to go to Mars.

As a place to live, it is not as nice as Earth, but we can live there. We have the technology to make water and fuel, and will be able to work in that environment.

Q. What is life on Mars or any other planet expected to look like?

Most people think—and it's reasonable to think so—that the most common type of life form to be found on another planet, if at all, is microbial life. Simple microbes—relatively simple compared to us—made up of single cells. One reason for thinking so is that over the course of Earth's history, the majority of life on our planet has been microbes. Even today, on a planet full of animals, microbes dominate the genetic diversity of life. Some people forget that we live on a planet of microbes. Humans are just a small part of the biosphere, though obviously an important part from certain aspects. So when we go to other planets, what we are looking for is single-celled microbial life. Will it be exactly the same as microbial life on Earth? We have good reason to think it might be. Science supports the logic of putting life inside a cellular membrane because that protects you from the outside environment and concentrates the molecules. So you can imagine some sort of a membranous cellular structure being the universal feature of a replicating and evolving life form, but we should always remember that we only have examples of life on Earth to look at. We should keep an open mind when we look for life elsewhere, but, at same time, there is good reason to think that the most primitive life forms on Earth reflect, in some way, the sort of life forms we might encounter on other planets.

Q. How is exploring any other planet going to advance life on Earth?

A classic example is the planet Venus. The greenhouse effect was first investigated on Venus. High levels of carbon dioxide warmed it up, and that was the first time humans saw the greenhouse effect altering a planet in a profound way. By going to other planets, we can develop a new perspective towards our home planet. We can learn new things about Earth. So we have no idea what we might learn about Earth by putting humans on Mars! Maybe by just landing on Mars and looking at the landscape, we will get new ideas about Earth. Perhaps just standing on a rocky planet like Mars, with its high radiation and lack of liquid water—perhaps just that experience would make us appreciate Earth more.

 **NOTE TO PARENTS**

Astrobiology is one of the newest research domains in science, which aims to unlock one of the oldest mysteries of humankind—the existence of life beyond Earth.

There is little doubt that in the next decade and beyond, mankind's biggest quest will be to live, literally, in the stars we see in the night sky. This will open up new avenues for the sector of astrobiology, and there is little doubt that this will become an aspirational sector in the future.

Besides doing research, astrobiologists can also have a variety of jobs. They can join the media industry by becoming a science journalist. They can write about the latest happenings and breakthroughs for websites, magazines, newspapers and books. They can also take up administrative posts and help the government in making well-informed decisions about new laws and funding for future projects.

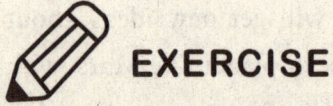 **EXERCISE**

You are about to settle down on Mars. Think of and list out all the essential items you would take along with you. Remember, the cumulative weight of all the items selected by you should be less than 3 kilogrammes, because of the baggage-weight restrictions on your spacecraft.

A few suggested items have been listed to help you decide. You can also rank them in order of importance.

ASTROBIOLOGY

ITEM	RANK IN ORDER OF IMPORTANCE
A thick (lead-lined) umbrella	
Goggles	
Fountain pen	
Face masks with air filters	
Fertilizers	
Compass	
Thin summer clothing	
Expensive wristwatch	
Warm winter clothing	
Solar-operated fans	
Mobile phone with SIM card	
Oxygen tanks	
Seeds of plants	
Space food	
Toothbrush	
Antiseptic lotion	
Sunscreen	
Petrol	
Tent	
Ball-point pen	

CHAPTER 7

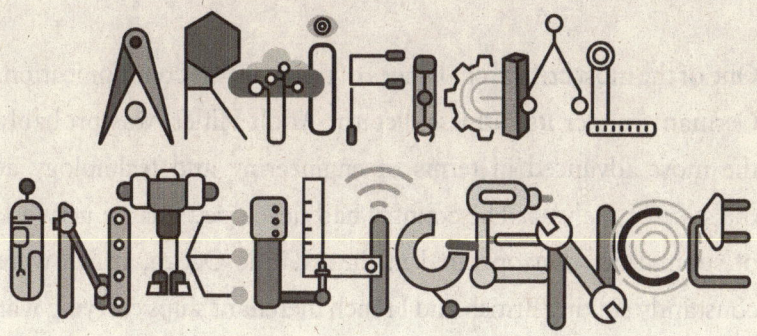

ARTIFICIAL INTELLIGENCE

In 1939, the Second War World broke out. It was the worst war to have ever occurred in human history. By the time it ended, in 1945, this war had claimed 80 million (8 crore) lives. Remember that in 1939, there were about 2 billion people in the world—that's almost a quarter of the population we have today. Hence it can be said that one in every twenty-five people were killed in this war.

The Second World War was the first war of technologies, during which jet fighters, missiles, radars, tanks, bombers, submarines, aircraft carriers and even atomic weapons were developed and deployed. On one side of this war were the Axis nations—Germany, Italy and Japan, along with smaller allies—and on the other side were the Allied forces—powers such as the USA, the Soviet Union, the British Empire (including India),

France and China. Both the warring sides had powerful armies and great strategy; hence the advantage to win kept flipping. Also affecting this was the emergence of new technologies.

One of the most critical challenges of this war was communication. Germany, under its ruthless dictator Adolf Hitler, was probably the most advanced in terms of engineering and technology at the start of the war. The country had developed a large network of submarines that operated in the Atlantic Ocean, which were constantly sinking British and French merchant ships carrying war supplies. These submarines were highly effective and sunk nearly 3500 British and American ships during the war, especially until 1942. In the early years of the war, the German air force, called Luftwaffe (meaning 'air force'), was dominating the skies. Both submarine and air force planners needed rapid communication technology that was not only operational but also secure from being hacked by the enemies. From this need was born the cipher machine E, better known as Enigma.

The Enigma machine, which was developed after the First World War, was improved upon even further in the early 1930s for encrypted communication. It had a typing pad, like an old typewriter, along with a set of three rotors that could be set to a particular key. Based on this key, whatever was typed was encrypted as a coded message and then transmitted using Morse code over a telegraph line to faraway places. At the receiving end, one needed another Enigma machine, set to the exact same rotor configuration, to accurately decrypt the coded message. Given the number of combinations the rotors could be set in, each word could be coded in 150 million (15 crore) different ways, making it impossible for the Allied forces to understand what was being said even if they managed to hack the Morse code.

Enigma was a truly revolutionary tool. It was, in fact, the most nascent form of computing technology developed for communication. Today, whatever password you type into your computer to access your mailbox goes through the same chain of encryption at your computer, then transmission via the Internet connection and, finally, decryption at the server end.

With the secure and fast transmission line of Enigma, the German army gained the upper hand by being far more effective than their enemies. Hence, in 1939, the world's first hacking project was established as a joint effort between the British, the Polish and the French, headquartered at a small mansion called Bletchley Park near London. It was headed by Commander Alastair Denniston, who spearheaded the project in the most unusual way. He formed a team of mathematicians, crossword-puzzle experts and chess masters to come together and solve the Enigma code.

One key member of this team was a twenty-seven-year-old Cambridge University mathematician named Alan Turing. He was the first to suggest the possibility of making a universal computing machine, which could solve all kinds of problems by way of algorithms in mathematics. This was the early idea behind modern computers.

Alan Turing's proposal was accepted and funded by the British government. Thus the world's earliest computer, the Bombe, was built, and, because of its colour, was often referred to as the Bronze Goddess. It was about 7 feet wide, 6.6 feet tall and 2 feet deep, and weighed over 1000 kilogrammes. It had dozens of dials and gears, which

Alan Turing

could rotate on their own to keep trying different combinations to match those on any Enigma machine. It was an electromechanical computer—noisy, clumsy but effective. By early 1940, Turing had delivered his first message via the Bronze Goddess. It took hours to crack a simple message, but it was an effort in the right direction. Turing got more funding to set up more such machines. Over 200 more were built. Turing's pace of decoding messages increased dramatically and, by 1943, he was decoding two messages every minute. On the other side, the Germans were so confident about their Enigma coding that they never even suspected the enemy decoding their messages on the Bronze Goddess in under a minute!

For his contribution to computing, Alan Turing is often regarded as the Father of Modern Computers. It is estimated that if Turing had failed to break the Enigma code, the Great War would have continued for several more years and another 21 million (2.1 crore) humans would have lost their lives.

Sadly, he met a strange end in 1954, when he committed suicide at the age of forty-one. He bit into an apple laced with cyanide that killed him instantly. It is often debated, though not proven, that the very same imagery of the bitten apple is the logo of a famous technology firm today. Can you guess which company it is?

Alan Turing's Bombe machine was considered to be the most important secret weapon of the British and their allies. It was the first machine that showed signs of something that we will now talk about—artificial intelligence. After all, the Bombe was a type of AI, trying different combinations of its own and arriving at a solution.

The future of artificial intelligence

From the time of Alan Turing till today, we have come a long way in the development of artificial intelligence and its power. Shortly after the Second World War, the world's first functional electronic computer was developed. It was called the Electronic Numerical Integrator and Calculator, or the ENIAC, and was used for solving numerical problems. It was invented by J. Presper Eckert and John Mauchly at the University of Pennsylvania. It occupied 1800 square feet, was as big as an apartment and weighed 30 tons. This generation of computers used glass transistors and hence consumed more power.

Then, in the mid-1960s, came the era of printing circuits on pieces of silicon, called integrated circuits. These tremendously reduced the size of the computer. Initially, these integrated circuits could accommodate only about ten transistors on a single chip and hence were called SSI, or Small Scale Integration. By the 1980s, this had become ULSI, or Ultra-Large Scale Integration, and over a million transistors could be fitted on a single chip. Today, an iPhone X chip has over 4 billion (400 crore) transistors built in!

This miniaturization of computers has led to an exponential increase in their processing power, which, in turn, has made computers more and more powerful but with a reduced size. In the 1970s, it was said that computers would never be able to solve complex mathematics as humans could—but by the 1980s, they could. In the 1980s, it was said that computers would never be able to 'remember' as much as humans could. In fact, Bill Gates, the founder of Microsoft, is said to have said in 1981, 'Six hundred and forty kilobytes of RAM are enough for any human application.' By the 1990s, computers were carrying RAM storage twenty times that limit, and today even mobile phones have a RAM capacity that is at least 10,000 times what Bill Gates thought was the limit for computers.

In 1997, computers broke another barrier that we thought was the limit for artificial intelligence—IBM's Deep Blue computer programme defeated the world chess champion Garry Kasparov. Since then, artificial intelligence has only grown stronger and more useful. Today, you can fully operate your mobile phone through a human-sounding AI or virtual assistant, such as Siri or Cortana. AI is performing the most complicated parts of surgeries as well, and they are also running trains and flying planes. In fact, for a standard commercial airline, on average, 80–90 per cent of the time the aircraft is being flown on autopilot by artificial intelligence.

In April 2015, a new robot was activated—a humanoid named Sophia. Sophia was designed by a Hong Kong-based company called Hanson Robotics and has become the most talked-about robot, and humanoid, of this decade. Humanoids are robots that look similar to human beings and can perform humanlike functions. Sophia not only looks human but she can also exhibit fifty different expressions on her face, which is governed by artificial intelligence. She has cameras in her eyes and a complex AI system that allows her to recognize faces, maintain eye contact and process speech. Sophia is able to crack jokes too, reply to questions and show emotions—artificial ones, of course. In October 2017, Sophia was awarded citizenship by Saudi Arabia, making her the only robot to receive this honour from any country. And in November 2017, Sophia was nominated as the first Innovation Champion of the United

Nations Development Programme. It thus became the first non-human to be given any United Nations title.

Sophia is essentially designed to assist old people, help them fetch things and aid in their medical needs. Its creators hope that some day Sophia can be taught complex medical processes so that she can help treat human beings.

The cost of humanoids like Sophia is very high—over 1,00,000 dollars (Rs 72 lakh)—but there is already a market for low-cost humanoids that are now selling in many countries to assist the elderly. Japan is already seeing a surge in the sales of the Sota robot, which networks with all the devices in the household and controls them to make life comfortable for its owner, even taking care to switch off the lights and fans. It is much smaller than Sophia, only about 28 centimetres in height, and can be placed on a table, from where it can respond to voice commands and give voice output. The cost of the Sota robot is merely 805 dollars (Rs 56,000).

In 2017, LG came out with its version of a humanoid robot, the Hub Robot. It is able to recognize facial expressions like nodding and hand movements and act accordingly. It is small in size and does a similar job as Sota or Amazon's Alexa. But LG is also building a larger version of it that can move around in airports and hotels. LG hopes that Hub Robots will be the future butlers and attendants in commercial places. Can you imagine a world where humans and humanoids coexist, often as equals?

How do I become an artificial intelligence expert?

Artificial intelligence is one of the most rapidly growing technological domains today. The use of complicated computer software and programmes, automation and robotics characterize a career in AI. Since it is an emerging field, three things are key to becoming an expert in AI: curiosity, perseverance and continuously keeping yourself updated.

An AI programmer needs to have problem-solving abilities, both creative and critical thinking, and a strong maths and computers background. You are expected to be well versed in different programming languages, like C, C++, Python, Java, C# and SQL. Currently no bachelor's degree is offered in AI. You would need to complete your graduation in computer science or engineering (mechanical, electrical, robotic, computer) and then enrol in a master's degree, offered by several universities abroad.

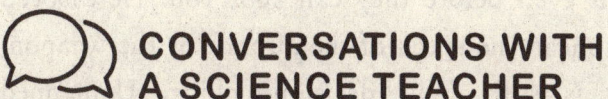 **CONVERSATIONS WITH A SCIENCE TEACHER**

What role does AI play in the defence sector?

AI is transforming the defence sector considerably. We have discussed this in greater detail in the chapter on weapons, but broadly, the following are the potential applications of AI that could interest the military forces:

First, the amount of data that the militaries deal with is no less in quantity than what is handled by companies or governments, and processing it fast has been a challenge for most of the modern militaries. This is where AI could take over; it could free up human labour for other tasks, along with speeding up the data interpretation process. For example, Project Maven of the US Algorithmic Warfare Cross-Function Team, which rapidly processes images and data to learn of potential enemy targets, could eventually be used to improve the efficiency of drone strikes on the battlefield. This type of AI application could help militaries in accurately interpreting information, which could ultimately lead to better decision-making.

Second, speed provides an upper hand in modern warfare. Think of it in terms of the military strategy of the observe-orient-decide-act (OODA) loop, or just the desire to attack the opponent even before they can spot you. Here speed doesn't only mean the speed of the aircraft or the weapon; however, it is still about decision-making. Unmanned aircraft piloted by AI have many advantages compared to the ones piloted by humans, in terms of both speed and manoeuvrability. For example, by using AI in the air defence system, we could enable a mechanism to protect the city against missile attacks more efficiently than a human. No matter how competent the latter is, it is impossible to match the reflexes of the former. This is the principle behind

Israel's Iron Dome, which is a defence system that spots and eliminates short-range projectiles.

How is AI impacting social media?

AI is influencing social media in many different ways.

Have you recently uploaded a photo with your friends on the social media platform Facebook? Have you observed how the faces of all your friends get detected and tagged even before you do so yourself? This is because of Facebook's facial recognition feature that is powered by AI. Besides this, another popular technology used by Facebook is called DeepText. This technology is currently operating only on Facebook Messenger, where it tries to recognize the needs of the user and accordingly sends them suggestions of services. Say, if you write to your friend, 'I need a ride', it would show you cab services like Uber and Ola. However, this technology still needs to work on nuances like slang and word-sense. For example, if I say, 'I like orange', this technology is currently not able to figure out whether I am talking about the colour or the fruit.

Instagram also uses DeepText technology in identifying and removing spam comments that are violating the application's community guidelines.

Further, Snapchat's lenses, more commonly known as filters, are perhaps the most childish feature of the app, but they have taken the world by storm. And the facial recognition technology behind this feature is driven by AI.

How is augmented reality (AR) different from virtual reality (VR)?

To explain the thin line of difference between AR and VR, let's first understand each one separately.

When we think of AR, the first thing that pops into our mind is Pokémon Go. This extremely successful AR game developed by Niantic Labs is based on the Japanese anime television show *Pokémon*. In this game, you need to catch as many Pokémon as you can while wandering around the city. In reality, there are no Pokémon in the city, but the developer has superimposed data and images on the real, physical world that can be seen through specific devices, in this case, any smartphone. This is AR, where a layer of digital information is overlaid on the real world. Another common example of AR are the facial filters on Snapchat and Instagram.

On the other hand, VR tricks the user's senses by transporting them to a completely different environment. You are required to wear a special VR headset to experience the simulated environment. These headsets can be connected to a computer (Oculus Rift) or a gaming station (PlayStation VR); they can even be unconnected (Google Cardboard). These unconnected devices work in combination with your smartphone—you need to insert your smartphone in the designated space and wear the cardboard to enjoy the VR world. Besides being extensively used in games, this technology also makes the 360-degree videos possible.

MEET THE EXPERT: NIKHIL RANJAN PAL

Nikhil Ranjan Pal is a professor in the Electronics and Communication Sciences Unit of the Indian Statistical Institute, Kolkata, where he has been teaching since 1995. He is also the president of the IEEE Computational Intelligence Society, the USA. His current research interests include bioinformatics, brain science, neural networks and artificial intelligence.

Q. You completed your graduation in physics. So how did you develop an interest in artificial intelligence?

My interest in artificial intelligence was not a straightforward transition from physics. After the completion of my undergraduate degree, I joined the master's programme in management at Calcutta University with a specialization in operations research. But I was not motivated to get a job. At that time, I was told that computer science (CS) had a great future. With my management degree, the only institution that allowed me to write an entrance exam for an MTech in CS was ISI. So that's what I did. Then I spent some time in two industries, but I realized soon that it was not for me.

So I joined the Indian Statistical Institute to do my PhD. My thesis was on image processing. Just after submitting my thesis, I attended a workshop on neural networks at the Indian Institute of Science, Bengaluru, and became interested in neural networks. That was the beginning, and with time I became more and more interested in biologically and linguistically motivated (nature-inspired) computing. This is how my journey in artificial intelligence or machine learning started.

Q. You have been working on bioinformatics. What exactly is it and what are its potential applications?

Bioinformatics is an interdisciplinary field to develop theories and methodologies for understanding biological data such as DNA sequences, amino acid sequences and gene expressions. Bioinformatics integrates knowledge of biology, computer science, chemistry, physics, mathematics and statistics to make sense of biological data.

It has many applications, particularly in medicine or health science, including the discovery of cancer biomarkers, drug discovery, the discovery of gene regulatory networks and personalized medicine. For example, using gene expression data, we can find the genes related to a particular cancer, and this will not only help diagnose the cancer more accurately but will also help us assess its stage and severity, which, in turn, may help to make a treatment plan. This is achieved in the same way that the understanding of the three-dimensional structure of a protein often helps us grasp the biology of a disease. For example, mad cow disease is known to be related to the misfolding of a protein. Knowledge of the three-dimensional structure of proteins also helps us find candidate drugs for a disease. Bioinformatics plays a key role in analysing the molecular biological data of patients to diagnose and prescribe personalized medicine (precision medicine). There are many more applications of bioinformatics.

Q. **Since you have also been working on brain–computer interfaces (BCI), according to you, how far are we from artificial general intelligence (AGI)? Will computers ever be able to perform all the intellectual tasks performed by humans?**

We are far from the so-called AGI or strong AI era. My short answer to the second question is, no, at least not in the near future. Why do I think so? In the next decade or so, I expect a tremendous advancement in the field of AI, leading to very successful applications that will beat humans in terms of performance and speed. But there will also be smart systems to fool AI. I also expect to see infrequent and unexpected major failures—failures that traditional machine learning systems usually do not face.

The realization of AGI requires the ability to perform intellectual tasks that humans can easily do. It demands explainable AI (XAI) systems with attributes like consciousness, ability of brain-like learning, common sense, reasoning and decision-making. Human beings do make mistakes, but in almost all cases, humans are capable of explaining the possible reasons behind such mistakes. But the present-day AI systems are not good at this. To achieve AGI, we must first develop explainable AI systems. Some of the successful AI systems (AlphaGo, Google Assistant) use deep neural networks, which are, at a macro level, inspired by the brain, but their computational processing is far from what happens in the brain. The human brain is one of the most complex systems in the known universe; and while there are more unknowns than knowns, many interesting and surprising discoveries have been made about it. For example, the conventional belief is that the cortex is organized based on different body parts, but a recent study suggested that the cortex is organized in terms of the functions performed by different organs. If further research reconfirms this, it may strongly influence the design of brain–computer interface systems. For example, people with a congenital missing arm often use other limbs to perform activities that would have been performed by the missing limb. Hence the computation in their brains is very different from that done by people born with all four limbs. Unless we look at the brain and exploit knowledge from brain science into our AI system, in my view, the realization of true AGI may remain a dream.

Q. There is a growing fear that robots powered by AI will replace humans. How valid is this fear?

I think there are two fears here: Will robots *replace* humans? And will robots *take over* humans?

There is some truth and validity to the first fear but not strong enough to cause alarm. Yes, in some areas, robots may replace humans—and this is already happening. Robots are certainly good for jobs that are of a repetitive nature; they also have an advantage in performing hazardous jobs. We all know of the Henn na Hotel Maihama Tokyo Bay, which is staffed by robots. So robots replacing humans is a reality. But how far will this go? Will all hotels be staffed by robots in time? No! Although robot or AI technologies will become necessary in some areas and will give rise to new jobs requiring specialized skills, uncontrolled use of AI may hurt the unskilled job market. Consequently, many may not be economically strong enough to buy the fruits of AI. This may constrain rampant robotization. Moreover, are we happy to be greeted by a robot in a hotel? Do we enjoy interacting more with robots than with humans? Will a robot be able to exchange thoughts about an ongoing football match in the way a housekeeping attendant or the concierge can? My answer to these questions is: NO! I believe government intervention (via formulation and imposition of AI policies, including AI ethics) as well as humankind's characteristics and preferences will ensure a balanced application of robots in human society.

Coming to the second question, I do not believe that robots will take over humans in the literal sense in the near future. For this, we need more sophisticated AI systems that possess consciousness and many other attributes explained earlier. However, there will be situations (maybe rare) wherein the behaviour of robots may make it seem like they have taken over humans. This will primarily be because of factors like a robot's black-box nature of reasoning, a failure of hardware or software components, inappropriate self-repairing activities, virus attacks and the inability to assess when it must not act.

 ## NOTE TO PARENTS

Artificial intelligence is one of the frontier sectors of human advancement. Every major product and service today is now deploying AI to enhance its efficacy. While this automation is reducing the number of traditional jobs, it is also causing an increased demand for experts who can design better, more robust and more effective artificial intelligence algorithms. In the future, every device will be connected to a network, whether they are home appliances, commercial enterprises, massive industries or even militaries. These networks will be operated by AI, which will be made and manufactured by leading AI designers.

A career in AI is very rewarding but, at the same time, it is a long-drawn, continuous education that requires investment and self-learning.

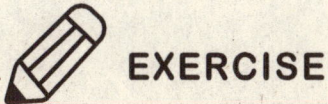 **EXERCISE**

1. Refer to the discussion on humanoids in this chapter. Now imagine that you have been asked by your organization to design a new humanoid to assist doctors in treating lethal communicable diseases. Think of and identify all the actions your humanoid is going to have to perform; also draw a diagram of the robot below. Think of how its voice is going to sound, what features it will have and so on. It is important that the robot is able to turn and bend its arms, so ensure you make the right joints at the right places.

(Hint: You might want to give it the ability to hold tools.)

2. Refer to the image of the humanoid Nadine in the collection of photographs in this book. Can you spot which one is the human and which one is the humanoid?

Answer: The humanoid is the one on your <u>left</u> and the human is the one on your <u>right</u>.

The Enigma cipher machine: It was a coding machine extensively used by the German Army during the Second World War (1939–1945). Every message could be encoded in 150 million ways, and hence it was near-impossible for their opponents to crack any.

The Bombe: This machine, developed by the mathematical genius Alan Turing, was 7 feet wide, 6.5 feet tall and 2 feet deep, and weighed over 1000 kilogrammes. These machines were the predecessors of modern computers and were able to crack the Enigma code. Historians believe that Alan Turing and his Bombe machines played a crucial role in the Allies (the USA, the UK and Russia) defeating the Germans in the Second World War.

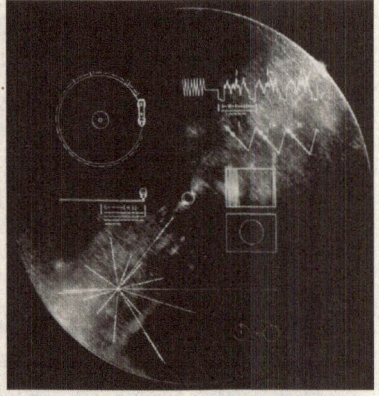

The Voyager Golden Record: This could be our first impression on an alien civilization. This record, containing sounds of Earth, is a collection of popular music, images and the sounds of nature on Earth as well as greetings said in fifty-five different languages. Do you think aliens would be able to understand at least one of these languages? On the back of the record is our planet's location. This is written using a space map, with the positions of the pulsar stars.

The Messerschmitt Me 262: Developed by the Germans towards the end of the Second World War, this machine is the world's first jet engine. Today, most commercial and fighter planes use the same technology.

Courtesy of Makarand Baokar

The Delahaye 135M: With only eleven cars to its name, this model was produced by the French manufacturer Delahaye. Only five have survived. The car in the image is presently owned by Maharaja Dalip Singh of Jodhpur.

Courtesy of Shreya Goswami

The Wanderer W24: This car was produced by the German manufacturer Auto Union for the middle-class market. Interestingly, it is associated with the history of Indian independence. This car was used by Netaji Subhash Chandra Bose to escape house arrest in Calcutta in 1941. It can be found on display at Netaji Bhawan in Kolkata.

Courtesy of ModelTMitch/Wikimedia Commons

Ford Model T: Manufactured in 1908, it was the first commercial vehicle made on a large scale, thanks to Henry Ford's assembly line manufacturing process.

Humanoids—the next generations of robots, who look like humans—are expected to be living among us soon. The science fiction of yesterday is becoming a reality of today!

Courtesy of Web Summit/Wikimedia Commons

Sophia: In 2017, she became the first humanoid to be given the citizenship of any nation—Saudi Arabia. She is able to show facial signs, respond to queries and strike up conversations with humans.

Courtesy of Nadiathalmann/Wikimedia Commons

Nadine: Humanoid Nadine with her human inspiration. They are both reading a book on computing. Can you spot which one is the human and which one is the humanoid? (The answer is at the end of Chapter 7.)

Laser Guns: These have been popular in science fiction and comics, and have now become a reality. Developed for the US Navy, this laser gun shoots a high-energy beam at targets and can destroy fast-moving missiles and planes by burning them up.

The Arable Mark: This unique instrument developed by Arable Labs, Inc. is like a small umbrella that can sense several parameters related to agriculture with utmost precision. It can sense rain, moisture, radiation, temperature, soil and wind conditions etc. and create real-time data that can be fed into a computer. This is ultra-precision farming, useful for not only our planet but also for when we settle on other planets. For more on this, read the interview with Adam Wolf in Chapter 4.

Europa: One of Jupiter's moons, it has oceans of water and a silicate-based surface similar to Earth. But it is very cold at −170 degrees Celsius.

Titan: One of Saturn's moons, it has no water but oceans of liquid methane. That should make this celestial body really smelly! The good part is that it seems to have carbon compounds. Remember, carbon compounds are the building blocks of life? Could there be methane-based life forms on Titan?

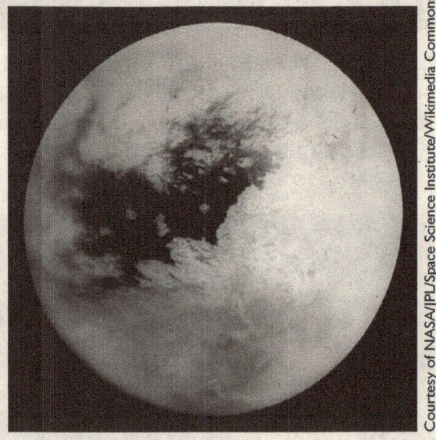

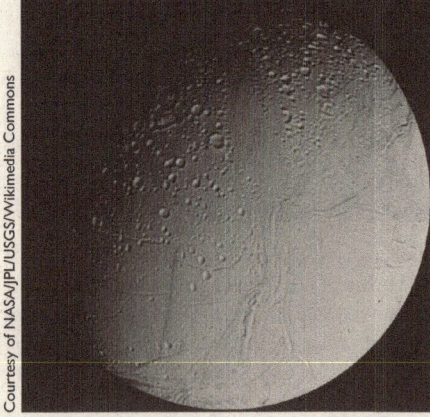

Enceladus: One of Saturn's moons, it is much smaller than the others, at only 500 kilometres across. The good news is that there are probably geysers of hot water jetting from its frozen surface. Scientists believe that there is a churning ocean of water below the frozen surface. This seems similar to our polar regions. Could marine life be thriving below the icy surface?

President Kalam's polio calipers: In the 1980s, President Kalam was developing Agni missiles. The team repurposed the material used in the nose cone of the missile to engineer calipers to help children affected by polio. The weight of these new calipers was less than one-tenth of that of the existing metal calipers. This is the cross application of technology.

The M61 Vulcan: This is an ultra-speed gun, which can fire 6000 bullets per minute. A critical issue arising from firing guns at high rates of speed is cooling the gun. Notice the large surface area of the gun and the spaces designed for wind to pass through.

The B-2 Bomber: Each of these bombers costs almost $1 billion (Rs 7500 crore). This aircraft is an example of extreme stealth. The B-2 Bomber is 21 metres long and 52 metres wide, but when detected by radar signals, it shows a cross section of no more than 30 centimetres (as long as a ruler). It weighs 71,000 kilogrammes. Here it is refueling while flying—a process called mid-air refueling.

CHAPTER 8

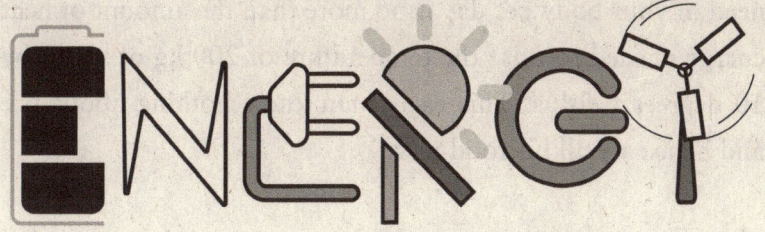

Let me take you through the historic journey of human beings and their need for energy.

One million years ago, in the forests of East Africa, roamed the early humans. They looked slightly different from us modern humans. They had smaller heads, and hence smaller brains than we have today. They did not have language, and they mostly roamed around, hunting for animals and foraging for fruit fallen from trees. Scientists estimate that the global human population back then was no more than 18,000. The entire population of prehistoric humans could fit in no more than four–five trains!

This early man had only a single energy need—biological energy needed for the functioning of the various organs of the body, about 2000 kilocalories (kcal) a day. Remember, one kcal is the amount of energy needed to raise the temperature of 1 kilogramme of water by 1 degree Celsius. So the biological need of your body per day is no more than the amount of heat energy needed to raise the temperature of 200 kg of water by 10 degrees Celsius. This early man knew nothing about fire and hence ate all his food raw.

Then about 60,000 years ago, an evolved human being discovered and started controlling fire. Fire allowed us to cook food and also light up caves. Occasionally, it became a weapon of defence against larger animals. Fire raised the energy consumption per person per day to about 5000 kcal—2.5 times the biological need. This new kind of energy was provided by wood; hence plants were technically the source of this new energy. Humans remained hunters until about 10,000 years ago, when we invented farming. We also started domesticating other animals and deploying them in agriculture. We built better houses and cooked even more. Our energy needs per day eventually reached 12,000 kcal with the addition of a new source—animal power.

Then about 4000 years ago, the wheel was invented. We now started travelling or moving around using non-human energy, mainly supplied by bulls and cows. We came up with the first exchanges based on trading and commerce. Another new dimension was added to our energy needs—transportation. Our mobility was still limited and slow; nevertheless, our energy needs per person per day had reached about 26,000 kcal by this time. The wheel more than doubled our energy needs, taking the figure up to more than ten times what we needed just to survive.

There was little addition to our sources of energy until we entered the Industrial Age (around 1760–mid-nineteenth century). Then we learnt to harness fossil fuel energy from dead animals and plants. We mastered engines, generators and motors. Man became motorized, and mass-manufacturing factories came up. Our energy intake per capita rose to over 77,000 kcal a day. We started spending a lot more energy in transportation as we moved between cities, travelling in the earliest railways and cars. The energy needed for food was less than 10 per cent of one's overall usage.

We finally reached the present day, when most houses are electrified and when we travel thousands of kilometres in airplanes in a matter of hours. We also air-condition our homes and offices. Today, each one of us spends almost 2,40,000 kcal of energy every single day. This figure is 120 times the basic biological requirement we started our journey with a million years ago.

Despite all the focus on clean sources like solar, wind and nuclear, even today much of the energy we use comes from fossil fuels.

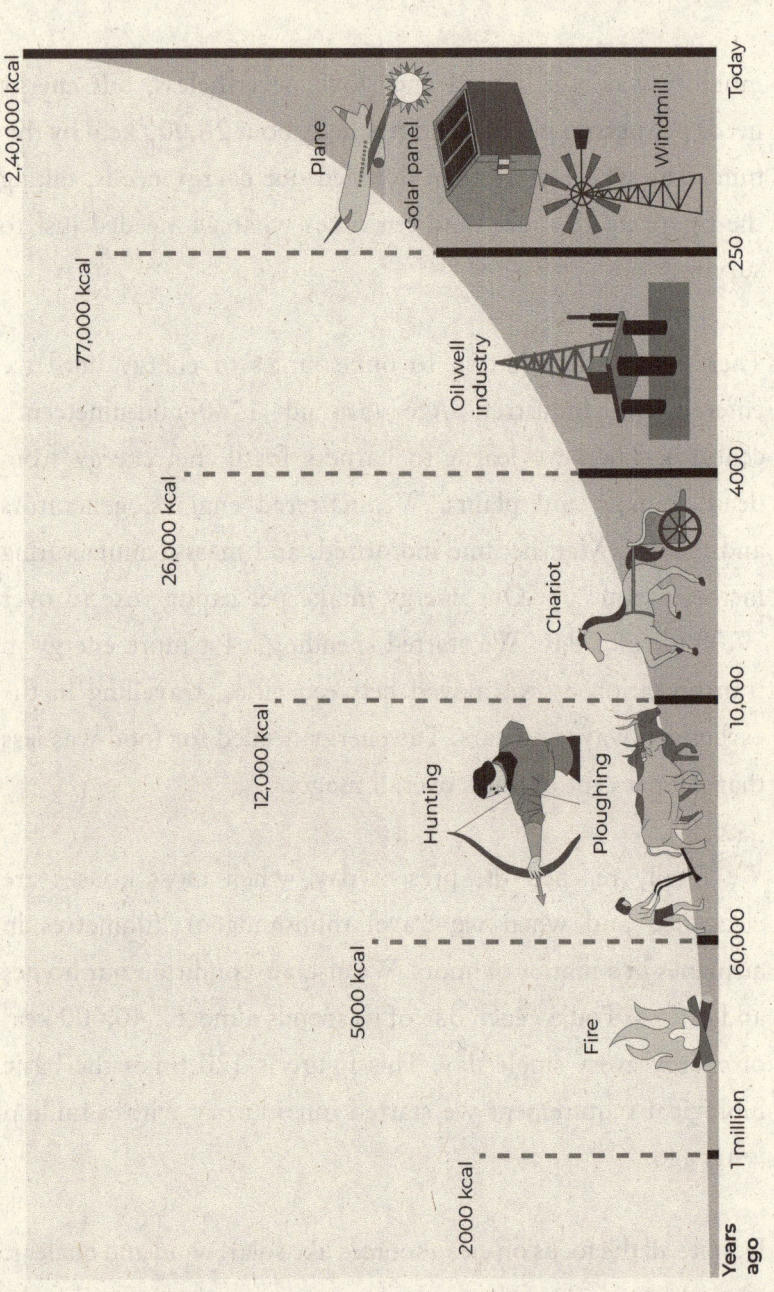

A timeline of energy consumption

Years ago

| 1 million | 60,000 | 10,000 | 4000 | 250 | Today |

2000 kcal   5000 kcal   12,000 kcal   26,000 kcal   77,000 kcal   2,40,000 kcal

Fire

Hunting

Ploughing

Chariot

Oil well industry

Plane

Solar panel

Windmill

Thirty-three per cent of the total energy we use is from petroleum oils; 29 per cent is from coal; and another 24 per cent is from petroleum gas.[1] Thus these environmentally harmful sources contribute to about 86 per cent of our energy consumption. The remaining 14 per cent comes from hydro or water-based plants (7 per cent), nuclear sources (4 per cent) and solar, wind and other green sources (about 1 per cent each). Of course, in the recent years, the growth rate of these green sources is promising and on the higher side, especially solar power.

Let me tell you the story of solar power, the energy we receive from the Sun.

● ● ●

How old do you think solar-power generation is? A decade? Two decades? Maybe half a century?

Most people are of the view that solar power is a relatively new invention in the energy sector. But that is far from the truth. Solar-powered machines and electricity is, in fact, older than diesel-, petrol- or gas-powered plants.

We wind the clock back to the year 1878 and travel to Paris.

This was a very different time. It was an age when human and animal power drove locomotion, and even the first form of the light bulb, by Edison, was to arrive in a year's time. And so electricity was an alien concept, and so was the combustion engine (an engine that generates power by the combustion of fuel). In September that year, the Universal Exhibition (*Exposition Universelle* in French) was held to celebrate the country's victory in the Franco-Prussian War. In this expo, organized in Paris, new goods and inventions were showcased over 66 acres of land. The prime attraction here was the completed head of the *Statue of Liberty*, which would later be finished and shipped to New York. However, many more marvellous goods were displayed there, and thousands and thousands of people turned up to view them.

In a small, obscure area of this grand exhibition was a schoolteacher who taught maths. His name was Augustin Mouchot. Everything about him was ordinary, except for his thin and spike-like moustache and, of course, his invention. His giant solar concentrator, shaped like a modern dish antenna, was capable of harnessing solar energy and converting it into mechanical energy. At the fair, he used this mechanical energy to operate an early form of the refrigerator. He made ice using the Sun! It dazzled the crowds, and Augustin declared, 'We may some day run out of coal, but the Sun will be there for us forever.' It was an accurate prophecy, and quite futuristic for those times.

Augustin was awarded the gold medal at the fair. But that did not help his cause much. Soon the price of coal dropped; its becoming a cheap commodity meant that no industry or government found solar power of any value. The world lost its first chance to steer clear of dangerous fossil fuels, which would not only damage the environment but also lead to several global wars.

Three and a half decades later, we got another chance. This time in Egypt, which was one of the most prominent ancient human civilizations.

Frank Shuman, born in 1862 in the United States, had only three years of formal schooling. But despite his lack of education, he was an inventor of the highest order. By the time he turned thirty, he had invented the wire mesh safety glass, which made broken glass less dangerous for humans. As the name indicates, this glass had a grid of thin metallic wires embedded within it to strengthen it. This invention made him rich. Shuman is also credited with designing the danger signal used at railway crossings, as well as the use of liquid air to run a submarine. But his true passion lay somewhere else—solar energy.

In 1912, he set up the world's first solar power station in Egypt. Several long rows of reflectors were employed to run a 70-horsepower motor. This motor was used to pump about 24,000 litres of water from River Nile to a barren land that was later turned into a cotton field. Shuman's dream was to turn deserts into lush fields and forests. He calculated that if he was able to build a bigger plant in the Sahara Desert, 250 kilometres on all sides, it could supply power to all the world. Shuman's dream was to see tropical nations, including India, which were mostly enslaved by European powers, use this new source of power they had in abundance to break the shackles of poverty, misery and colonization.

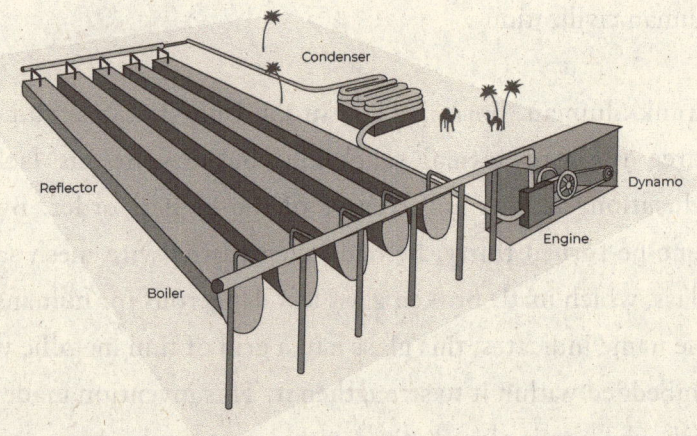

The earliest solar plant, built by Frank Shuman in Egypt in 1912

The Sun would have become the liberator for these countries. Shuman's invention had made solar power even cheaper than coal. The world was on the cusp of an energy revolution. But then two events happened.

First, a new liquid fossil fuel, petroleum, took over the market. It would take 100 men a week to extract a ship full of coal. With liquid petrol, one man could do this in a single day. The second, and perhaps more significant, event was the First World War, which broke out a year after Shuman's solar power went into operation. In this war, which engulfed the world, there was a great shortage of glass. So Shuman was ordered to shut down his plant, and the glass from the solar panels was recycled and made into weapons.[2] This was a sad end to humanity's opportunity to steer away from all the pollution that would go on to haunt us for the next century and even today.

Today, more than a century after Shuman's dream was literally shattered, just like the panels of the world's first clean solar plant, we are back on track. Today, solar power is almost as cheap as coal or oil. The Sun is abundant, especially in nations near the equator, like ours. Most scientists agree that the global climate change is a result of the poor energy sources we have chased for a century. Global industries are finding investment in solar power to be profitable. And, frankly, this is our last chance to avert a climatic catastrophe. As energy scientists of tomorrow, your goal will be to amplify clean power sources like solar and discover new sources of energy.

What could they be? Can you think of any?

The future of energy science

Solar and wind energy are the most talked-about candidates for future sources of energy, and already a lot is being done to develop them further. But solar and wind sources have a limiting factor: they depend on natural cycles. On a cloudy day, solar energy output can go down by 60–70 per cent, and nobody can really predict the speed and direction of winds. Hence energy scientists are constantly looking for new and more stable ways to generate power. I will discuss three of them here with you; of course, there are many more. All of these are in the ideation or development stages and, as of now, we have not been able to find a proper and economical path to harness them for power. But then, much of the science around us today blossomed from our courage to challenge what once seemed impossible.

1. Nuclear power from thorium: Every single atom in the universe carries an unimaginably powerful battery at its core, called the nucleus. This form of energy, often called type-1 fuel, is hundreds of thousands, if not millions, of times more powerful than the conventional type-0 fuels, which are basically dead plants and animals existing in the form of coal, petroleum, natural gas and other fossil fuels.

Now, imagine a kilometre-long train, with about fifty freight bogies, all fully laden with the most typical fossil fuel— about 10,000 tons of coal. With this development, the same amount of energy can be generated from 500 kg of type-1 fuel—naturally occurring uranium—which would barely fill the boot of a small car. When the technology is fully realized, one can do even better with naturally occurring thorium, in which case the amount of material required would be much less—about 62.5 kg, or even lesser, according to some estimates, and thus compact enough to fit in a small bag.[3]

In 1945, the human race learnt how to split an atom and generate massive amounts of energy from it. Our first application of this new skill was, unfortunately, the killing of hundreds of thousands with atomic bombs, which wiped two cities off the face of the planet. In 1954, in a place called Obninsk, just outside of Moscow (the Russian capital), the world's first nuclear power plant was built. Since then, nuclear power has been developed considerably and, despite some alarming accidents, several major countries are on the path of nuclear power.

But there is one problem with our approach to nuclear power. Humankind started pursuing nuclear power with the aim of developing it into a weapon, and once that was accomplished, the weapons technology inspired the power plant application. Then there is another serious drawback: we followed a path using uranium as an input fuel. Uranium is an extremely rare element that is highly fissile. This means that it rapidly disintegrates into smaller elements and releases a lot of heat energy—a very difficult process to control. Hence, while it is perfect for a bomb, it may not be the best choice for a power plant, where one needs to control the rate of reaction to be able to create limited and consistent heat. Thorium, a much better choice, is fertile, which means that you can convert it into fissile material using certain processes, but it will not decay on its own and be used as a bomb.

Moreover, there is four times as much thorium than there is uranium on our planet. Thorium is a safer, more stable alternative to uranium, and future energy scientists would definitely find it a promising fuel to develop. Given that India has the world's richest reserves of thorium—almost 50 per cent of the total—it is likely that an Indian scientific team will be the first to solve the thorium challenge.[4]

2. Antimatter energy: Have you heard of the equation $E = mc^2$? This is the famous equation coined by Albert Einstein, one of the most brilliant human minds to have ever existed. The equation says that matter and energy are interconvertible. That was a revolutionary thought in its time. Here, 'E' is the energy in joules (1 kilocalorie = 4200 joules); 'm' is the mass in kilogrammes; and 'c' is the velocity of light (3×10^8 metres/second).

Now, let me present a problem. Imagine that you were able to annihilate and thereby convert 1 kilogramme of matter into energy. How much energy would you have produced?

Let us solve this together.

We know $E = mc^2$
Now $m = 1$ kg and $c = 3 \times 10^8$ m/s
Hence $E = 1 \times (3 \times 10^8 \times 3 \times 10^8)$ joules
$E = 9 \times 10^{16}$ joules

This is equal to about 25 billion units (kWh) of energy, or about 25 terawatt-hours.

What does this mean? The world consumes about 20,000 TWh of electricity in a year. So if we could find a way to destroy about 400 kilogrammes of matter by mixing it with exactly 400 kilogrammes of antimatter, it would supply the whole world with all the power it needs for a full year.

So how do we do that? We are not completely sure, but we have a very strong clue. The closest answers lie somewhere in space, in the rings of Saturn and the spaces between Mars and Jupiter, which are our nearest sources of the particle called antimatter.

Antimatter is, as the name suggests, the particle opposite to matter. Antimatter particles are almost identical to their matter counterparts, but they carry the opposite charge and spin. When antimatter and matter meet, they immediately convert to energy. This is governed by the same equation: $E = mc^2$.

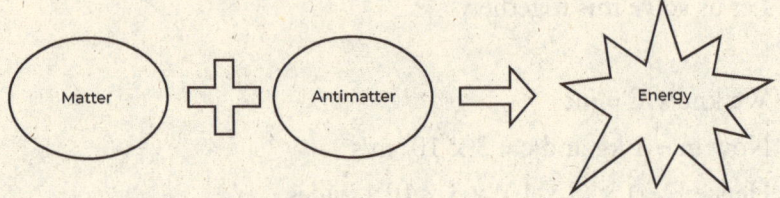

Matter combined with antimatter produces energy

Theoretically, when the Big Bang happened and the universe was born, all the antimatter should have combined with equal parts matter and both should have been completely annihilated, leaving behind only energy. But there was a small excess of matter over antimatter, about one extra particle of matter for every 1 billion pairs of matter–antimatter. Why? We do not know that yet. But this deficit is what helped create *all* matter: the celestial bodies, humans and even this book! During this intense Big Bang, a very small amount of antimatter also escaped the reaction and is locked in vacuum in space. How much antimatter is it? We do not exactly know, but it is extremely less. NASA estimates that while only about a kilogramme of antiprotons (the most basic form of antimatter) enters our solar system every second from all over the universe, only a few grams reach the vicinity of Earth in a year. This makes it very hard to track and capture. In fact, it is such a difficult project that we are more focused on finding ways to manufacture antimatter than harness it from space. And currently it is the most expensive particle to manufacture. Making 1 gram of antimatter will cost about 1000 trillion dollars! That's more than the annual GDPs of all the countries put together. But that should not deject you—technology, for most applications around us, was exorbitantly costly in the beginning and the costs rapidly fell as manufacturing processes evolved. The same thing should happen in the case of antimatter.

3. Zero-point energy: Helium-4 is a non-radioactive isotope of the element helium, which makes up about 25 per cent of the matter in the universe (by mass). This helium isotope remains in a gaseous state till −267.95 degrees Celsius, beyond which it turns into liquid. This is when the isotope starts to behave strangely. When we bring the temperature further down, to −273 degrees Celsius, a level called the absolute zero (the temperature at which all motion in the universe ceases), the helium still remains liquid. It doesn't freeze even at the absolute zero due to a mysterious force that we call zero-point energy, which is present in the atomic spaces. This means that all the spaces in the universe, including the tiny spaces between electron and electron, and electron and proton, have energy. It might appear that this energy is zero, but in reality it is not. Even vacuum possesses a certain amount of energy, and that energy is called the zero-point energy or vacuum energy.

How much of this energy is in existence? Well, we don't know. Theoretically, since space is infinite, this energy is also infinite. According to some scientists, if not all, there's so much energy in the empty spaces of the universe that if we could find a way to harness it, we would gain access to a never-ending supply of energy. This is a source that has the potential to power our planet with the strength of multiple suns and could solve all our energy woes forever.

However, physicists disagree on the exact amount of energy actually contained in vacuum. According to Richard Feynman and John Wheeler, this energy is so powerful that just a small cup of it would be sufficient to bring all of Earth's oceans to a boil. But according to Albert Einstein's theory of general relativity, these radiations gravitate—scatter throughout the universe—and hence would be very weak.

In other words, currently we don't have the necessary technology to predict the strength of this energy. However, if the beliefs of some of the scientists are true and we do develop a way to tap this energy, it would end our quest to find an alternative source of energy.

How do I become an energy scientist?

Essentially, there are three ways to approach a career in the field of energy. First is the most obvious choice: pursuing engineering in electrical or similar fields. Such engineers work on improving modern energy sources, such as solar, wind, geothermal and nuclear power. There are several colleges both in India and abroad that offer courses in this domain. The Indian Institute of Science in Bengaluru, IIT Bombay, IIT Delhi and the Birla Institute of Technology and Science (BITS) in Pilani are some of the good colleges to pursue electrical engineering. MIT, Cambridge University, ETH Zurich and the National Institute of Singapore are some of the globally renowned colleges that are working on energy sources.

The second approach towards a career in energy is the field of scientific research, primarily in the subject of physics, wherein one gets to deal with antimatter, zero-point energy and similar concepts. The University of Illinois, the University of Edinburgh, Harvard University and the University of Tokyo are some of the leading universities abroad that are working on different sources of energy, including zero-point energy. All the research related to antimatter is conducted at the European Organization for Nuclear Research (popularly known as CERN) in Switzerland.

In either case, you will need a solid foundation in physics, mathematics and chemistry. You need to keep yourself updated on the latest developments related to energy generation and storage methods. There are plenty of free online resources available, such as *IEEE Power & Energy Magazine*, *Energy Digital* and many others. You can also subscribe to the publications of the Institute of Electrical and Electronics Engineers (IEEE), which is one of the foremost professional organizations for electrical engineers.

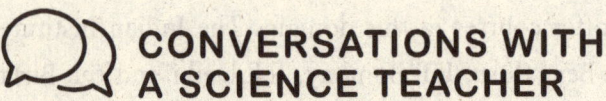

CONVERSATIONS WITH A SCIENCE TEACHER

How much power does a lightning bolt have? Can we extract and harness it?

A single bolt of lightning contains around 1400 kWh of energy (we are assuming zero loss in transfer and storage), which is enough to power a household in Delhi for five months. When a single bolt of lightning is so powerful, why are we not extracting this energy?

The answer lies in the logistical problems involved in harvesting this energy. First, we need a dependable source to meet our steady energy demands. And thunderstorms are spontaneous, followed by a sudden strike of lightning, which makes them unpredictable.

Second, to capture the energy associated with each and every lightning strike (land strikes only), we would need to install a grid of tall towers, each around 1.5 kilometres apart, across the globe. Imagine the havoc these towers will wreak on air traffic! Also, these towers need to have equipment to convert the extreme amount of charge that flows only for about 30 milliseconds (the approximate duration of a lighting strike) to electrical energy. Even though currently we do not have such a technology for the storage of electrical energy, let's assume we have created one and that it is 100 per cent efficient. Then the cost of each tower, along with the storage system, can be estimated to be around Rs 3,14,00,000 ($4,57,000). This is just the construction cost of a single tower, excluding the installation cost and the cost of regular maintenance. Now, just imagine the total cost of the grid of towers required to capture all this energy. Therefore, with currently available technology, harnessing energy from lightning seems to be an unfeasible task.

Can we harness energy from footsteps?

Harnessing power from the footsteps of people as they go about their everyday tasks is not a new concept. It is being used to light up advertisement hoardings and ticket machines at railway stations in Tokyo, Japan, since 2008. This energy harvesting works on the principle of the piezoelectric effect, which means converting the mechanical energy of footsteps to electrical energy. The railway stations are installed with a special type of rubber flooring in front of the ticket barriers. Every time a passenger steps on the mat, it triggers a vibration that is stored as energy. An average person weighing 60 kilogrammes would generate only 0.1 watt in a second (in the time it takes to cross the tile). So, on an average day, around 4 million users cross the Tokyo station, producing enough energy to power its electronic signboards!

How much energy can waste produce?

The whole idea of producing energy from waste stinks! But the process of converting waste to energy is not so unappealing. The solid waste collected from municipal corporations and industrial units is heated at a very high temperature to produce steam. This steam then drives the turbine to produce electricity. This not only decreases the amount of waste that reaches landfills but also reduces carbon emissions by reducing the burden on fossil fuels to meet energy requirements.

Let us take an example. Delhi produces 9620 tons (96,20,000 kg) of waste per day. This waste is further divided into dry solid waste and wet solid waste. The energy conversions of the two types of waste employ different methods. First, let's discuss dry solid waste. Delhi produces 48,10,000 kg of dry waste per day (50 per cent of the total). In India, the average net calorific value of dry waste is estimated to be 900 kcal/kg. This means that the potential energy content of the dry waste produced per day is about 5000 megawatt-hour. If we assume that we are able to effectively convert only 25 per cent of the energy, we are left with 1250 MWh of energy.

Now let's come to wet waste. It is assumed that only 30 per cent of the total wet waste is organic and biodegradable, which leaves us with 14,43,000 kg of waste. Now, assuming the efficiency of digestion to be 60 per cent and that of biogas production to be

80 per cent, we are left with about 6,92,000 m³ of biogas. The net calorific value of biogas is estimated to be about 5000 kcal/m³. Hence the potential energy content of wet waste is 4000 MWh. Assuming conversion efficiency to be 30 per cent, we are left with 1200 MWh of energy.

Adding both the figures, we get 2450 MWh of energy from the waste produced in Delhi in just a single day.

MEET THE EXPERT: ABHILASH THIRUPATHY

Abhilash Thirupathy is the co-founder of Gold Farm and Surya Power Magic. He is a dentist by qualification and also holds a master's degree in business administration from the Indian Institute of Management (IIM), Lucknow. Coming from an agrarian background, he is working towards creating effective ecosystems through technology and innovation to catalyse the growth and sustainability of farmers.

Q. In ten–fifteen years from now, we will surely see a spike in the global energy demand. What are the sources that could help meet this demand?

As far as I can see, through my line of work as well as outside it, new energy sources and technologies will establish the missing link between consumption and sustainability. I strongly feel that, today, the world is going through a consumption-driven phase, wherein we are going crazy about consuming more and more. This whole generation is going to be all about consuming more and more energy.

With technology taking over, the next decade will see a more energy-hungry world. By this, I am indicating the number of devices that we are going to carry or install in our homes in the name of IoT (Internet of things). Automation and smart gadgets will be the new sinks of energy that are going to make the world energy-hungry.

And to further amplify the problem, the sources of energy that we have today will not be able to meet this new demand that we are about to generate, as about 29 per cent of the greenhouse gases generated today are because of electricity production. So we definitely need a paradigm shift towards green alternatives, or we will be living in a very hot world.

According to me, we will see a major chunk of energy coming from individuals and organizations. This basically means that an independent unit will set up a micro power plant and generate its own energy. For instance, solar panels are installed on top of houses to generate green energy for household consumption.

Furthermore, the future will see some major innovations being done in the production as well as storage of energy.

This could be something like a battery that is a thousand times more efficient than what we have today. Or it could be a solar panel that has an efficiency of 90 per cent, as compared to the 13–17 per cent that we get today. These would be the new sources that would help us meet the energy demand.

Q. Which countries are going to be the leaders in using and developing non-conventional sources of energy?

When I think of the energy leaders of the world, the only names that come to my mind are China and India. There is no other country in the world that has greater scope and urgency than these two countries. This is largely because of the fact that, with the increasing population, the demand in these countries is going to be huge. And to meet that demand for energy, they will have to innovate and shift to non-conventional sources. Also, other countries will shift to these green sources of energy too, but their urgency to do so will be far less compared to these two countries.

Q. What are your views on the International Solar Alliance, started by India?

Any great leader is recognized in retrospect, because when there are so many people involved in decision-making, it becomes very difficult to predict the results.

Coming back to your question on the International Solar Alliance, which was started by the current central government in 2016. It is an alliance initiated by India, with the sole objective of working on the exploitation of solar energy to reduce the dependence on conventional energy sources (fossil fuels). Today, this alliance has the participation of more than 121 countries, most of which are what we call the 'sunshine countries'. This term is used for the countries that lie between the Tropic of Cancer and the Tropic of Capricorn. This project is still in its nascent stage and looks promising, but it's too early to comment on its success.

Let me put this differently: The University of Stanford derives its value from the alumni it has produced. In the same way, the parameter for judging any organization or alliance is the number of great leaders it has produced in the past. And for that to happen, we need to give the organization at least twenty-five years. So the success or failure of this alliance can only be judged after at least twenty-five years.

 **NOTE TO PARENTS**

Energy is the basis of all advancements we have made in all sectors, from transport to healthcare and from space to entertainment. In the future, there will be a job shift in the sector. Coal and oil plants will reduce in number, while gas ones might still grow. Green energy plants like solar and wind are well on their way to growing exponentially, and even nuclear power is gaining traction. Hence the world will see tremendous demand for new-age energy scientists. Moreover, there is great scope for expanding into new realms of energy sources for humankind, which will see a demand for researchers in the domain of quantum physics and energy particles. This is a sector that will, quite literally, never go out of power.

 **EXERCISE**

This exercise requires an Internet connection or access to a library. So make sure you have access to either before you start.

1. Encircle the country that is the largest producer of the particular source of energy:

- Solar energy: India, the USA, China, France, Germany
- Tidal energy: India, China, South Korea, the USA, the UK
- Wind energy: the USA, Switzerland, India, China, Brazil
- Geothermal energy: Argentina, the USA, India, China, Brazil
- Biogas: France, Germany, Brazil, India, China
- Hydroelectricity: the USA, India, Russia, China, Brazil

2. Classify the following sources of energy as renewable or non-renewable. Sort them into two columns in the table below:

Solar energy	Coal	Tidal energy	Geothermal energy
Wind energy	Hydroelectricity	Biogas	Wave and marine energy
Nuclear energy	Shale gas	Petroleum	Natural gas

RENEWABLE SOURCES	NON-RENEWABLE SOURCES

Acknowledgements

First and foremost, I would like to express my gratitude to my teacher President A.P.J. Abdul Kalam, who will always inspire me and many millions like me across the globe. This book is only a humble attempt at continuing the legacy of *Reignited*, the book that emerged from his wisdom and unparalleled futuristic thinking. He remains a beacon of hope for the citizens of India and the world; his life story is something today's youth should absorb, emulate and narrate to others.

A large portion of the thoughts expressed in this book are essentially the extensions of the dreams, imaginings, fears, ambitions, hopes and challenges of the nation's youth, many of whom have been giving me ideas and suggestions in person and via social media. I thank them all.

I would like to especially express my gratitude to the learned contributors of this book—Professor V. Ramgopal Rao, Professor Charles Cockell, Mr Gautam Sen, Professor Nikhil R. Pal, Adam Wolf, Colonel N. Ramachandran, Lieutenant Colonel Satyendra Verma and Mr Abhilash Thirupathy—who helped me with the expert sections and also with many other ideas that shaped the contents of the book. I also thank Professor Hongkun Park and Professor Vinothan N. Manoharan from Harvard University, who, in 2011, were very kind to open up their laboratories and work to President Kalam and me.

I would like to thank Ms Sohini Mitra, who played a key role in all stages of this book—from the writing to its production—and whose wise ideas led its editing. My gratitude is due to Ms Arpita Nath and Ms Kankana Basu for their untiring effort in editing and improving the content. I'd also like to thank Mr Neeraj Nath for his excellent cover design and Ms Rujuta Thakurdesai for her wonderful illustrations. I am indebted to the always helpful Ms Piya Kapur for ensuring that the copies of the book reach the right channels at the right time.

I would also like to thank Ms Hemali Sodhi for her support and leadership. My gratitude is due to Mr Kanishka Gupta, whose thinking was critical to the genesis of this book.

I also acknowledge the contribution of Ms Preksha Sethia, who untiringly assembled all the research needed to put this book together. Her contribution to this book is indeed immense and imperative. I would also like to thank Mr Agam Khare, Ms Vishakha and Dr Ashok Patil for their help in putting some of the facts together.

I appreciate the efforts of Mr Saurav, of the Kalam Library Project, towards the mission, which provides free education to underprivileged children.

Finally, I want to express my deepest regards to my parents and teachers for the values they instilled in me. They enabled me to work with President Kalam and learn from him every day of our time together.

Notes

Chapter 1: Automobile Technology

1. Ran Prieur. 'Ivan Illich on Cars: Excerpts from Energy and Equity.' Accessed on 30 January 2019. http://ranprieur.com/readings/illichcars.html

Chapter 2: Environmental Science

1. Cosmos: The Science of Everything. 'The Big Five Mass Extinctions.' Accessed on 30 January 2019. https://cosmosmagazine.com/palaeontology/big-five-extinctions
2. Data from the National Climatic Data Centre, USA.
3. *Target 3 Billion*. A.P.J. Abdul Kalam and Srijan Pal Singh. Penguin Books. 2011.
4. National Geographic. 'Save the Plankton, Breathe Freely.' Accessed on 30 January 2019. https://www.nationalgeographic.org/activity/save-the-plankton-breathe-freely/
5. IANS. 'Kalam's Dream "PURA" Project To Get a Push.' *The Hindu*. 17 March 2010. Accessed on 6 March 2019. https://www.thehindu.com/news/national/Kalams-dream-PURA-project-to-get-a-push/article16573247.ece
6. *Target 3 Billion*. A.P.J. Abdul Kalam and Srijan Pal Singh. Penguin Books. 2011.

Chapter 3: Nanotechnology

1. Srijan Pal Singh accompanied President Kalam on this visit, and they were shown around the labs of professors Park and Manoharan together.
2. Srijan Pal Singh accompanied President Kalam on this visit, and they conducted a course at the University of Kentucky.

Chapter 4: Agriculture

1. Culinary Lore. 'Is Color an Indication of Which Berries Are Edible?' Accessed on 30 January 2019. https://culinarylore.com/food-science:is-color-an-indication-of-edible-berries/

2. Wikipedia. 'History of Agriculture.' Accessed on 30 January 2019. https://en.wikipedia.org/wiki/History_of_agriculture

3. K. Kris Hirst. 'Dog History: How and Why Dogs Were Domesticated.' ThoughtCo. 12 December 2017. Accessed on 30 January 2019. https://www.thoughtco.com/how-and-why-dogs-were-domesticated-170656

4. History. 'Fertile Crescent.' 20 December 2017. Accessed on 30 January 2019. https://www.history.com/topics/pre-history/fertile-crescent

5. University College London. 'DNA Traces Cattle Back to a Small Herd Domesticated around 10,500 Years Ago.' ScienceDaily. Accessed on 30 January 2019. https://www.sciencedaily.com/releases/2012/03/120327124243.htm

6. Rich Cohen. 'Sugar Love.' National Geographic. August 2013. Accessed on 30 January 2019. https://www.nationalgeographic.com/magazine/2013/08/sugar-love/

7. National Research Council. *Lost Crops of the Incas: Little-Known Plants of the Andes with Promise for Worldwide Cultivation*. The National Academies Press, 1989.

8. J. Molina, M. Sikora, N. Garud, et al. 'Molecular Evidence for a Single Evolutionary Origin of Domesticated Rice.' Proceedings of the National Academy of Sciences of the United States of America. Vol. 108 (20), 2011.

9. Melissa Islam. 'Tracing the Evolutionary History of Coca (Erythroxylum).' *Ecology & Evolutionary Biology Graduate Theses & Dissertations*. Boulder: University of Colorado, Spring 2011. Accessed on 30 January 2019. https://scholar.colorado.edu/cgi/viewcontent.cgi?article=1015&context=ebio_gradetds

10. Press Information Bureau: Government of India, Ministry of Water Resources. 'Shortage of Water.' 20 July 2017. Accessed on 30 January 2019. http://pib.nic.in/newsite/PrintRelease.aspx?relid=168727

11. The Guardian Datablog. 'How Much Water Is Needed to Produce Food and How Much Do We Waste?' Accessed on 30 January 2019. https://www.theguardian.com/news/datablog/2013/jan/10/how-much-water-food-production-waste

12. Ralph Thomlinson. *Demographic Problems: Controversy over Population Control*. Encino: Dickenson Publishing Company, 1975.

13. Vaclav Smil. 'Harvesting the Biosphere: The Human Impact.' *Population and Development Review*. The Population Council, December 2011.

Chapter 5: Defence and Weapons

1. Srijan Pal Singh accompanied President Kalam on this visit.
2. Chris Hedges. 'What Every Person Should Know about War.' *New York Times*. Excerpted from *What Every Person Should Know About War* (Free Press, Simon & Schuster). 6 July 2003. Accessed on 30 January 2019. http://www.nytimes.com/2003/07/06/books/chapters/what-every-person-should-know-about-war.html
3. Ibid.
4. Srijan Pal Singh accompanied President Kalam on the visit wherein the question was raised.
5. Mary Bellis. 'The History of Sonar.' ThoughtCo. Updated 1 February 2019. Accessed 10 February 2019. https://www.thoughtco.com/the-history-of-sonar-1992436
6. International Institute for Strategic Studies. *The Military Balance*. London: Routledge, 2018.
7. *Advantage India: From Challenge to Opportunity*. A.P.J. Abdul Kalam and Srijan Pal Singh. HarperCollins Publishers. 2015.

Chapter 8: Energy

1. 'BP Statistical Review of World Energy June 2016.' Centre for Energy Economics Research and Policy, Heriot-Watt University, 2016. Accessed on 30 January 2019. http://large.stanford.edu/courses/2017/ph241/albokhari2/docs/bp-2016.pdf
2. Jonathan Gornall. 'The Promise of Solar Power, Made a Century Ago.' *National*. 22 January 2011. Accessed on 30 January 2019. https://www.thenational.ae/business/technology/the-promise-of-solar-power-made-a-century-ago-1.389398
3. A.P.J. Abdul Kalam and Srijan Pal Singh. 'Nuclear Power Is Our Gateway to a Prosperous Future.' *The Hindu*. 6 November 2011. Accessed on 30 January 2019. https://www.thehindu.com/todays-paper/tp-opinion/nuclear-power-is-our-gateway-to-a-prosperous-future/article2602677.ece
4. US Geological Survey. 'Thorium Statistics and Information.' 27 September 2018. Accessed on 30 January 2019. https://minerals.usgs.gov/minerals/pubs/commodity/thorium/index.html#mcs